PENGUIN CRIME FICTION

BLOODY MURDOCK

Robert Ray was born in Amarillo, Texas, and lives in Irvine, California. He has taught tennis, college literature, and writing, and has completed a second Matt Murdock mystery, called *Murdock for Hire*.

BLOODY MURDOCK

Robert J. Ray

PENGUIN BOOKS

PENGUIN BOOKS
Viking Penguin Inc., 40 West 23rd Street,
New York, New York 10010, U.S.A.
Penguin Books Ltd, 27 Wrights Lane, London W8 5TZ
(Publishing & Editorial) and Harmondsworth,
Middlesex, England (Distribution & Warehouse)
Penguin Books Australia Ltd, Ringwood,
Victoria, Australia
Penguin Books Canada Limited, 2801 John Street,
Markham, Ontario, Canada L3R 1B4
Penguin Books (N.Z.) Ltd, 182–190 Wairau Road,
Auckland 10, New Zealand

First published in the United States of America by
St. Martin's Press 1986
Published in Penguin Books 1987

This is a work of fiction. Any resemblance of any character
to any person, living or dead, is purely coincidental.

LIBRARY OF CONGRESS CATALOGING IN PUBLICATION DATA
Ray, Robert J. (Robert Joseph), 1935–
Bloody Murdock.
(Penguin crime fiction)
I. Title.
[PS3568.A92178B5   1987]   813'.52   87-2330
ISBN 0 14 01.0284 1

Printed in the United States of America by
Offset Paperback Mfrs., Inc., Dallas, Pennsylvania
Set in Baskerville

*For my mother
Lillian M. Jenkins,
who taught me about work and tenacity*

PROLOGUE:
The Killing of Gayla Jean

She was putting on the finishing touches for Philo's party when Mr. Dean rang the buzzer. She took a look at herself in the mirror, saw the purple dress shouting down the brilliance of her rich, shining hair, and decided it wasn't quite right. Then when Mr. Dean came in carrying purple orchids it was too much color, so she made him watch her in the bright mirrored door between her bedroom and the living room while she stripped, slowly, down to the buff, and dressed in the new white jumpsuit.

"I liked the dress," Mr. Dean said, as she came out of the bedroom, electric heels clicking on white tile. The dress made Mr. Dean glassy-eyed, took him back to that scorching day last fall he'd paid $500 to shoot photographs of her in and out of the dress. Men always wanted to seal a girl in Saran wrap, keep her dust-free, like a little doll. The purple dress stoked Mr. Dean's little burner right up to high.

"You can button me up, Mr. Dean." She stood in front of him, resting slender wrists on the shoulders of his jacket. Sweat dotted his forehead when his careful accountant's fingers brushed against her bare skin, the smooth curved slopes of her breasts. His hands shook. She squirmed, laughed. Blinking like a mole, he handed her a slim black box containing a gorgeous diamond bracelet. "Sweetheart," she purred, as he locked it on her wrist.

"I'm terribly pleased you decided to ride with me," Mr. Dean said as he steered his Saab Turbo into the rain down Pacific Coast Highway toward Laguna Beach and Philo's party. "I like walking into Philo's parties with a beautiful girl on my arm."

Corn, she thought.

"Silky platinum rain," she said, leaning over and blowing in Mr. Dean's ear. She couldn't drive her own car, a darling red BMW Alpina, because Philo had taken her keys away yesterday in a snit. Philo was pissed at her for partying up in L.A., where a jowly man had promised her a screen test. Soon.

Philo stood at the front door, greeting guests, looking huge, when she sauntered into the cushy entryway in the big house in Bluebird Canyon. When she became a movie star she'd buy Philo's house right out from under him—statues, tennis court, Jacuzzi, swimming pool. She'd keep the crystal, the oriental rugs, the parquet floors, the paintings, the houseboy. The bed, she'd sell.

Philo's diamond stickpin winked at her, viciously, as he shook hands with Mr. Dean. Wearing his purple coat and the white slacks with the sharp crease, Philo made believe he was the King of Bluebird Canyon. Naked, in bed, he reminded her of a hairy white sea lion. Philo was a wallower.

2

"You little bitch!" he whispered, glancing down the front of her jumpsuit. "Why ever did you wear that?"

She smirked. "I knew you'd hate it, daddy."

"Careful of flying blood," he said, squeezing her bare arm.

She didn't blink. "Give me back my keys, daddy."

"If you're good," Philo said, and turned back to his guests.

And then she was into the swirl of Philo's party, flirting and passing around a joint as she stood at the edge of the miniature arena to watch the first pair of fighting cocks stab, rip, and tear. Chicken blood spurted on the pale blue frock of the woman next to her, who didn't budge, or scream.

Sidestepping, she hugged herself. Death screams from the cocks gave her goose bumps. Fred J. Johnson, the cowboy from Vegas, handed her a bloody feather, grinning. Fred J. wanted into her pants. He was always crowding her, feeling her up. She hated pushy rednecks. Fred J. smelled.

"Split with me, baby," Fred J. said. "I'll put a smile on that sassy puss with a dose of Dr. Fred's White Root Tonic."

"Don't you ever wash, honey?" she asked, digging into his bicep with sharp red nails.

Around midnight, she sent twerpy Mr. Dean off to dance with Lucinda, who was looking old and tired. Mr. Dean couldn't take his eyes off Lucinda's breasts, with their Acapulco tourist tan. She danced some more, snorted some coke, then around two in the morning, after Philo had lost a ton of money betting on three chickens in a row, she spotted Jaime Modesto, the Latino movie star. Oh, God. Did he make her shiver! She knew it was Modesto right away, because she'd seen *Tijuana Rose* three times with one of the girls from work. Off the screen, in person, Jaime looked short, but his smile brightened the basement room and he was from Hollywood, that golden land where she longed to go.

"Daddy," she said to Philo. "Thank you scads."

"Hmmm?" Philo said, turning to her. "What for, my dear?"

"For finally getting a name down from Hollywood to meet me. What else?"

"Who?" he asked.

She indicated Modesto, wearing a frilly Mexican shirt and skintight leather pants that showed off his bulge. "That's Jaime Modesto," she said. "Don't tell me *he's* not invited."

"Of course," Philo said, and moved away from her.

This was her chance. She could feel it. She smiled. Jaime smiled back. She was dancing with smelly Fred J. Johnson when Modesto strutted up like a regular fighting cock to cut in.

"Watch it, greaseball," Fred J. growled.

"Split, Fred J.," she said. "This is a friend of mine, from Los Angeles." And she began dancing with Jaime.

"You have mucho booty," he said, grinning. "Madre mia."

"And you," she said. "Are Jaime Modesto."

He grinned, flashing his teeth. "Si. You have seen the moveese?" It rhymed with "geese."

"Five times," she said. "What are you doing here, anyway?"

"I have the business with El Senor Thick Lips," he said.

"Business with Philo?"

"Si. Es verdad."

"I thought *Tijuana Rose* was the absolute greatest," she said.

4

"Thank you. Muchas gracias."

"And I just love your cute accent."

He kept telling her she was beautiful, which she liked, and she kept waiting for him to ask her to visit him in Tinsel Town, and then Butch Denning, Philo's fairy handmaiden, came to take Jaime upstairs to talk. She watched the cocks stab and slash with gleaming razors. People with chicken blood on their clothes smiled at her, touched her. "We saw your film," they said, making it sound like they'd been saved. She loved feeling religious.

Upstairs, she leaned against a wall, smoking weed from Colombia. The door to Philo's study was closed, and smelly Fred J. Johnson stood outside, big arms crossed. After awhile, the door opened and Jaime Modesto came out, looking smug. She followed him downstairs. In the billiard room, she tapped Jaime's shoulder.

"Hi."

"Hey, mi corazon," he said. "I found you again."

"Hope I made it easy enough." She knew "corazon" meant "heart," in Espanol. Coming from him, it sounded sweet.

"You are so bootifull," he said. "You could be in peetchers."

"Pictures" had a golden sound. She pushed close in, sliding her pelvis against his tight leather crotch. "Those are some britches, amigo," she whispered. He grinned at her, showing a gold tooth.

"I gotta spleet ahora," he said. "You come with me, corazon?"

His sudden invitation made her sweat. "Where to?"

"Holeywood," he said. "Manana, we go to big party in Bel Aire. Many producers. Many deals."

He said "Air" wrong, because of his accent, but she

5

thought it was charming. She had only seen Bel Air from a car.

"You mean it?"

"Es verdad," he said.

"I know a secret way out of here," she said, and without saying goodbye to Philo or Mr. Dean she took Jaime by the hand and led him past the bloody sandpile where the fighting cocks were screaming, to a door that opened out into Philo's rock garden. Behind her, Mr. Dean called out, but then she and Jaime were running hand in hand through the chilly California morning to his car.

It was a Trans Am, low slung, with racing stripes. A gaudy oversize Saint Christopher hung from the rearview mirror. There was an empty Corona bottle in the passenger seat. She tossed it at Philo's house, heard it splatter with a harsh tinkle of glass against a wall.

"Hey!" he said, and plucked a chicken feather from her hair.

As they turned out of Goldfinch Lane where Philo lived onto Bluebird Canyon Drive, the brights from a car behind them splashed the inside of the Trans Am with light. Jaime grinned at her and goosed the foot feed, making the Trans Am leap ahead, into the darkness and beach fog. She squealed in delight. Danger turned her on. Trembling, she leaned over to kiss him and put her hot hand on his thigh. Visions of Hollywood excited her, made her sweat inside the jumpsuit. The high beams behind them went out of sight as the Trans Am slid around the curve beside Bluebird Park. The maneuver threw the car into a skid, slamming her against the door. Jaime brought the car back on track and continued on down toward the sea. Hollywood, here we come!

It was 3:22 by the dashboard clock.

They reached the corner at Coast Highway and turned

right, toward L.A. and all her dreams. Behind them, through the rear window, she saw headlights against the fog. He dug into his leather pants, brought out a bill. It smelled new.

"See this, corazon?"

"Whatcha got there?"

"A C-note," he said. "Ciento dolares."

Money was one of her weaknesses. "Where did you get that?"

"From El Senor Thick Lips."

She laughed. "What have you got on Philo, anyway?"

Instead of answering, Jaime pulled out a white handkerchief. "Tie up the ice," he said. Then he stuffed the hundred dollar bill back down the front of his tight leather pants.

For a second, she didn't understand what he meant. Then she grinned and tied the handkerchief around her eyes.

"Now what?" This was one crazy dude!

"You got the money, mi corazon," he said.

"You just want me to feel you up," she said, and ran her hands over the outside of the leather pants.

"Madre mia," he said, groaning. "You are mi corazon."

Her hand was down inside the pants, and she could feel a thick money belt strapped around his body. All hundreds? Sweet Jesus! She gave him a quick squeeze, and that was what he wanted, and he rolled his eyes at her. Jaime was getting excited, revving the engine, slipping through the gears as the Trans Am tore through sleepy Laguna. Making him groan made her hot. Her palms were all sweaty. This was fun. She liked him. She was about to suggest they stop at her place in Newport Beach when he swerved, throwing her against him, hard.

7

The squealing brakes scared her, and she tore off the blindfold.

"Hey!" The diamond bracelet snagged as she jerked her hand free. "Take it easy, pal! I've got a future, you know!"

"Cabrones!" he shouted, in Spanish. "Hijos de las putas!"

"Watch out for that pickup!" she yelled.

Some road hog S.O.B. in a red pickup was trying to run them off the road, crowding them over. Then she knew. The pickup belonged to Fred J. Johnson, the jealous cowboy from Vegas. Fred J. wanted to scare her. Then she saw the second set of headlights, as Philo's Land Rover pulled up on their left.

"Butch!" she yelled at Jaime. "It's Butch Denning. He works for Philo!" She knew these guys. Something had happened, back at the house. Emergency.

Jaime glared at her and let out a stream of curses in Spanish.

"Stop!" she cried. "They want us to stop!" She made a grab for Jaime's keys.

"Cabrones Putas Pendejos!" he shouted, as the Trans Am ran off the road and sank its right front fender into the side of the hill.

She pitched forward, slamming her head, and she was knocked out for a minute. When she revived she was coughing and the car was full of smoke. Flames licked up the rear windows. Jaime was thrust back against the seat, leather pants open. A man's hand was pulling a money belt off Jaime. Then a pair of eyes looked at her and a voice she knew said: "Had yer chance, sweet bitch." She coughed, almost passed out, used her last burst of strength to kick at the door on her side. She got free of the car just as the flames caught poor Jaime Modesto on fire. She lay on the ground, coughing, weak, and just then she looked up and saw Butch running to help her. In his hands, he cradled a tank with a nozzle, and as she cried his name he stopped and pointed it at her and she remembered in a sickening flash that Butch had always been jealous of her because she had taken Philo away from him.

She was too weak to roll aside. She cursed Butch. It was her final act before the flames stole her oxygen and she died.

1

I read about the death of Gayla Jean Kirkwood on page one of the *Tribune,* Orange County's largest newspaper, on a rainy Sunday in March. Her photo—a pretty, smiling girl framed in newspaper black and white—looked familiar, so I read the whole story.

She'd been to a Saturday night party in Bluebird Canyon, a snappy upscale section of Laguna Beach, where she'd apparently met a young dude from Hollywood named Jaime Modesto. The party had been at the home of a Laguna Beach art dealer named Philo Waddell.

Gayla Jean and Modesto had left the party together around 3:20 A.M. Sunday morning, and started driving north on Highway 1, the Pacific Coast Highway. At approximately 3:31 A.M. Modesto's Pontiac Trans Am had slammed up against a wall of rock just on the outskirts of Laguna. The car had caught fire, the gas tank had exploded, and both Modesto and Gayla Jean Kirkwood had been killed. The photo, which covered a third of the front page, showed some cops, a couple of emergency vehicles, a smoking wreck, and a fire crew fighting a fire that was spreading up the hill. Burning up was not a good way to die.

The reporter was careful about documenting how hopeless it had all been, and how quickly the emergency units had responded. The journalist's name was Teresa Aiken, and she was an ace at laying out chronology.

The Laguna Beach PD had arrived seven minutes after the accident. The fire department had arrived two minutes after the police. Two cars from the Orange County Sheriff's Department had arrived at 3:52 A.M. And the paramedics, who weren't needed at all, arrived at 4:01.

The fire had spread from Modesto's car up the hill to ignite some dry brush, and had done a hundred thousand dollars' worth of damage to a house that was probably worth close to a million, because of the spectacular ocean view. The rain had started at 4:30, the paper said.

The story didn't mention any witnesses.

Down below the picture of the scene of the accident, there were photos of Jaime Modesto and Gayla Jean Kirkwood, side by side, smiling into the camera. Modesto was what some women would call handsome—sad eyes, open face, Valentino grin, though with a better set of teeth than old Valentino. The paper said Modesto had made three movies in four years, the last one being *Tijuana Rose,* a story about Mexican illegals and their problems getting across the border.

Modesto himself had "emigrated" to the U.S. seven years ago. His hometown back in Mexico was Guanajuato. His present address was Marina Del Rey. When he'd got himself burned to death on PCH on a dark Sunday morning in March, Modesto had been twenty-six.

The picture of Gayla Jean Kirkwood showed a girl in her early twenties, strawberry blonde or light redhead, with intelligent eyes and a smile that turned out just lopsided enough to make her interesting. She'd died young, and died pretty.

Gayla Jean's residence was Newport Beach, where she was also employed, as a waitress. Her hometown was Fort Worth, Texas. She was twenty-three, the paper said. She was "survived" by a sister, Margaret Kirkwood, also of Fort Worth. I looked at the picture again and felt sad. Two kids were dead. They had probably smoked a joint at the Bluebird Canyon party, decided to share a bed for the night, and had wound up in a surprise funeral pyre on a dark road in the clammy beach fog of Southern California.

Maybe I'd seen her around. She'd lived in Newport Beach, where I lived. Newport Beach was a small town, snug, smug, cramped, on that edge of America about halfway between Kansas City and Honolulu. Maybe we'd passed one day on the pier. Maybe we'd locked eyeballs across a room, a bar, a restaurant. Maybe she'd served me a beer, or some fish and chips, or some spaghetti and meatballs. Maybe I'd made her day with a tip, on a sunny summer Sunday when I'd had money.

Now, looking at her lopsided smile, I wondered what Gayla Jean's hopes had been, what she liked for breakfast, how she handled sorrow and frustration, whether she was neat or sloppy, what made her happy, what kind of men she chose, what made her sad.

Something—the look in her eye, the pretty, lopsided smile, the short, terse formality of the obituary—made you think of Gayla Jean as a butterfly, with only one summer to live.

So what do you do when you're alone on a beach in

California on a rainy Sunday and you read a newspaper story about two kids burning up in a car in the dark and the fog on a twisting coastal highway?

Well, you try not to react. That's what. You shut death out.

You drop the paper and you try to forget the eyes filled with fierce energy and youthful promise. You heave yourself out of the canvas director's chair and you go through the motions of assembling another mug of coffee. This is the way you brew your coffee these days, French style, a plastic Melitta coffee cone, number 4 filter papers, boiling water. You make only one cup at a time. It's one of the few good things you brought home from the Viet Nam war, and brewing it this way gives you the feeling you're a major part of California cafe society. Once the coffee is brewed, you stand at the window and stare out at the rain and the tossing sea and you think about the jungle and the killing, and how you almost bought the farm yourself. Then, to forget, to stop yourself from thinking about death, you open the paper again and read the scores from the sports pages.

So I did that. Only it didn't help much, so I put on some old shorts and my Nikes and went out into the rain for a run along the beach.

That didn't help, either. It was okay as long as I kept my eyes straight ahead, on the wet asphalt. But when I glanced out to sea, the waves turned into green jungle and in the center of the jungle was a mound of earth with a little white cross sticking up from it. It was a grave, and on the white cross was a small shiny plate with my name on it. And some fat words, filled with hot air. Inside my head, the metal plate winked in the tropical sun.

*　　*　　*

MATT MURDOCK, SOLDIER, ADVENTURER,
DREAMER, BUILDER, LOVER.
R.I.P.

If there had been a woman in my life, I would have phoned her and tried to forget my troubles in her warm and comforting presence. But there wasn't, not right then, so I ran back through the rain to my place, above Wally's Surf Shop at the beach end of Newport Pier, and I showered away the chill and opened a can of Bud and fixed some eggs and sausage and cut some green two-by-fours for Jerry Monaghan's patio cover over in Costa Mesa.

2

My phone was ringing when I came in from dinner. It was after ten, the beach was buttoned up for the night, and walking back from beer and fish and chips at the Blue Beet, I'd been humming "Oh, it's beer, beer, beer, that makes you want to cheer"—a song sung by college boys gearing up to conquer the world and all its beautiful women. The streets were wet and shining. There was a cold, raw wind whipping in from the sea. All I could think of was a warm bed and a deep, dreamless sleep.

Then I heard the phone.

The guy on the other end was a Laguna Beach resident named Ellis Dean. The way he said his name, "Ellis Dean," with lots of authority, gave me the idea he was used to giving orders to secretaries and other corporate underlings. His voice was overcontrolled, nervous, on the edge of panic. "Is this Mr. Murdock, the investigator?"

"That's me. Who's this?"

"Mr. Murdock, my name's Ellis Dean. I'm calling on

the recommendation of Mrs. Adrianna Califano. I hope it's not too late, but I'm . . . in need of some advice and . . . ah . . . information."

There are women you can never forget. They stick inside your head like sea creatures on your hull—humid, undulating, salty. Adrianna Califano was one of them.

"How is Mrs. Califano these days?"

"Oh, fine. Just fine."

"She back in the country?" Adrianna had an expensive life-style—winter in Hawaii, spring on a Greek island, summer in the Swiss Alps, autumn in Paris.

"Well, I don't know, you see. I got your name from her last October. In Paris."

Ellis Dean was giving me a clear picture of how he lived, of how organized he was—get a name in October, wait until March to use it—but I was thinking of Adrianna Califano, the dark, the sultry, the dangerous.

She had hired me back in August, on the recommendation of her attorney, J. Benton Sturges, who sometimes referred lost people my way. She'd invested $100,000 in some so-called "energy condos" out in the desert, beyond Palm Springs, and the builder, a friend of hers from Lido Island, had taken off with his secretary, Adrianna's hundred grand, and maybe a million more gleaned from other suckers dumb enough to try and double their money in half a year. For a forty percent salvage fee, I'd followed the builder to Mexico. When I found him, in a smelly second-class hotel in Acapulco, he was drunk and sad and alone. The secretary had run out on him, taking a bundle of money with her, and all he had left from his million-plus was $47,000 and change. I left the builder there, crying in his Carta Blanca, and I brought back the $47,000, minus my forty percent.

Adrianna is a woman of spirit. She's been married twice, that I know of, and she's used to coming away from men carrying silver buckets dripping with dollars. Her instinct for survival—and her natural sense of competition for any prize—told her to go for a chunk of my forty percent. I had finished my obligatory drink and was walking out the door when she brought up the heavy sexual artillery. Adrianna was thirty-five at the time. She'd been fat once, she told me, but then she learned to keep those groceries under control and to stay in shape by working out at a local spa. The workouts worked. We'd be walking down the street and people who thought they knew her from one of the nighttime soaps—"Knots Landing" or "Dynasty"—would rush up asking for her autograph. Adrianna loved signing her name, which was what got her in trouble with the "energy condos" in the first place.

For me, Adrianna was tanned, experienced, ruthless. In bed, she maneuvered her muscles like a four-star general bucking for a seat on the Joint Chiefs. The bedsheet was her battleground. The victory prize was my forty percent.

But us Irish detectives have a life-style to protect, too. Work is always scarce, even when the Republicans are in office. Tracking people is dangerous and tedious. It tests your staying power. Being the relentless hunter takes energy. And after a torrid week of torrid Adrianna, I took the money and walked away. She made a loud scene, straight from a nighttime soap—tears, keening, threats, the works. On legs made unsteady by sex and drink and discovery, I advised Adrianna Califano to trim the fat from her life-style the way she'd trimmed it from her elegant bones.

"Spend a fall here instead of in Paree," I'd told her. "Save on the exchange rate. Cheat the money changers."

We hadn't spoken since. Adrianna hated to lose. She thought she could outwit any man between fifteen and eighty-three, and with me she'd gone all out. Remembering Adrianna made me wonder about Ellis Dean.

"She speaks highly of you," Ellis Dean said.

"Great," I said. "Fine person."

"Are you occupied at the moment, Mr. Murdock?"

"What's on your mind, Mr. Dean?"

"Adrianna—Mrs. Califano—said you sometimes worked as a security consultant?" He had a way of ending his sentences with a question mark when there was no question. He meant bodyguard, but he said security consultant. It was a fifty-dollar phrase.

"That's correct, Mr. Dean. Mind telling me the situation?"

He hesitated. In the short time I would know Ellis Dean, I'd see him hesitate a lot. Hesitation was built into his personality. It was Dean's way of controlling situations. It probably worked great at the office. "I'd rather not say . . . on the phone. Is there someplace we can meet? I'm calling from a . . . pay phone."

I checked my watch. It said 10:32, Sunday P.M. The Blue Beet would be closing. It had been a nothing day. I was fading fast. "How about tomorrow, Mr. Dean?"

"I'd rather get started immediately, at whatever retainer you think necessary. This is a . . . sort of . . . emergency. Perhaps I could . . . ah . . . drive over to your . . . ah . . . office?"

I'd been in the PI business since the late seventies. One of my first lessons was you don't let frightened prospects come to your place late at night. People go crazy at night. They drink. They kill haphazardly. They feel sorry for themselves on your floor. If someone's after them, your home can get blown to bits. It's better to meet in public, among witnesses, spread out the risk. I wanted to wait until daylight to begin bodyguarding Ellis Dean, but I smelled a client, and I hadn't worked in a month.

18

"There's a bar in the Ancient Mariner, on PCH. How soon can you get there?"

"Fifteen minutes. How will I know you?"

I almost said I'd wear a red rose in my lapel. But smarting off is bad for business. "I'm six-two. I weigh one eighty-five. I'll be wearing a yellow slicker, jeans, boots."

"Mrs. Califano mentioned you had a beard."

One of my weaknesses is a woman with a memory. I used the beard to tickle Adrianna's flat, brown, athlete's belly. The feel of it made her laugh, made her cry. And when I was finished teasing and pleasing, she still went after my forty percent like a shark whiffing raw meat in the cold sea.

"Still do," I said.

"What do you charge . . . may I ask?"

"I get forty dollars an hour. If the job runs over seven hours, I get two hundred and fifty dollars a day."

"I find that . . . agreeable," Mr. Dean said.

"See you at the Ancient Mariner."

"I'll look forward to it," he said.

I have two land vehicles. One is a '73 Ford pickup with an inflated book value of $650. It came to me as part of a deal when I still had one hand in the construction game. It is a muscular, useful vehicle that reminds me of my working-class heritage.

The other vehicle is a Plymouth V-8, 1969 vintage, with dual carburetors and a super charger that boosts the horsepower to just over 500. She's blue, with a white interior, a handsome German stereo, a two-way radio, and a police band scanner that allows me to tune in to law enforcement efforts along my strip of beach. Four years ago, I traded a mechanic named Patrick Vallejo some construction work for a pair of Rocaro seats and now the Plymouth rides like the Queen Mary on a glassy sea. Freddy Heidegger, an engineer buddy who's moved back east, installed some electric windows plus some remote control side mirrors—my idea of total automotive luxury. Her in-town mileage is twelve miles per gallon. On the freeway, with the wind behind her, she cruises at seventy and gets seventeen miles per gallon. She's made for OPEC, that Plymouth, but I dig her mightily.

I drove the Plymouth across the Newport bridge and turned right onto PCH. I parked in the lot in front of the Ancient Mariner and walked through the puddles to the bar. The rain was down to a fine drizzle. I was tired, but the scent of money and the sight of the waitresses revived me.

The waitresses in the Ancient Mariner are mostly heart-breakers who wear costumes intended only to inflame the mind and encourage exorbitant tips. Tight red tank tops that hug the torso and lift the breasts and leave arms bare and shining. Sarong-style skirts that call attention to long, athletic legs, kept fit by summer volleyball. For some guys, I know, waitresses are fair game. For me, they're just people. They work. They laugh. They hope. They get tired. Some waitresses, like Gayla Jean Kirkwood, die young.

I knew one of the waitresses who was working that evening. Her name was Donna. She was a brunette, at least twenty years younger than my forty-odd, tall, with elegant legs and a good smile. We were chatting when Ellis Dean arrived.

He was short, with close-cropped graying hair and an edgy nervous look about the eyes. His shoulders were tense. His right hand kept clenching, then unclenching. He stood at the entrance, like Jimmy Cagney in an old gangster movie, staring around at the room while trying to appear calm and in control. He wore a natty blue business suit, uniform of the corporation, a white shirt, and a conservative striped tie. His Burberry, which was thrown open to billow in the coastal breeze, retailed for at least $500.

I signaled him from the bar and went to one of Donna's tables. Ellis Dean's hand was cold as we shook. Short men like to impress you with their muscle, so he squeezed extra hard.

Donna slid up, bare arms gleaming, with a whisper of silk and slim promises of love in the soft rain, but Ellis Dean didn't seem to notice. When a guy doesn't respond to a woman like Donna, that's when you know he's afraid. He ordered gin and tonic, then turned to check me out. His knotted brows spoke disapproval. Maybe I should dress better, carry embossed business cards, trim the beard.

"Are you armed, Mr. Murdock?"

"Not for consulting. What's up, Mr. Dean?"

He shook his head like he had me under contract. "Yes. Yes. I . . . assumed you'd understood that." His eyes kept darting to the door, to the bar, then back to me. A cowboy came in, slapped the rain from his carefully rolled Stetson, and took a seat at the bar. Ellis Dean's eyes fluttered, and some color drained from his face. He stopped looking at the cowboy and turned back to me. "They have this reserve police program in Laguna. It's volunteer work, nights, mostly, and weekends. You go through extensive training at one of the local academies. I thought about it a long time, and even talked to some friends on the city council, but still, when I . . . vuh . . . vuh . . . volunteered, they turned me down. I'm a strict law-and-order person. I was very disappointed at being rejected. I could have served . . . I'm sure."

"Tough, getting rejected."

"I've never fired a weapon. I was certain I could learn. I'm very tenacious. I . . . hang in there."

He was trying to tell me something about bravery,

about weapons and the rituals and trappings of manhood. Tough, brave talk was common among men. I rank it one cut above locker-room humor. I didn't answer.

"Adrianna—Mrs. Califano, I mean—says you're an expert with weapons, Mr. Murdock. Is that true?"

He was asking for my credentials. They always do. Especially after they see me in my working clothes and find out I don't carry business cards.

"I was career army," I said. "I worked for a year training a S.W.A.T. outfit, up in L.A. After that, I taught small arms to recruits at the Orange County Police Academy."

"Oh?" He seemed surprised and impressed. "For how long? At the academy, I mean?"

"Six years."

"You seem to be well qualified, Mr. Murdock."

"Thanks."

Donna arrived with Ellis Dean's gin and tonic and a fresh beer for me. He grabbed his glass and gulped at it nervously. When half the drink was gone, he set the glass down with a thump and leaned across the table. I smelled gin, and something sour. "Did you happen to read about the accident last night? The one near Laguna, on PCH? It involved a Mexican movie actor and a girl named Kirkwood?"

Them again. The smiling youths with the hopeful faces. "I read about it."

"What did you think?"

"A bad way to go."

"They were murdered, Mr. Murdock. Murdered in cold blood."

Now we were getting to it. "How do you know?"

He looked around the room furtively, like a small animal searching for a place to hide. Over at the bar, the cowboy had turned to watch us. Dean's face lost more color.

"I . . . observed it. I have . . . photographs."

"Did you call the cops?"

"No. Not . . . yet." He grabbed his glass and drained the rest of his drink, then motioned impatiently to Donna for another. "I need . . . time to think. I need some . . . breathing space. That's why I called you." He leaned closer. "Do you know that man? The young one, at the bar. Dressed . . . like a cowboy?"

"Never saw him before."

"Did he come in after I did?"

"Yes. Is he the one you're worried about?"

"I'm not sure." He pulled out a checkbook and a gold ballpoint. "Two-fifty a day, you said?"

"That's right."

"I'll make this for six hundred. That should cover two days, plus expenses. At the end of two days, we'll re-negotiate. Fair enough?"

I needed the money. He wanted to give it to me. But there were things I had to know. If the cowboy was after him, I'd want reinforcements or at least an equalizer. The cowboy was fifteen years younger, forty pounds heavier. He filled the tight western shirt with no trouble. Probably a weight-lifter. Dean was no help. Maybe Donna would take the cowboy from behind with a beer bottle if he came for me. "Starting now?" I asked.

"Yes." He ripped off the check and handed it to me. I took it, then set it on the table, between us.

"There are things I need to know, Mr. Dean."

"What things?" He scowled at Donna for not getting here fast enough with his refill. Deep worry-furrows creased his brow. Man under stress.

"Evidence things," I said. "If you've got evidence in a felony, you're required to turn it over to the police."

"I'm not sure it's evidence, Mr. Murdock."

"You said you had pictures."

23

"I do. But they—they aren't all that clear."

"They're clear enough, Mr. Dean. You're jumpy as a cat in a roomful of rocking chairs."

He looked at me with wide, red-rimmed eyes. "Is it that obvious?"

"Afraid so."

"I was hoping I had it well under control."

We paused while Donna set down fresh drinks. I refrained from saying anything more about the law, the cops, the reserve police program he hadn't been able to get into. Donna smiled, left us alone. Dean gulped his drink quickly, and a trickle of liquid ran down the left side of his mouth, onto his chin. Random gin dribbles were not a part of Ellis Dean's tidy world. He wiped, clumsily, with one hand. His eyes blinked back tears. "If I tell you what's going on—or rather, my sense of what's . . . going on—will you help me?"

"I'll do my best."

"You'll need to be armed. That's a . . . precondition."

"The gun's at my place, near Newport Pier. Five minutes."

He stood up, whipped the skirts of his Burberry aside, and dug for his wallet. It was a leather job, dark brown, smooth, expensive. He laid a crisp new twenty on the table without consulting the check, which I knew to be about twelve bucks. I had the feeling Mr. Ellis Dean didn't make a practice of overtipping. He was an accountant, maybe an engineer. If he hadn't been under pressure, he'd have figured out a precise twelve percent tip. The extra would make Donna's night.

"Let's take your car over. I'll ride with you, if that's all right. We'll pick mine up on the way back . . . if that's all right with you." Hesitation, hesitation.

"Where to after that, Mr. Dean?"

"My place," Ellis Dean said. "It's on a hill in Laguna."

24

3

After getting into the Plymouth, I started up, turned on the defroster, and waited for a couple of minutes to see if the cowboy followed. Ellis Dean wasn't saying much, so that gave me a minute to analyze my motives.

They were mixed.

Bodyguarding isn't my favorite job. The hours are long. The clients are usually unsavory, or terrified, or paranoid plus. Lots of times, they're running from something I can't handle. In addition, the conversation in close quarters can put you to sleep. The food, however, can sometimes be a surprise. Three years ago, I'd been hired to head a three-man team guarding John Jake Appleton, a liberal Southern California Congressman who was also a gourmet. Wherever John Jake went—hotels, restaurants, farm-country cafes, eateries in Mexican Town—the food was spectacular. John Jake weighed 275. Guarding John Jake, my weight jumped ten pounds in twelve days.

But bodyguarding is steady work, if mindless, and getting paid is always a number-one motive. Also, it can lead to other gardens, other trees, other fruits. In this case, Ellis Dean's photos—if there were photos—might help turn over a rock covering up some evil snakes. Snake-killing is a favorite activity of mine. It helps me think I'm doing good for society. So motive number two, I told myself, was idealistic—cleaning up the world. At the same time, there was a chance I could one-up the cops, and I'm not above a little professional competition.

Motive number three was the dead girl. I'm one of those people who thinks there's a shortage of beauty in the world. A lady college professor told me once I was a romantic. She also told me I wasn't much on art and literature. The professor was right. Books aren't my thing and art is something my upscale clients call a collectible. But when a pretty girl gets killed, it leaves me feeling empty, like I was back in Nam, on patrol, watching for an ambush, shooting rats.

And that's why I sat with Ellis Dean in the rain-soaked parking lot of the Ancient Mariner on PCH on a chilly night in March.

"What kind of work do you do, Mr. Dean?"

"I'm comptroller, for . . . Infokorp."

"What do they do?"

"High tech." He paused. "We design . . . for aerospace."

"Design what?"

"Classified things, mostly."

"Weapons?"

He glared at me for probing into government secrets. "Satellites, mostly. Why are we sitting here, Mr. Murdock?"

"Checking out your cowboy," I said, and eased the Plymouth out of the parking lot onto PCH.

I drove across the bridge to my place. Coming off the bridge, I did notice a pair of headlights in the rearview. They hung back there, turning when we did, never getting close. The lights sat low to the ground. If it was a tail, he was behaving himself. I figured the car for a Porsche.

Back at my place, Ellis Dean sat on the edge of a director's chair, watching me strap on the leather shoulder holster. For him, this was the action big time.

The first couple of dozen times, strapping on a shoulder holster can be an exacting ritual. The smell of leather and mansweat. The flat emptiness before you insert the pistol. The knowledge that this is a harness of death. I don't like shoulder holsters, especially in summer heat, when society forces you to wear a jacket to hide the straps. But they are the way of civilization. I knew an old Chinese dude in Saigon who put everything into symbolism. Politics was the dagger up the sleeve, he said. Government was the gun beneath the armpit.

The gun I chose was a .357 Magnum, six-inch barrel, with half a box of extra ammo. If I slept that night, it would be at Ellis Dean's house in Laguna, so I packed a bag.

The low-slung headlights weren't there as we drove back across the bridge to pick up Dean's car. It was a Saab Turbo, four doors, late model, with a power antenna that slithered up as the car coughed into life. I told him to drive slow, so I could keep up, and then we started for Laguna, exhaust gray against the light and the black, rain-slick streets.

The time was ten minutes to midnight.

Ellis Dean might have been a conservative dresser in a

27

corporate straitjacket, but behind the wheel of his turbo, he drove like Andy Granatelli at the Indy 500. He zipped south down PCH, making me hit 60 mph to catch up. We slid past Le Club and Newport Bay on our right, past the tall white high rises of Promontory Point, past the fancy import car dealers near the entrance to Balboa Island. I was busy keeping up with Dean on the wet asphalt, and watching for traffic cops, since we were over the limit, so I didn't spot the Porsche headlights right away.

They were coming fast. I saw the lights in my rearview mirror, on high, so I shifted in the seat sideways and flipped the Plymouth's rearview mirror to Night, to cut the glare. We drove along that way for a half mile, Dean leading, me behind him two car lengths in the Plymouth, and the Porsche holding steady behind us, like a sleek hound tracking us for a gang of bloodthirsty fox hunters.

We came out of Newport Beach, climbing the hill leading to Corona Del Mar, with the signs for the Fashion Island Mall back to our left. Dean stopped at a red light in Corona Del Mar. The Porsche swung in behind me, lights still on high beam, engine revving.

I could feel something about to happen. I loosened the .357 in the shoulder holster. My hands started to sweat and I could hear death hovering.

We were almost out of Corona Del Mar when the pickup appeared. It was a big red Chevrolet with oversize tires, a roll bar, and a set of hunting spots mounted on top. The pickup came ripping past me in the left lane. I was doing fifty-five, so the pickup must have been doing seventy. He went by fast. I didn't see the driver's face. I swung out from behind Ellis Dean and goosed the Plymouth until her nose was half a car length away from the red Chevvy, and at the same time the pickup brushed

28

up against the rear fender of the Saab, nudging Dean toward the shoulder.

At the first touch, Ellis Dean accelerated, and you could see that turbo power kick in as the little foreign job shot ahead. The pickup lurched, then skidded across the wet pavement before straightening out again, one wheel off the shoulder of the right hand lane. The speedometer of the Plymouth read 75 mph. I hit the toggle switch to lower the window on the passenger side. The Porsche swung in behind me, with the high beams in my eyes, just to keep me occupied. Then I pulled almost even with the pickup, and I fired two quick shots low, at the engine compartment. You can't shoot straight from a speeding car, especially when you're driving, but at the sheriff's academy, where I taught rookies the fine art of small arms, I used to deliver this speech about how often in real life you couldn't use the two-handed FBI shooting stance, and after the speech I'd demonstrate, with targets, how to shoot while diving or falling or driving at high speed.

All that practice helped, because the shots hit something under the hood that brought forth smoke and bright sparks. That got the attention of the driver, who swerved off the road, across the shoulder, barely squeezing between two palm trees. The last I saw of the red pickup, it was heading straight toward a security gate of one of the carefully guarded and extremely well tended condo compounds that line the private beaches of Southern California.

Now, engine roaring, two wheels spurting roadside sand, the Porsche swung around me and zipped down PCH after Ellis Dean. I couldn't see the Saab lights anywhere, but up ahead were three cars—two in the right lane, doing forty, one in the left lane, passing—with the Porsche headlights blinking from high beam to low beam and back to high and the sound of its horn wailing against the night. If the cars kept on slowpoking, I had a chance to catch the Porsche, maybe ask the driver a couple of questions about following too close and shining his brights into my eyes in the rearview.

I was three car lengths away when the slowpoke blocking the left lane sped up, leaving a slot wide enough to go through. The sleek Porsche slipped through it and was over the hill and gone at 130 mph.

I caught up with Ellis Dean on Coast Highway outside Laguna Beach, just about at the place where the two kids had been killed the night before. He was parked at the side of the road, lights off. When he saw me drive up, he flashed his lights once and then led me down the hill and into town.

We turned left about four blocks past the center of town where the Hotel Laguna sits on the edge of the beach and headed along a narrow road away from the sea. We made several turns, climbing slowly, and all the houses were dark. Then we made a right and a left and another left and when I came around the corner I saw a garage door opening. Ellis Dean drove the Saab in, then got out to examine his car. I parked beside him. He was squatting down, running his hand over a foot-long scrape. He looked at me, and I thought I saw him wink back another tear. While I was getting out of the Plymouth, he pressed a button to close the garage door.

"What happened back there?" His lips were tight, his voice controlled. Anybody could see the bad guys were after his ass, but Ellis Dean needed a corporate report bearing ten signatures.

"The guy in the pickup tried to bump you off the road."

"A red pickup?"

"Yes. You figure it was the cowboy driving?"

"What cowboy, Mr. Murdock?"

"The one that made you antsy, back at the Ancient Mariner."

"He is not known to me, I assure you."

"How come you knew it was red?"

"It looked red," Ellis Dean shivered. "Come inside, please. I need a drink."

Carrying my canvas bag, I followed him. It was a nice house. Picture window facing the sea, so you could get inspired watching the waves on sunny days. Medium-sized living room, with a fireplace, andirons, an expensive brass fire screen. The fireplace, I noted, was clean. Not a stray ash anywhere. That meant we were back in the tidy, controlled world of Ellis Dean, comptroller for Infokorp. The furniture was pale wood with white cushions. It looked Scandinavian and expensive.

"What would you like?"

"Scotch," I said, breaking a rule.

Ellis Dean busied himself at the bar. Clink of glasses. The sound of whiskey being poured into a glass. I went around checking doors, planning how I'd defend this place if the bad guys came for us with guns blazing.

I came to the conclusion that contemporary houses out of *Sunset* or *Architectural Digest* are not designed to withstand attack from marauders, crusaders, tattooed bikers, bandits. Maybe, I thought, we were headed back to the middle ages. What we needed tonight was a castle, high walls, an army of crossbowmen, a moat filled with crocodiles.

31

He handed me my drink and took a long pull of his. The way he drank told me Ellis Dean didn't understand how liquor could hurt a guy. Or maybe he just didn't care.

"What did you do, Mr. Murdock? Back there, I mean?"

He was asking me if I'd earned my money.

"I put a couple of rounds into the pickup."

"Did you kill him?"

"I doubt it."

"Too bad," Dean said. "I wish you'd killed him."

I drank the scotch. It wasn't the best, but still okay on a cold night in March.

"Who was it, Mr. Dean?"

"Do you think I should get a gun, Mr. Murdock?"

"Not if you haven't been trained to use it."

He nodded, stared at me, then at the floor. He walked over to the window and looked out at the night, the scudding clouds, the sea. I watched his head tilt back as he drained the glass. Three belts since he'd walked into the Ancient Mariner, and no telling how many before that.

"I knew the girl." He spoke without turning to face me.

"Which girl is that?"

"The one who was murdered last night. Gayla Jean Kirkwood."

"How well did you know her?"

"Not well. She—I might as well tell you this—she posed for a modeling session. For several sessions, in fact. Did I tell you I was an amateur photographer?"

"No. You didn't." I sipped the scotch. "Where was the modeling session?"

"In the apartment of . . . a friend. Over near your place. On Lido Island."

Lido Island is near me in a geographical sense only. In

a real, or economic, sense, it is light-years away from my humble home on the pier.

"Who else was there?"

"Two other photographers and myself. And a . . . sort of, well . . . bouncer."

"How many other models?"

"Only one. Gayla Jean. She was . . . more than . . . sufficient."

"How long ago was this, Mr. Dean?"

"Last, er, fall. It was . . . innocent. But then my wife saw some of the photos, and that's when things started going . . . wrong. And then it was no longer . . . innocent." His voice had dropped to a rattly whisper.

His house had a woman's touch, and he was your typical family guy who'd screwed up. "Where is your wife, Mr. Dean?"

"Gone," he said, his voice cracking. " She's left me. She took my daughter and they left. They were both . . . terribly . . . angry." And then he slumped down in the nearest chair, put his face in his hands, and cried.

4

When I cry, it sounds to me like an animal in pain.

But Ellis Dean held it down to a whimper. His shoulders shook. He squeaked, almost blubbered. A couple of times, he blew his nose on a big, white handkerchief. When he was finished, the room got real quiet, until the only sound was our breathing, the clink of ice as I made fresh drinks. A couple of sips and he was ready to tell me about how he'd fallen in love with Gayla Jean.

"I have this friend . . . Stephen Marx. He's an amateur photographer, like I am, and one of his interests is taking photos of young women, in the . . . ah . . . nude." Dean sniffed the air as if to say that nudity was a crime. "Stephen's always after me to go along to one of his sessions. He thinks I'm a prude, I suppose." Dean blew his nose. It was one of the few things he did full out, with no hesitation. "Maybe that's why I went—to prove I wasn't. A prude," he added, shaking his head and sighing.

"This was September, you said?"

"Yes. The middle of the month. September. During one of our famous Santa Anas. My wife was . . . out of town. It was awfully hot . . . I remember. Scorching, she called it."

He blew his nose again.

"Where on Lido Island was the session?"

"On Lido Soud. A condominium called Lido Landing. Do you know it?"

"Only from the outside. Who else was there?"

"Stephen Marx. Another man. Gayla Jean, of course. And Butch Denning."

"Who's Butch Denning?"

"He acted the role of guard or bouncer. Butch is one of your muscle beach types, blond, very tanned. I remember, during most of the session, he stood against the wall, watching, with his arms folded. He had an odd smile on his face . . . most of the time."

"How long did the session take, Mr. Dean?"

"Oh, counting our setup time, two hours and a quarter. There were breaks, of course, while the model went to change her costume." Dean rubbed his knee nervously. "It was . . . a very good session. I'd never photographed anyone quite like her. She was . . . extraordinarily beautiful. And she had . . . something. Something indefinable."

"What did she get out of the deal?"

"Stephen and I paid five hundred dollars each. I presume the other man did, also."

Fifteen hundred wasn't bad for a couple hours of work, especially if the lady enjoyed the power, making the camera boys sweat. I wondered how much went to the model, how much to the house.

"This other guy. Remember his name?"

35

"Only his first name. Ken."

"Age?"

"Late thirties, I should guess. Thirty-nine?"

"Description?"

"Is this really necessary, Mr. Murdock?"

"You never know. If the question bothers you, forget it."

"No. No. It's just that . . ." his voice trailed off. He rubbed the back of his neck before going on. "He was a heavy man, with large brown hands. He wore corduroy trousers and a shirt open at the neck. Around his neck, there was a gold chain. His equipment was an old Zeiss."

"What kind of camera do you use, Mr. Dean?"

He stared at me as if he hadn't understood the question. "I have several," he said. "I have a Linhof 220, for outdoor work. A Hasselblad 500C/M and a Rolleiflex SL 66, which do about the same for me. A—"

I cut him off. "Remember what you used that day at the session?"

"The Mamiya."

I didn't know much about cameras. Ellis Dean talked as if he knew a lot. Camera buff fit his profile.

"What happened at the session?"

"She posed. We shot film."

"You mentioned something about her posing in the nude. Did she?"

"Not totally." He closed his eyes and leaned back. Outside, a car wound down the road in low gear. Ellis Dean spoke without opening his eyes. "The session began with Gayla Jean wearing a full-length terry cloth robe over a very brief bikini. The idea—Stephen explained it to me ahead of time—was that we were to pretend it was a fashion show. The reason given for her posing was to create a portfolio, you see, to launch her modeling career. She

36

was to pretend we weren't there, that she was alone in her bedroom, or dressing room, so that if an occasional peek were allowed, well . . ." He paused. "You understand."

I nodded. "It wasn't your crummy strip show. It had class."

He went on as if he hadn't heard me. "There was one moment that was absolutely electric. The model entered the room where we were shooting wearing a lavish creamy fur—a fitch, I believe—under which was a lavender dress. On her feet, she wore high heels. Silver. During her change, she had applied a very pale lipstick, of an almost identical shade, so that the eye moved from her lips down to the shoes and back again. When she removed the fur and passed between us and the light, it became clear that she wore a garter belt, stockings, but no other underthings, and that added to the excitement. The session was almost at an end, and my only thought was that I had to see her again. You must understand, I am not a terribly passionate person. I live in a world of numbers and electronic spreadsheets, and while I appreciate a beautiful woman along with the next man, I am not ordinarily given to moving without a lot of thought. But this girl, this woman, was maddening, and maddeningly beautiful. The way she moved made you want to touch her, just to make certain you weren't dreaming. Have you ever felt that way about someone?"

His voice hung in the room while I considered the question. I had the feeling he didn't want an answer, so I sat there, holding what was left of my Scotch, and waited for him to go on.

"She did her last round of poses wearing the lavender dress. You used the word 'class' before, Mr. Murdock, and that's what it was. And then she did something that made me respect her no end."

"What was that?"

"She sent Butch, the bouncer, out of the room."

"How?"

In the dim half dark of the living room that faced the sea, I saw Ellis Dean smile at the memory. "It was elementary, and quite an elegant move. She marched up to him and handed him the fur and told him, in a quiet voice, to hang it up in her closet. He grinned his muscular grin, took the fur, and went away. And do you know what she did then?"

I knew, but Ellis Dean was going to tell me anyway. "Shoot," I said.

"Then—" His voice was choked with emotion. "Then, she slowly disrobed."

It was clear to me that Ellis Dean had fallen in love with a girl half his age. The feeling had been strong enough to run Mrs. Dean out of the classy house in Laguna. Where was she now? My watch said it was after one in the morning. I was bone tired. I stood up, stretched, and was about to ask him where the bedroom was.

"Watching her was . . . magnificent. I had never seen anything quite so beautiful or so . . . erotic. That's not the right word. She was innocent. She was beautiful. Yet her eyes, staring into the camera, were so sad, so filled with pain. There was that moment, while I hung there, focused on her eyes through the Mamiya, and I saw the sadness, and I knew I must photograph that. But just as I was tripping the shutter, her face changed and she lifted one leg to rest her foot on the edge of the glass-topped coffee table and began to undress. I felt suffocated. When I was a child, back in Chicago, I used to have the same feeling when following my mother through a revolving door. Suffocation is what I felt. Terrible, pleasurable suffocation." He stopped, stared at me. Mothers can do that to a guy. Then he went on, his voice choked with the memory of that moment. "And as her long fingers began to unhook the snap of the silvery garter belt, the lavender dress fell open and I was alone in the universe with her naked. . . ." Ellis Dean paused. His delivery was heavy, a memory weighted with lead. He finished in a whisper, ". . . her naked sex."

He said it like a naughty boy.

Ellis Dean was a shy, prudish little man who'd lived his forty-odd surrounded by numbers, budgets, dollar signs, the trappings of corporate accounting. But down under the $500 Burberry and the Savile Row power suit there lurked an artist, a painter, a preserver of beautiful things. And one of the things he wanted to preserve was this girl in the purple dress lifting her leg in a classic girlie mag beaver pose while she stared at the camera with professional innocence. I liked the story. I felt sorry for Ellis Dean. And since I thought I was getting to know the girl better, I was starting to wonder how I would have reacted on that hot autumn afternoon. For one thing, I told myself, I wouldn't have had the 500 bills to toss away.

I stood at the window for a couple minutes, letting the scene sink in, before I asked him more questions.

"When did you see her next, Mr. Dean?"

"She called. After she'd seen the photos. We met in Long Beach—she worked as a cocktail waitress there, on the beach—and she told me how much she liked the photos, which pleased me. And then she said how embarrassed she sometimes got, while exposing herself. And somehow we began to talk about motivation—about why she did that—and she told me she owed money to some people and this was the only way she had of paying it off, and . . . that's when things started."

"You gave her money?"

"Um. Yes."

"What else?"

"I helped her obtain a position down here."

"Where was that, Mr. Dean?"

"Grogan's Grogerie. That's the lounge at Le Club. Do you know it?"

"Not for a year or so," I said. "Anything else?"

"I . . . ah . . . tried to aid her in making connections with people in . . . ah . . . the world of film. From Hollywood."

"How did that work out?"

"It was a . . . disaster. I'm terrible at that sort of thing. She—" He paused to look at me with red-rimmed eyes. "When she discovered I could not help, she became derisive."

Hollywood, show biz, and glitter. Maybe that's why she went off with Mr. Jaime Modesto. "Were you intimate with her?"

He nodded. "A few times."

It didn't sound supersexy. I swung back to money talk. "So you helped her pay off the money she owed?"

He nodded. "Yes."

"Mind telling me how much?"

"Just over seven thousand."

"Who did she owe it to?"

"She wouldn't tell me. She said it would be better if I didn't know."

I could hear her speech now, in my head. Poor Ellis Dean had been suckered. "This muscle type, Butch. Did he have anything to do with who she owed it to?"

"No. I . . . ah . . . don't think so." Mr. Dean swiveled his eyes away from me. He knew, all right.

"And what about the photographs? The ones you say prove she was murdered. Who's in those?"

"I'm not at liberty to tell you. Not yet."

I turned away from staring out at the dark to look at Dean, slumped back in the chair, eyes closed. His right hand rubbed away slowly at his trousers, just above the knee.

"Mind telling me what you're planning?"

"Not at all," he said. "I have retained you as my security consultant for the next two days. When that time is up, I may wish to retain you further. At the same time, I may have no more need of your services. After what happened on the way down here, you should be aware of what precautions to take. As you are the expert, I rely on you. In addition, I have faith in your capabilities to protect me. Is that enough? Or would you like more detail?"

I wanted to shake him, wake him up.

"Cut the crap, Mr. Dean. You're scared, and the more I know about it, the safer you'll be."

"I feel perfectly safe . . . now that you're here." He stood, wearily, and turned toward the stairs. "There's a guest bedroom. Left, at the top of the stairs. The sheets are fresh."

I grabbed him by the arm as he was starting up. "I need to see those pictures."

He shook his head. "No. Not yet." And then he climbed slowly up. At the top of the stairs he turned and said, "Tomorrow, I'd like you to accompany me to a memorial service."

"The Kirkwood girl?"

"Yes." His face was pale.

"Pretty fast. She just died."

He tried a sad joke. "The word came out from Texas. Perhaps it's a custom of swift burial, because of the heat."

Pretty organized, too, I thought.

And then he walked upstairs and left me alone.

5

I slept heavily, but did not dream of Gayla Jean Kirkwood in silver heels and see-through purple dress. I woke next morning to the smell of fresh perked coffee—one of the few good reasons I know for waking—so I got up, checked the .357 to make sure it was still loaded, showered, dressed, and walked downstairs carrying my boots in one hand, the shoulder holster in the other. Ellis Dean's face was pale. He looked to me like he'd slept in his clothes from last night. He stared for a moment at the shoulder holster, which I set on the breakfast table. Matt Murdock, confidence builder.

Over coffee and croissants, Ellis Dean told me about Philo Waddell's party. There wasn't any sugar in the Dean house, just some honey with a health food label from a farm in Northern California. On my first try, the coffee wasn't sweet enough. On my second, it was too sweet. One more trick I hadn't mastered on my journey through life.

"I don't know whether I told you I played tennis or not, Mr. Murdock, but Philo and I have this . . . sort of . . . rivalry. He's huge, with a terrible killer instinct. When he's angry, he tends to overhit. I, on the other hand, play the terrier type of game. I retrieve the ball until I can work my opponent out of position. Philo and I met playing doubles at Le Club, and we have a fairly regular match on Saturday afternoons on his private court."

Dean stopped and looked past me out the window. The kitchen where we were sitting faced south, past a drop-off and along a stand of small trees and thick underbrush clumped along a red dirt cliff. Through the trees, you could see the dull, orange patches of a couple of neighboring roofs. From here, the beach was invisible. The coffee wasn't bad. Not as good as what I brewed, French style, at my place. But not bad.

"We were playing when he received the phone call."

"Which phone call is that, Mr. Dean?"

"This is only an assumption, you understand. But I think it was the young Mexican . . . Modesto . . . the one who was killed with Gayla. I have . . . been piecing it . . . together."

The rain had stopped and outside I watched a slow drip descend from the roof line. The sun was out. It was a morning for assumptions. I nodded at Dean and gave him a half smile as I sipped the coffee. Sleep had not refreshed me.

"What made you think so?"

"I'm . . . not sure. It was . . . just a feeling. Philo was called to the phone. He has an extension right there on the court. He spoke to someone briefly. I thought I heard him say something in Spanish, but I'm not sure. When he hung up and turned away from the phone, he was furious. Philo is overweight. When he gets angry, his face becomes terribly red and his neck gets all blotchy and he stalks about like some sort of great beast. He growled at me when I asked the score. He made two great backhands out of sheer rage. He missed several easy ones. I started winning. But before we finished the match, he smashed his racket against the net post and marched into the house. Those rackets retail for at least three hundred dollars. I didn't see him again until that night, at the party."

"How was he then?"

"All smiles. And full of apologies for the way he'd acted. Philo was born poor as dirt, but he does have a small bit of charm about him when he tries."

"Did you go to a lot of his parties?"

"Only since Mildred—that's my wife—only since Mildred and I separated."

"How long has that been?"

"She left three days before Christmas. It was the worst time of my life."

"Because she found out about you and Gayla Jean?"

"Yes. Mildred's naturally suspicious. And then she found one of the photographs. I was carrying it in my briefcase. Mildred looked inside. C'est fini."

"Did you go alone to the party, Mr. Dean?"

"No. I escorted Gayla Jean. We had . . . plans. To . . . ah . . . spend the night together."

"Here?"

"No," he said. "Her place. At Lido Landing."

I had read in the paper she'd gone off with Jaime Modesto, the movie actor. But I wanted as clear a picture of

44

the party as I could get, so I kept on with the low profile questions.

"What happened to that plan?"

"The Mexican—Modesto—showed up." Dean's jaw was clenched as he said Modesto's name.

"Remember where you were? What time it was?"

"Of course. It was precisely one fifty-three A.M., and we were downstairs, in this huge basement, attending a cockfight."

I grinned, in spite of the early hour. "A cockfight? In fat cat Bluebird Canyon?"

"You find that amusing." Dean pursed his lips, like an old-fashioned schoolmarm about to deliver a lecture by rapping her ruler on some kid's knuckles. "And that's precisely why Philo's parties have become so popular. The room was like a furnace. Society page people were screaming, sweating, even sniffing cocaine. Philo has a portable fighting arena, complete with sand, like a miniature bullring, and half of Orange County society encircles this . . . this miniature coliseum to watch chickens stab each other to death."

"I take it you've seen more than one."

Dean nodded. "It has a certain . . . ghoulish attraction. I told myself I went because it excited her so—Gayla Jean, I mean—but then at the New Year's party I found myself betting with a woman wearing one of those rubberized suits you see in fetishist magazines, and the next thing I knew I was screaming myself hoarse, shouting for a rooster with a red comb."

It was a new side of Ellis Dean. The poor guy had been bottled up so long he had to cut loose. So he bet on Philo's chickens. I wondered if he'd won any money.

I was still trying to get a picture of Philo Waddell's

45

friends. All trails kept leading back to the house in Bluebird Canyon, and I had a feeling I'd be paying the great
man a visit, but before I went in there I wanted some
background. That's the way they taught me when I
played cop for two years in the Army CID. You spend a
lot of time on background, on knowing your pigeon, on
memorizing the layout. And then when you charge in,
guns blazing, you have a better chance of not shooting
yourself in the foot.

"This woman you bet with. Is she a regular at Philo's?"

"Very. Lucinda Smith-Travis. She's very prominent.
The Art League. The Hospital Advisory. She's . . .
around a lot." Dean gave me a funny look for not recog-
nizing the name. It's a habit I get into with society folk.
They don't know me. I don't know them. Sometimes they
hire my services. Life is simpler that way.

"A rubber suit," I said.

"Mmm," he said. His coffee cup was half empty. Mine
was totally empty. I got up to pour myself some fresh.
When I gestured with the pot, Dean shook his head. I
wondered if he'd had a drink already this morning.

"Must have been hot, screaming at the roosters, wearing that rubber suit."

"Several areas were unzipped, for ventilation, if I recall. The lady is nothing if not well displayed."

"When did you spot Modesto?"

"Just before the cockfight came to an end. And then he
invited Gayla Jean to dance."

"Where was Philo all this time?"

"In and out. One minute he'd be there, watching the
cocks stab each other to death. The next minute, he'd
vanish."

"How many people at these parties, anyway?"

"I'd estimate two hundred."

I whistled. Philo had some bucks. "Every Saturday?"

"More like every third Saturday. There's a lot of informal partying . . . during the week—Philo keeps his house filled with these runaway beach types—but the formal gatherings are more for the society people who get bored driving up to Los Angeles."

"Remember the first thing Modesto did?"

"I saw him staring at Gayla Jean across the sand of the fighting arena. I was in perfect position. She recognized him, and began to flirt . . . with that terrible magnetism. I felt . . . pain."

"What happened then, Mr. Dean?"

"The cockfight was over. Some men came to add fresh sand. Someone ran a huge industrial vacuum. The music started. They danced."

"What did you do?"

"I danced, too. First, with a girl from the beach. A very pretty girl. Her name was Cindi or Teri or Cheri. Something with an i. And then with Lucinda Smith-Travis."

"Was she wearing her rubber suit?"

"No." Dean looked away from me, then dug into his watch pocket and pulled out a grandfather watch. He checked it, wound it like it was a normal day in Laguna, and put it back. "That night, she wore a black blouse with hardly any front and some of those baggy pantaloons, from France. She . . . ah . . . seldom wore a brassiere. And she is . . . ah . . . very tanned."

"How long did Modesto and Gayla Jean dance?"

"Oh, several times, I'd say. Then one of Philo's men tapped him on the shoulder, and Modesto followed the man out of the room. The cockfights started again. A woman vomited. She was from Newport Beach, I believe. I didn't see Gayla Jean for awhile."

"Had she ever known Modesto before?"

"I don't think so. How could she?"

"She could have been a movie groupie," I said. "What did you do then?"

"The next time I saw her she was in a corner, talking with Modesto. His face was sweating and his smile was sardonic, like he had just put one over . . . on dear Philo. I know now Modesto was persuading her to come with him. It made me sick. They left together, through a door into a rock garden. I followed."

"You wanted her back, right?"

"She had awakened me. I was helpless before her."

"What happened then?"

"I saw them getting into Modesto's car. Before I could reach my car, a second . . . er . . . car pulled out and followed them. I was hurrying, so I dropped my keys, and then my Saab slid off the road at Bluebird Park. I had to wait for a red stop signal in town. By the time I . . ." He stopped, shook his head, wiped his bleary eyes.

"What kind of car was it, Mr. Dean?"

"A van, I think. A large van."

"Do you know who owns it?"

"No." He looked away.

"What did you do then?"

"I followed them through town. I had no idea what I would do when I caught up with them—Lido Landing is a security building, and I knew she wouldn't let me in—but once you've been deserted by one woman, you don't somehow relish being deserted by another, especially by one so young. The town was deserted at that hour. My dashboard clock said three twenty-six, but it . . . ah . . . runs consistently behind, which meant the time was actually three thirty-one. I rounded the last curve before leaving town when I saw the glow of the fire, magnified by the fog. I knew it was a horrible accident. My heart told me it involved Gayla Jean. I slowed down for the curve, and for a thick bank of fog. When I came through that patch of fog, I saw the fire."

Ellis Dean stopped, buried his face in his hands, started sobbing. He stood up jerkily and walked to the sink to splash his face with tap water. He blew his nose with the big handkerchief. While he finished his story, he leaned wearily against the sink.

"There's a low hill right there, so that you can look down on what's happening. I saw the car, in flames. I knew without any doubt that it was Modesto's. I cried her name aloud, and then I saw the flame, shooting out from the middle of the highway in a long arcing stream, and I knew from television footage about guerrilla warfare it was a flamethrower and that someone was murdering her."

Dean shook his head. Crying had made his eyes red and weepy again. He looked like a drowned rat. "I acted mechanically. If I had been a law officer, I would have been armed. As it was, all I had was a camera. I cannot tell you how defenseless and ineffectual I felt, taking pictures. I had time for only five. Perhaps I acted wrongly. It was . . . all I could do."

I let the silence build before I asked him.

"Who was in the pictures, Mr. Dean?"

"I . . . I told you. I'm not sure."

"Somebody tried to kill you last night, Mr. Dean. Who was it?"

He shook his head, pulled out the big gold watch again, checked the time. When he spoke, staring at the floor, he was talking mostly to himself.

"I have . . . a plan. It's already in motion. If it works, I will have—perhaps this sounds silly—I will have avenged her death. Nothing can bring her back. But I have to be free to attempt this on my own."

"I might be able to help."

He glanced up. There was a slight ironic smile on his lips. He was one sad-looking dude.

"You already have. You saved my life last night. You listened to my confession."

"They mean business, Mr. Dean. We need to check with the cops."

"No. No police. Not yet. There's not enough . . . the evidence is purely circumstantial, as they say."

He was standing firm. I argued with him a couple more minutes, but he wouldn't budge. He was a short guy out to prove himself a man by taking revenge on the killers of Gayla Jean Kirkwood, the girl who could raise the dead. I had a feeling old Philo Waddell was mixed up in it, but, like the man said, we didn't have much proof.

Dean let out a long sigh. "I think I'll sleep now. The memorial service is at twelve-thirty." He looked at my outfit. "You'll probably want to change."

"We can swing by my place," I said. "Where's the service?"

"Sonderson's," he said. "Over in Laguna Hills."

"We can leave early," I said, wondering about the state of my single dress shirt. "I may have to buy a shirt."

He eyed me, a little guy checking out a bigger guy. "Too bad we're not the same size," he said. "I have dozens."

"Yeah," I said. "It is."

He left me sitting there, watching the last of the rain drip off the eaves, and went to get some rest. I poured more coffee, buttered another croissant, and thought about helping him with his revenge.

6

Every head turned to stare at Meg Kirkwood when she entered Sonderson's Funeral Chapel. The scorched remains of her sister rested up front, in a closed coffin. The coffin was buried under a mountain of California springtime flowers.

Everyone else stared. But my client Ellis Dean came close to dropping into cardiac arrest.

"Gayla Jean—my God!" Dean's face went white. He broke into a sticky sweat, choked out her name. And before I could grab him, Dean was up out of the pew and running on wobbly legs toward Gayla Jean's sister.

"Gayla!" Dean cried. "Gayla Jean!" His arms were spread wide for a welcome-home embrace. He was half running, half walking, as if his legs hadn't made up their mind how fast to close the distance between himself and the lady in dark tweed. For her part, she had stopped moving to look at Dean. For support, she leaned on the arm of her companion, a big fat-faced jowly dude with mean eyes that were too close together. He reminded me of a right guard gone to fat, weight about 240, and he was still hanging onto his leisure suit—a pale blue polyester job that was probably right in style back home. As Dean approached, Leisure Suit patted Meg Kirkwood on the arm and moved forward for the intercept.

Dean figured it out before he got there. He wasn't a dumb guy, but getting involved with Gayla Jean had strung him out, like wet washing on a sagging clothesline. Other folks looked at her as if she was a ghost, sniffing the air for a welcome break in the burial routine we will all have to endure one day.

Dean stopped, stumbled, almost fell. Leisure Suit was ready to kill. I was eight steps away, behind Dean, and not looking forward to tangling with Leisure Suit.

"Oh, dear God," Dean said, mournfully. "You're not Gayla Jean." He said it again. "You're not Gayla. She's dead."

Meg Kirkwood touched poor old Dean on the arm, murmured something that I didn't hear. Over his bowed head, she looked at me. I saw something there that I liked. Decision. Purpose. Brains. Then she and Leisure Suit kept on moving toward the pew reserved for family of the deceased.

White-faced and gulping for air, Dean stumbled back to slump down in the pew. He used up about a minute doing the terrible shakes. Sonorous music pumped across the room. Then he looked at me with tears in his eyes and shook his head.

I felt sad for him. But I understood what he was going through. He had given up the good life in Laguna for Gayla Jean and she had left him hanging at Philo's while she skipped out with the Mexican kid, and now Meg Kirkwood appears, sedate and beautiful, looking like the apparition of her dead sister, and Dean goes bananas.

I wondered if she knew how she affected folks, looking that way.

Dean and I were sitting four rows back, on the left. In front of us were three pretty girls who I guessed were waitress pals of the deceased. Meg Kirkwood was up front, on the right, and as she turned her head away from Leisure Suit, I had a long look at her profile. It was superior. Good mouth. Eyes of Pacific blue. Cheekbones that could have put her on the cover of *Cosmo*. Except the lady from Fort Worth didn't look like a carefree *Cosmo* girl. Behind the careful walk and the carefully composed face, I sensed vulnerability, magic, a sense of doom. I couldn't put my finger on it. The severe hairdo was right. The dark tweed suit was perfect. The hand she'd reached out to Ellis Dean was real, warm, human. Yet, there was something about the way she moved that—

The lady had radar. Because just as the preacher walked in wearing his black robes, she felt me watching her and turned to see who it was and our eyes locked across the heads of the mourners of Gayla Jean Kirkwood. I had the strong sense her sister was trying to send me a message.

That was all there was. She turned. Our eyes met. She held my gaze for a quick instant, then turned away to whisper something to old Leisure Suit. He nodded heavily, looking thick and protective.

The memorial service was brief. The minister, a young-ish reverend with a beach tan and a carefully trimmed mustache, talked to us about the awful waste of youth. He had thick red lips and the only thing he did well was read something from the Bible. "Ashes to ashes," the line reads, "Dust, dust, dust."

Sonderson's Chapel is located in Laguna Hills on the ocean side of the San Diego Freeway, near a retirement community called Leisure World. Today was not my first trip. Sonderson's has what funeral marketeers call the "traditional" look. They've done the place up with hardwood paneling, highly polished, and shiny brass fittings that give it a nineteenth century feel. You have to hand it to them. Sonderson's has kept the Age of Plastic to a minimum. The music is semiclassical instead of warmed-over Lawrence Welk. And when you come in, they hand out black armbands. Some funeral parlors have forgotten about armbands.

The reason I had been there before was that Sonderson's gets a lot of out-of-town trade and some of them had been clients, or relatives of clients. I'm not sure why they chose Sonderson's. Maybe Sonderson's belongs to an undertaker's association, and relatives of people who die out of town call home and get referred. Or maybe out-of-towners who end their days on the sunny California coast are pulled to Sonderson's by occult forces. The pews are padded. There's always a heap of flowers. If you have to wind up in a coffin when you're twenty-three and reaching for Hollywood and the silver California moon, it might as well be at Sonderson's.

After the service, we drove in a cortege over to Harbor Lawn, in Costa Mesa. The sun was out, for a change. I drove Dean's Saab Turbo, a sweet piece of iron. Dean took the passenger seat. A little color had come back to his face. We were the last car. The car in front of us was a superdoop Mercedes 450 diesel. "That's Philo," Dean said. "In the Mercedes."

"Nice car," I said.

"Philo lives the good life twenty-four hours a day."

"I didn't see him inside."

"He wasn't there," Dean said.

The good life was showing on Philo, especially when he turned corners, taking these wide fat cat swings across the yellow divider and out into the other lane. I figured him for a big dude, and they drive like that. Big dudes get used to taking more than their share of everything—food, money, liquor, road. I didn't even know Philo Waddell, and I was already mad at him.

At the gravesite, I stood across the opening from Meg Kirkwood, Leisure Suit, the covey of slim-hipped waitresses, and an old party in a blazer and red ascot who gazed at the flower-covered coffin with sad, bleary eyes. He was old money, Spyglass Hill, Ritz Carlton Hotel, Corona Del Mar. During the service, Meg Kirkwood looked at me twice, and I looked back. Who was this statue lady? Every so often, she'd shift her weight ever so slightly. The third time she did it, I knew what it was—Meg Kirkwood had an artificial left leg, probably from the knee down. To compensate, the right leg curved like perfection itself. There is a God, after all.

Some folks leave the grave as soon as the burial words have died on the wind. They get depressed. They need to lie down, to mourn, to drink, to eat, to forget. But Meg Kirkwood had come to stay awhile. She asked Leisure Suit to bring her a chair, and while the shoveling machine cranked away, filling her sister's grave with California dirt, she sat staring into space, ankles crossed, a white hankie pressed up against her nice wide mouth.

Watching her sitting there, you'd never know about the leg.

Dean left me for awhile to have a chat with his tennis pal, Philo Waddell. Waddell was dressed in an expensive business suit, gray, with a conservative tie. More like Vegas Mafia than Laguna Beach art dealer. I was about to march over and introduce myself and tell Meg Kirkwood how sorry I was about her loss when Webby Smith arrived.

Webster Smith is a lieutenant and watch commander in the Laguna Beach PD. Webby looks like a young version of Harry Morgan, the actor who played Jack Webb's sidekick on "Dragnet." I was an army brat who grew up on "Dragnet."

Webby's short, about Dean's size, only thicker across the chest and heftier. To stay sane in police work, he runs marathons. Last year, at the age of forty-two, he decided to train for the Iron Man, that triathlon killer event they hold in Hawaii. He was in better shape than any guy his age around. He won the bike part, but was way down in the swimming.

"Hello, there, Ironside," Webby said. "You must be working. Nothing else would bring you out at this hour."

"You owe me a lunch, Webby. For that case I cracked for you at Christmastime."

"Let's subtract that one from the five you owe me. Now you only owe me four. What say the Ritz, this time tomorrow? Or maybe the Chanticleer. It's my day off."

"Your accountant is blind, Lieutenant."

"That's the best kind, Murdock. You know the deceased? Or have you taken to chasing hearses?"

I figured I didn't have anything to lose, so I told him. "That's my client, over there, talking to one of the two sumo wrestlers at this party."

"Ellis Dean? You working for him?"

"The same. You know Ellis?"

"Sure, I know Ellis. The department broke his heart when we turned him down for our reserve officer program," Webby said. "We had all these applicants with military experience, MP's and the like, and in comes this guy with an MBA and a three-page résumé that took us all the way back to his mama's tit."

"He could have done phone duty," I said.

"Not him. These reserve boys crave action. Most of them are married—unhappily—and they need an excuse to get out of the house and play cops and robbers. What are you doing for Dean?"

56

"Bodyguard."

"Who from? His shadow?"

"Good guess," I said, grinning.

"Have you ever thought about taking up some honest work, Murdock? Even back at the academy, you loafed along. How long have you been on Dean's dole?"

Before I could come up with an answer with some teeth, a lady appeared at Webby's elbow. She was a trim little brunette, five-four or so, with horn-rimmed glasses and a turned-up nose that probably got her elected cheerleader back in high school. For her, high school had to be about six years ago. She had a good California tan, dark eyes, and a way of talking that made her stand about six inches too close. Webby Smith was between us, but I still caught the strategic drift of perfume. "Hello, lieutenant. How are you?"

"Hey, it's Brenda Starr. You don't give up, do you?"

"You have your official opinion, lieutenant. I have my reporter's nose."

She was standing next to Webby, studying me with a critical eye. Reporters are not all smart, but most of them are cynical and world-weary, which makes them seem smart. The smile on her face as she looked at my funeral outfit was amused. So as not to embarrass my client, I'd changed into an old tweed coat and some halfway decent cords. I was wearing the brown knit tie and a white shirt. I'd gone to some trouble dressing, but it probably didn't cut much ice with the brunette. Maybe she was used to corporate Orange County types.

"You're Matt Murdock, aren't you? The famous private eye?"

Webby grinned. He liked that. "Mr. Murdock, meet Teresa Aiken. She writes for the OC *Tribune*. Weddings. Funerals."

"Murders," she said.

Webby's smile dimmed. The trim brunette held out her hand. I took it. It was a nice warm hand, and she held on longer than she needed to. "You don't remember me, I'll bet."

"No," I said. "But I read your stuff in the Sunday *Trib*. You have a way with a tight chronology."

Teresa Aiken didn't bat an eye. "Six years ago—no, make that seven—you gave a talk to my senior class at Fullerton High. I interviewed you afterward, for the school paper."

I vaguely remembered the faces, smooth youth, sighs of boredom, acne, gleam of teenage knees. "What was the talk on?"

"Law enforcement as a career," she said. "You influenced seven boys, as I remember. Two of them are in law school, studying to be FBI agents. Three became cops. Two work for drug enforcement."

"Hooray for the law," I said. "How did I affect you?"

"My story won second prize in a regional journalism contest. I still have my little silver plaque."

"You should have sent me a copy."

"I did."

Webby Smith was grinning, enjoying the lady as she worked on me instead of him. "Murdock, the guru of law enforcement. I didn't know you were on the lecture circuit, Murdock."

"Weak moment." I studied Miss Teresa Aiken. Behind the lenses, her eyes were sharp, probing. And from what I could see, she had a nice tight beach-girl ass. She turned to face Webby Smith.

"Anything new, lieutenant?"

"On what?" Webby gave her his Official Police Look.

"You know on what. The Modesto/Kirkwood accident—so-called."

58

Webby stared at her. "Nothing. It's on the books as an accident, Miss Aiken. Pure and simple. Cut and dried."

"Let me see the reports, lieutenant. You owe me one."

"Those are classified. You know that. Go back to your weddings."

"But there's something there. Can't you smell it?"

"No," Webby said, and walked off to speak to Meg Kirkwood.

Over against a small tree, Ellis Dean was still locked in conversation with Philo Waddell. The three waitresses were picking their way through the wet grass, high heels stabbing the earth. They were all tall, leggy, with terrible blank faces and unison hips.

Teresa Aiken turned to me. "Are you working, Mr. Murdock?"

"I'm a government spy." I had been, once.

Instead of following that one up, she shifted ground. "One of my pals on the paper covered the Kamrath case. Jane Birch. I caught up on your noble profession by reading Jane's notes. Remember Jane?"

Sure, I remembered Jane. Redhead in her mid-thirties. Sassy. Freckles across the bridge of her nose. Couldn't stay too long in the sun. Favorite drink was stingers. Ate Texas chili for breakfast, which was why we got along. Divorced. One child. Liked to make love wearing knee-boots. A pleasant memory of sex on Saturday afternoons, when the kid was out playing. I remembered Lady Jane.

"Sure thing," I said to Teresa Aiken. "She still at the paper?"

"No. She remarried and now she lives in Seattle."

"Nice lady," I said, feeling a stab of jealousy for something lost, something irretrievable.

"Jane thinks you discovered the real killer in the Kamrath case. She says you showed up the police."

"The butler did it," I said.

"She wanted to write about it, about your part in it. But you wouldn't let her."

"Get too famous in this business and you're no good. People know your face, and you can't get information."

"That's what Jane said you said."

Teresa Aiken was biting her lip when I turned to look at her. She was a brassy kid, pert, bouncy—the kind of girl who grows up on California beaches, playing volleyball, smoking a little pot, not knowing much else besides sun and more sun—and now she was clawing her way along the world of words and hot news they called journalism. Even Californians grow up.

I didn't want to be news. I also knew she wanted something from me. You could smell ambition on her.

"Sounds like you and Lieutenant Smith disagree about how those folks died."

"I was there within an hour after it happened. I saw the car after it got burnt up. You could almost smell the evil. Did they tell you she tried to crawl away?"

"No."

"That's why there was more of her. She tried to crawl away from the burning car."

"I didn't know that."

"You didn't answer my question, Mr. Murdock."

"Which one is that?"

"Are you working?"

"If I tell you, will you print it?"

"Not if it's off the record."

"I'm working."

"Who for?"

I knew she'd find out when she saw me drive off with Ellis Dean in his Saab, so I told her I was a security consultant for Dean. She looked past me to where Ellis was talking with Philo. She moved a step closer to me, and I felt body heat. She was a sexy little number. I wondered how far she'd go to see those pictures by Ellis Dean. The thought made me smile.

"Security consultant?" Her voice was packed with disbelief.

"That's right." I crinkled my eyes and gave her my Clint Eastwood smile.

"Did you say security consultant?"

I nodded.

"Who's after him? And why?"

"Sorry. Privileged info."

She laughed. It was an involuntary explosion, and if there had been a grape between her teeth, it would have plunged between my eyes as she let out a whoof. I watched her laugh. Pretty to watch. Feisty. But too young for me.

She whipped out a business card. "You're fibbing to me. I don't know why, but a girl can tell, especially if she's in this line of work. I think maybe you and I can help each other. That's my number. Call me anytime. If I'm not there, leave a message."

"Okay."

"You don't buy it, do you?"

"Buy what?"

"My idea. That they were murdered."

"Say they were. Where would you go from there?"

"Where would you go?"

"Back to bed," I said.

She laughed again, a throaty sound, from a young lady with experience. "You're too much."

"Thanks."

"But do me a favor first?"

"Okay."

"Make sure you *want* to call, okay?"

"Just business, right?"

"Sure," she said, turning to go. "Just business. Or a talk. Or lunch. Yes." She paused. "Lunch."

Teresa Aiken walked away from me, giving her hips that extra little swing that means a woman has read your masculine intent and has maneuvered pieces on the board so that it's now her advantage. I never know how it happens. Until I see the hips swinging, I'm not even sure it has. Hips tell more than eyes.

Over across the green lawn, Dean stood alone while Philo Waddell moved like a great mastodon toward his Mercedes. Clutching his fists together in frustration, Dean motioned for me to get moving, and I was reminded of the way he'd signaled Donna last night for more drinks. Ellis Dean got power from buying people. Just then, Webby Smith came up with Meg Kirkwood.

"Matt Murdock, I'd like you to meet Ms. Kirkwood." Webby was trying to be nice. For the time being, he'd dropped his watch commander's voice. "Ms. Kirkwood is the sister of the deceased."

I held out my hand. "Sorry about your trouble, ma'am."

"Yes. Thank you." Her hand was cool and her pale blue eyes stared at me out of an expressionless face. One strand of strawberry blonde hair had broken loose from the tight capped arrangement on her head and was blowing in the breeze.

I'd seen her use the handkerchief and I'd assumed she'd been crying. Now, up close, I didn't see any evidence of tears. What I saw was a super good-looking woman, unsmiling, out of her element. A woman a little uncertain of herself. A woman hunting for something.

"Lieutenant Smith says you might be able to help me, Mr. Murdock." Her voice had a trace of Texas. Echoes of my lost childhood—Fort Hood, Fort Bliss, Fort Sill.

I gave Webby the eye. He was using the woman to ease out of that lunch he owed me.

"What seems to be the problem?"

"It's—it's my sister, Gayla Jean. She lived—" Meg Kirkwood stopped, looked around. "I don't know anything about her life out here. The lieutenant seems to think you could help me—investigate—and I was wondering what you might charge for a couple of days . . . of your time."

Over Meg Kirkwood's left shoulder I saw Ellis Dean. Ellis Dean was my client. Meg Kirkwood was a beauty, but I have a certain code of conduct. One client at a time. Maybe there was a way out.

"When were you thinking of getting started?"

"Soon. Today. This afternoon. Billy Bob—I mean, Mr. Marshall—we have to get back to Fort Worth. I wanted to spend a couple of days, sort of, well, just looking around at what she. . . ."

I sighed. "Wish I could help, ma'am, but I've got a client right now. And he's full time."

"Oh!" Her voice registered disappointment, but the muscles in her face didn't change. "Are you sure?"

I nodded, threw another look at Ellis Dean. I still wasn't ready to give in. I could call Tommy Joe Breed, my Indian pal, switch him over to bodyguard duty on Dean. Then I could work for the lady. "Tell me where you're staying. Maybe I can work something out."

"The Newporter. It's on—" She looked at Webby.

"Jamboree Road," he said.

"Yes," she said. "Boy Scouts."

"Murdock!" Ellis Dean called. "Murdock! Come on!"

"That poor man," she said. "He knew my sister, didn't he?"

"Yes."

"Perhaps I could talk to him about her?"

"I'll check," I said. I took one last look at Meg Kirkwood's eyes and then moved off to join my client in his Saab Turbo.

7

Back at Ellis Dean's comfy hillside home above Laguna Beach, I drank a Heineken's with my ham and cheese sandwich while Dean, who said he wasn't hungry, locked himself in his study. In the service, I learned you should eat whenever you had a break in the shooting. The second beer made me sleepy, so I closed the miniblinds against the afternoon sun and stretched out on the couch. I dreamed about Meg, mirrors, cameras, and gorgeous Gayla Jean.

In the dream, I was alone in a room full of mirrors with a camera in one hand and a .45 automatic in the other. I was sitting on a white couch, dressed in a tuxedo, and then one of the mirrors slid aside and I realized it was a doorway and beyond, through the doorway, I could see rows and rows of costumes, and then a woman stepped through and I saw it was Meg Kirkwood, on crutches. She wore silver shoes, dark stockings and a clinging, filmy purple dress that accented the fine curves of her figure, and as the door closed, I had the impression that she was there to have her picture taken, so I set the .45 automatic on one of the couch cushions and raised the camera to my face and began snapping photos, and after each one the room would blaze up because of the white flash, and the bright light would linger a half minute or more, making my eyes water, and then, after the sixth or seventh shot, Meg Kirkwood threw the crutches down and began to take the pins out of her hair. The way she stood made it seem like she had two good legs, but then a voice whispered it wasn't Meg standing there, but her sister. I wasn't surprised. From behind me, I heard a bell ring, once, then again, so I looked around because I didn't remember seeing a telephone anywhere, and when I turned back Meg was leaving the room, wearing nothing but the silver spike heels and the dark stockings. She was almost through the mirrored doorway when I caught a glimpse of bare curved bottom. Unleashed, her golden red hair fell to the middle of her back. The purple dress lay in a puddle on the floor, where she had dropped it. The crutches were nowhere to be seen. I dropped the camera and picked up the .45, which I aimed at the doorway. I fired, the mirror shattered, and I came awake, sitting up on Dean's couch, grabbing for my shoulder holster.

Nothing moved. The sun was low in the west. Shadows slanted across the room. I stood up, shakily, holding the .357, and moved to the door of Dean's study, which was still closed. He was on the phone with someone. I pressed closer to the door. His voice was sharp-pitched and afraid. He was trying to threaten and push whomever he was talking to, and he wasn't having much luck. There was a pause at our end of the phone while Dean listened, and then he set a time for some kind of meeting.

"All right," he said. "But no later. I warn you. Don't keep me waiting."

I didn't hear any hesitation now, just anger. And maybe defeat.

Through the door, I heard him hang up the phone. When he unlocked the door and swung it open, I was back on the couch, scratching my head, stretching. Matt Murdock, Oscar nominee.

"I trust you had a restful afternoon."

"Not bad." This time, I yawned for real.

Dean walked over to where I sat and handed me a folded check. I opened it. The check was for $200. Today's date.

"What's this?"

"For services rendered." His voice had the finality of a pink slip. "As of this moment, they are no longer required."

It was too much, guilt money, getting me out of the way. I tried to hand the check back. "You sure about this. Those hard guys are still out there."

"Things have changed, Mr. . . . ah . . . Murdock. Things are coming . . . to a head. Now, if you don't mind, I have some things . . . to attend to."

He was showing me the door. I shook my head. Dean was on a suicide mission. "Who was on the phone?"

He stopped, sucked in his gut, bantam fighter, ready to hit the ring. He thought he had the bull by the balls. "That's none of your business. Now, please?"

I sighed, pulled on my boots, stood. In five minutes, I was out of Dean's house, sitting in a cul-de-sac at the bottom of the hill where the Saab had to come out. One of the beauties of a hill town like Laguna Beach is that what goes up has got to come down, the same way. The dashboard clock said 5:15. I figured I'd give him an hour to show, but I didn't have to wait that long. At 5:29, the little Saab eased down the hill, so I followed it through town to the Laguna Canyon Road.

There are three ways out of Laguna Beach. Heading north, you can take Coast Highway up to Newport and Corona Del Mar. Heading south, you can take Coast Highway to Dana Point and the freeway to San Clemente. Heading east, away from the Pacific, you take Laguna Canyon Road inland through El Toro to the San Diego Freeway.

Dean took the Canyon Road. Incoming traffic from the freeway was heavy, but Dean was heading northeast, and he kept the Saab at 55 mph all the way. I had no idea where his rendezvous was, but I owed him for a couple more days' work, and Murdock's Code kept me tailing him. I kept three vehicles as a buffer in between the Saab and my Plymouth. I could see him up ahead about fifty yards, red taillights heavy in the gathering gloom, and after we passed the El Toro turnoff, the road went straight to the freeway.

A couple of miles this side of the San Diego Freeway, two sweet boys in a red open-top MG decided to pass because the middle-aged traffic was too slow, and when they were even with me, giggling and straining ahead and showing teeth, a truck appeared in the right lane, bearing down on them and blowing its air horn, so they swerved my way to save their butts from becoming peanut butter, and I swerved off the road, jockeyed the Plymouth across a construction culvert, stalled her out, and by the time I got back onto the road, Dean's Saab was out of sight.

I punched the accelerator, wound the mill up to seventy-five, passed a couple of cars like they were tied to a tree, and made the San Diego Freeway in less than a minute. No sign of Dean. Southbound traffic, heading toward Mission Viejo, Carlsbad, and San Diego, was crawling like a metal snake, but the northbound stream to Long Beach and L.A. was zipping along. I had the feeling Dean had to go north, so I did the same, but it was no use. I lost him, somewhere between the Laguna Freeway and MacArthur. I exited at the 55 freeway and headed back to the beach.

I was almost home when I decided to check out Grogan's Grogerie, where Gayla Jean had worked. Grogan's was part of the posh outfit called Le Club of Newport Beach, a combined tennis and yachting facility that catered to the rich and the nouveau riche and gave old guys with money someplace to take hard-body girls for a drink and some images of the good life. I'd been a regular at Grogan's a year or so ago, as the guest of a potential client named Charles Vardeen, who had wanted me to locate some ex-business partners who owed him money. This night, I used Vardeen's name going in. The uniform at the gate gave my venerable Plymouth a suspicious look, but let me go on through to the visitors' lot. I was still wearing my funeral regalia—white shirt, knitted brown tie, tweed jacket—and I figured that's what really snowed the guard.

Walking across the parking lot to Grogan's, I encountered a foursome coming off the courts. Two gals in their early twenties, two gray-haired fellows in their mature years. The gals were slender and coiffed and sported sleek Acapulco tans. The boys had money and the latest in tennis gear. One of the boys looked familiar, but his old eyes slid off me like a fish off Alaskan ice. I followed the foursome into Grogan's.

They had remodeled since I had been there with Chick

Vardeen—new carpet, more glass, higher prices, skimpier costumes on the waitresses. I sat at the bar and ordered a beer, and when it came I drank off the first half before deciding I didn't need to drink alone, so I went to a phone and called Meg Kirkwood first, to tell her I was free and could now accept her gracious offer of employment, and when Meg didn't answer I left a message. Then I pulled out the card with Teresa Aiken's phone number on it and dialed. She answered on the sixth ring.

"It's me, Murdock. Your favorite private eye."

"Oh, hi!" She sounded breathless. "I just walked in and I was afraid it was you."

"Afraid?"

"Sorry. I meant 'hope.' I hoped it was you."

"That's better. I was wondering if you'd like to assist me in my investigation."

"What are you investigating?"

"The disappearance of a client," I said.

"What does that mean?"

"It means," I said, "that I have been dismissed, pistol and all, by one Ellis Dean, who has ventured off on his own private crusade, and that I am starting an investigation in which I desire your help."

"Murdock, are you drunk?"

"No. But I intend to get that way."

"Where are you, anyway?"

"Grogan's Grogerie, in the heart of Le Club, located just off Pacific Coast Highway, across from—"

She didn't let me finish. "Isn't that where Gayla Jean Kirkwood worked as a waitress?"

"The same."

"Le Club's private," she said. "How did you get in?"

"Power of the press," I said. "I used your name."

She laughed. Over the phone, it sounded good, and I

had the feeling the lady was impressed. When you've just been fired, my dad used to say, the sound of a woman's laughter helps you forget the lumps. He should know. After the army, he was fired a lot.

"Give me half an hour," she said.

"Use the name Vardeen," I said. "Chick Vardeen. He's a member."

"You devil."

It started to rain while I was waiting, so I moved to corral the last table from wet tennis players drifting in from the courts. My waitress was named Lenore, according to her nameplate, and she had not been at the funeral. Lenore said Gayla Jean had been very popular with the customers, and that she was always talking about quitting and making it big in the movies. As Lenore was bringing my second beer, a man about sixty came in, wearing an Ellis Dean-type Burberry, and took a seat at the bar. His gray hair gleamed from an expensive razor cut. He wore a blazer, gray slacks, a red ascot. This afternoon, he had stood across from me at Gayla Jean's funeral, at Harbor Lawn. Monday night at Grogan's was looking like old home week.

Teresa Aiken came in with the last of the tennis crowd. Under a plastic raincoat that had seen better days, she wore the same Girl Reporter tweeds she'd had on at the funeral. She spotted me before I stood up to wave her over. As she sat down, she gave me a quick, sisterly kiss on the cheek. I smelled fresh girl, rain, tweeds, newsprint.

"You're not drunk," she said.

"Soon."

"That was an act, over the phone. To get my sympathy."

"What are you drinking, lady?"

70

"Martini on the rocks, please. It's been a grueling day."

"You must want to catch up fast."

"Um," she said.

I waved at Lenore, who took our order. Teresa brought out a man-sized handkerchief and wiped the rain off her glasses.

"How do you feel about rain, Murdock?"

"In Southern California, it's okay. In Viet Nam, a good rain can get your ass shot off."

"I like rain," she said, shifting herself in the seat. "When were you in Viet Nam?"

"1964 to 1968," I said. "Just over three-and-a-half years."

"1964?" she said. "Wasn't that kind of early?"

"They needed heroes," I said.

"Ha ha. Tell the truth."

"I went over as a small-arms trainer. I had a house trailer, all the booze I could drink, and a fresh Hollywood starlet every two weeks." I grinned at her and drank some beer.

"How much of that is true?"

"On the record, boss," I said. "Print it on page one."

"How many beers have you had, anyway?"

"Enough to ask you a favor, boss."

"Don't call me that, okay?"

"Okay."

"What's the favor?"

I looked at the old party at the bar, in the blazer and ascot, and then I said, "I thought I might listen in while you asked questions about Gayla Jean Kirkwood."

"You want me to quiz the waitresses? The way they're not dressed, I thought that might be more your style."

"I can quiz the waitresses. But the gentleman at the bar

was at the funeral. I thought you might try your luck with him."

Her face clouded in disappointment. "Don't tell me you brought a nice girl like me out in the rain for this?"

I spread my hands, an Irish gesture I learned from my grandfather Murdock. "Just a suggestion. Might produce a lead. Might not."

"Murdock, you're a rascal."

"Just earning a living."

"What do you get out of this?" She was frowning at me, trying to make up her mind.

"Fighting evil, always," I said. And then, in a whisper: "Meet you outside in half an hour."

She sat there, not moving, staring at me, her pretty mouth half-open in astonishment. Then her face took on a shrewd look, and I knew she had taken the bait. Ambition wins out, every time. A good reporter can be seduced by the mere whisper of a story.

"Well," she said, loudly, to the room. "Have it your way, Jack." She stood up, suddenly, snatched her raincoat, and intercepted Lenore, who was coming with Teresa's martini. "Bring my drink to the bar, will you, hon?"

I was impressed. The lady was an actress.

Lenore gave me a look, then followed Teresa Aiken to the bar with her drink on a tray. The reporter took a seat one down from the old party. I paid my tab and wandered to the men's room. After that I wandered to the foyer, where a slick-haired dude in a tuxedo with a frilly shirt was presiding over a gold-embossed reservations list. The dude gave me the fish eye.

"Have you a reservation, sir?"

"No."

The dude consulted his list, frowning. "I have very few singles, sir."

"No problem. I'll just wait here for a table, if that's okay with you."

The dude sniffed the air. "Very good, sir. It might be awhile."

"No problem." I sat down and folded my arms.

"Might I have your name, sir?"

"Vardeen," I said.

"Really? Are you related to Charles Vardeen?"

"Chick's my baby brother," I said. "I'm Roy Vardeen." I held out my hand, Texas style, and hoped he wasn't an ace with accents. He wasn't. "Howdy," I said.

"In that case, Mr. Vardeen, I think we can seat you sooner. I'll have a table set up right away."

I smiled. "Thanks, partner. I'm starved."

The tuxedo hustled off, leaving me alone. He was gone awhile. In this business, you get used to waiting. You either get good at it, or you get into another business.

He came back at the same time Teresa Aiken walked out of Grogan's. She was alone. She moved right up to me with a reporter's gleam in her eye.

"Take me home. I have lots to tell."

And at the same time, the dude said: "We have your table, Mr. Vardeen."

"You want to eat, babe?" I asked Teresa.

She gave me a look. "Not *here!*" she said. She was busting with news. She wanted to talk. So we waltzed out of there, and she followed me in her little yellow Toyota across the bridge to my place near the pier, where we feasted on Budweiser and garlic bread and homemade chili from Joe's Place down the street. Joe is from Gonzales, Texas. His real name is Josef. He's part Mexican and part German-Czech and part something else that's wilder than both, and he makes the best damned chili in the southwest. Over the meal, Teresa Aiken told me what she'd learned from the old party. It wasn't much. Or maybe it was, and she wasn't telling me everything.

"His name is Jack D. Downs, and he's a stockbroker. He used to work for Merrill Lynch, but now he owns his own agency, with offices in Newport Beach. Mr. Downs met Gayla Jean at Grogan's, 'squired her around,' as he calls it, and was very sad when she died."

"How old do you figure he is, our Mr. Jack D. Downs?"

"Oh, sixty, sixty-five. But when he shook my hand, he made a very smooth run at me. Did I mention he sails?"

"Did he take Gayla Jean out on the boat?"

"Yes. Several times. To meet some people from Hollywood," he said.

"Happen to get their names?"

"I tried, but he wouldn't give. A girl can only probe so far."

"Did he mention going to a modeling session that starred Gayla Jean?"

"No. Where did you learn that?"

"She did some modeling. If we find out who went to those sessions, we might know more about why she died."

"What if she died because she was with Modesto?"

"Then we need to find out why Modesto died."

"This is your trade. What do you think?"

"I think this is the best chili in the world," I said, and stood up to refill my bowl. "You?"

"I'm stuffed," she said, looking around. "This is a nice place, even though it needs cleaning. How long have you lived here, anyway?"

74

"Five years last Christmas," I said. "I inherited it from my Uncle Walt."

"You got a great deal. My place is a hundred miles from the beach."

"It was a good deal," I admitted.

"Why did he leave it to you?"

"Uncle Walt and I got along," I said. "He taught me to build stuff when I was a kid, and when I got out of the service I used to stop by for a beer. Building these cabinets kept me from going crazy." I indicated the kitchen cabinets, a solid testimony to stability and craftsmanship.

"Somehow, you don't look to me like a builder of cabinets."

"What does a builder of cabinets look like?"

"Not like you."

"I have also been known to build a house or two."

"Man of many talents. Tell me more."

"I was also a crime reporter for *The New York Times*," I said, grinning. "In my youth."

"No kidding? When?"

"Oh, back in the thirties. During the Great Depression."

Recognition dawned when she computed that and discovered that Irish fib would have made me even older than I was, and the next thing I knew she was pounding me on the chest with her small brown fists, laughing and calling me a bum and a rascal and before I caught her wrists she landed a couple of shots to my head and grazed my nose, and then we were on the couch, and she was laughing even harder and squirming and I smelled the fresh scent of her, and then her eyes got that hooded look that signaled a smooth feminine gear shift and she

75

got her mouth set for the kiss she knew was coming and I tasted her lips.

They were young and sweet and less innocent than they should have been, a legacy of coming of age on the golden beach in California. We kissed for a moment and she shifted her body beneath mine in a practiced motion, and when she felt me getting hot because of her, she relaxed, feeling the age-old power. Her eyes got wide and shiny, and then they narrowed, reminding me of crossbow slots in the hooded turret of a medieval castle. At the same time, her mood made a hundred and eighty degree shift and she asked me to let her up, please.

"I better go," she said.

"Are you sure?"

"Yes."

I was disappointed. I helped her to her feet, then into her plastic raincoat. She was trembling as she shook hands and said good night. I walked her to the door and she stepped out into the drizzling rain. It was drifting down slowly now, but when she reached the bottom of the stairs the wind came on suddenly from the sea and the heavy downpour started up again. I grinned. The cosmos was on my side, for a change. I kept the door half open. I waited. In a minute she was back, breathless from her fast climb, glasses wet, dark hair plastered to her forehead.

"I changed my mind," she said. "Brrr."

She wanted to shower, so I showed her to the bathroom and handed her an old bathrobe left behind by some other lady from the misty past, and while she showered I made up my couch for the night. Then I sat in the director's chair and drank another Budweiser. Bud is not my favorite beer, but I hadn't worked since Christmas and the price is right. Some of my pals in the trade have shifted to Bud Light, a clear admission that you are over the hill. No light beer for Murdock.

From the bathroom came sounds of the toilet, the shower, an occasional humming. I decided I liked having her here, under my roof. The rain slanted at the window, slacked off, then slanted in again. When I was halfway through the beer, the door opened and Teresa came out. She was barefoot, something that always turns me on. Around her hips she wore a white towel, sarong style, and one of my blue Levi workshirts on top. The shirt was unbuttoned and as she moved toward me, slowly, I saw glimpses of soft breasts and belly and ribcage. She was a primitive, earthy island beauty from Bali, and without the tweeds and the horn-rimmed work glasses she seemed much more feminine. We touched fingers and then she planted herself with a soft purr in my lap and buried her face in my neck. With practiced teeth, she nipped the edges of my beard. I put my hand beneath her shirt to caress one breast. The flesh was smooth, sweet. The nipple was erect. She murmured something I could not understand. I moved my hand to caress her flat smooth belly. The caress made her squirm even more, and then the towel fell away, revealing slick shaved thighs and the dusky echoes of tan from a distant summer. She put up her face for a kiss as she parted her legs in hesitant invitation, and then we both stayed that way for a long moment, hovering on the brink of sex, and I thought briefly of Gayla Jean, and how her death by burning had brought Matt Murdock together with this California beach girl, here and now, for an instant on a rainy evening, and then Teresa Aiken, girl reporter from Fullerton, stood up without shyness and undressed me slowly and led me with a touch of night magic to bed.

It was what we both needed that chill March night.

8

The smell of coffee woke me, and when I opened my eyes it was morning and Teresa Aiken of the OC *Trib* was sitting on the edge of the bed wearing the white terry cloth robe while she held out a mug of coffee. I took it from her, sat up, sipped, nodded. I like coffee in bed in the morning. It's the one good reason I know for hiring a live-in servant.

Teresa came back with a cup for herself. She plumped up a pillow on her side of the bed, settled herself. "Let's talk."

"Minute," I said.

But the lady wasn't in a waiting mood. It was daylight on the beach, and time for business. No more night magic for girl reporters.

"This Kirkwood/Modesto thing woke me up, and I have the feeling you know something you're not telling me. What is it?"

My mind was not ready for this, not at this hour. It had

been a long, heated night, full of grunts and sweat and basic animal pleasures. I wanted to wake up slow and easy. "You know as much as I do. They met at that party at Waddell's. They left together. They ran into a mountain and burned up."

"No," she said. "Something stopped Gayla Kirkwood from crawling away from the wreck. That's what sticks in my head. She was trying to crawl away and something stopped her. Or someone."

"Have you checked with the fire department?"

"Of course." She gave me a weary look. "Nothing there."

"This is good coffee," I said, trying to shift her off the topic, "but I've been fired from the case that would have given me access." I didn't tell her about Ellis Dean's alleged photos, or about Meg Kirkwood. "What do you want me to do?"

"Promise me you'll keep me informed, okay?"

"Of what?"

She set her coffee cup down. Then she took my coffee cup away from me. I let it go regretfully. She set that down too. Then she opened up her robe to show me she was naked underneath, and I decided she looked even better in the morning than she had the night before. She locked eyeballs with me and threw one bare leg over mine, so that she was sitting astride my legs. This morning, she seemed heavier, which is another vote for night magic. While I watched, she let the robe fall down behind her back, like a model posing in the nude. She had good shoulders. Photogenic. Paintable. "You like me?"

"I like you."

She lifted herself up so she could take away the wool army blanket and sheet separating us, and then she settled back in place, warmly. Flesh to flesh. I liked it. "I like

79

you, too," she said, "but I wasn't born yesterday, as they say."

"I'll vouch for that," I said, feeling my response begin as an electric tingle in the mind, and then expand to a tingle in the crotch.

She put her hands on my chest and began to rock slowly back and forth. The tingles grew sharper, mounted briskly toward pleasure-pain.

"Remember what Jane Birch said, Murdock?"

"No," I grunted. "What did Jane Birch say?"

"Jane said you smelled crime. She said you had a radar for tracking criminals. She said you led her right to the bloody heart of the Kamrath story."

"And I thought you liked me for myself alone."

For her answer, Teresa grinned, raised up, centered herself, and then sat down again. I was inside. Whoo. "I do," she said, catching her breath. "Oh, I do."

I didn't believe her. She was being too obvious about what she wanted from me. But I was lost in the enthusiasm of the moment. "How old are you, anyway?"

"Old enough," she said.

"What if there's no case?"

Her eyes were closed as she began to swivel, and I knew she was enjoying it as much as I was. "Then," she said, her voice gravelly with passion. "Then we'll just have to be satisfied—with this."

Amen, I thought. This is better than a gallon of coffee.

Three minutes later, we were finished, barely, when the phone rang. Teresa was fetching fresh coffee. I answered. It was Webby Smith, my cop friend from Laguna Beach.

"Murdock? Hope I didn't interrupt your beauty sleep?"

"No problem. What's up?"

"It's your client, Ellis Dean. He was found about an hour ago in a parking garage at South Coast Plaza."

South Coast Plaza is the world's largest covered shopping mall, where they do more business than any mall in the country. The plaza is three miles or so beyond where I'd lost Ellis Dean yesterday.

"What was he doing there?" I asked, remembering the phone call Ellis Dean had just before I was fired.

"Dying," Webby Smith said. "Unpleasantly."

I wasn't surprised, mentally, but the idea of Ellis Dean dead slammed away at my emotions, and my eyes started to water. I had failed another client. Make that ex-client. I was alive. An ex-client was dead. I felt responsible. I also felt relieved it hadn't been me. Relief rhymes with grief. My hand shook.

"How?" I asked.

"Murdered," the lieutenant said. "We'll have to wait for the autopsy, but there were several puncture wounds in the upper body. Preliminary thinks it was a pitchfork."

"You're kidding," I said.

"Wish I was. It's in Santa Ana PD territory, so I've only been briefed because Dean lived here, in Laguna Beach, and they wanted a profile. I still had his résumé on file, from when he wanted to be a reserve officer. I'm asking to be kept informed, and since he was your client, I thought you should know right away." The lieutenant paused. "Where were you around nine last night?"

"Drinking," I said, looking at Teresa, who was standing in the bedroom doorway, sipping coffee. She had slipped into the robe again. Love-making had softened her face. "With a lady." Then I said: "Dean fired me yesterday afternoon, Webby. Five o'clock or so. Then took off in his Saab Turbo. I tracked him to the San Diego Freeway."

"Have any idea where he was headed?"

"None. He said he didn't need me any more. I would have stayed with him, but he lost me in traffic."

"Where?"

"Between Laguna and the 55 freeway."

"Well, we know where he was headed now."

"Yeah," I said.

"I hate it when one of my people gets it," the lieutenant said, sighing. "It mars my image of Laguna Beach as a real fun play place. Stop by the office sometime. I may have more details."

"Thanks," I said, and hung up.

"What was it?" Teresa asked.

"Police business," I said, throwing off the covers and sitting up on the side of the bed. I felt tired and old. Relief was still on a seesaw with responsibility.

"What about our deal?" she asked.

I stared at her. She was a good lay and a tough lady and at that moment I wanted her out of there. "Ellis Dean was murdered last night. South Coast Plaza. Around nine o'clock. There were puncture wounds. His body was found this morning in a parking garage."

"The same Ellis Dean who hired you?" Her face had gone hard.

"The same." My throat was tight.

"South Coast Plaza?" she said, turning away from me.

"Yes."

She threw the robe down and started to get dressed. "Damn!" she said. "I knew there was a connection! I just knew it!"

I went into the bathroom and splashed my face with water. Poor Ellis Dean. When I came out, Teresa was dressed and ready for battle in the world of hot news reporting. Her eyes were sharp, like needles, and when she kissed me her mouth was all business.

"Thanks," she said. "I'll call you as soon as I find out something."

"Do that," I said.

She gave me a flat-eyed look, walked out the door. I

heard her heels on the stairs. And then I was alone. For Teresa Aiken, the death of Ellis Dean meant a hot story. For me, it meant I was a lousy bodyguard.

I was on my fourth cup of coffee when the phone rang. It was after ten, I hadn't eaten anything, and I was thinking about shifting from coffee to beer, and then from beer to boilermakers. I let the phone ring a long time before I got up to answer. It was Meg Kirkwood, returning my call from last night. I was surprisingly glad to hear from her, and I thought perhaps looking across a table at her face might lift my spirits, so we made a date for Coco's, near Fashion Island.

She was waiting for me when I got there, dressed in a khaki sports jacket, blue blouse, and matching khaki skirt. She wore soft calfskin boots that looked expensive, and her black mourner's armband. When she stood up to shake hands, I was impressed by the firmness of her grip. The hand was cool and without jewelry. Her hair was pulled back from her face in the same tight hairdo from yesterday, at the funeral. It gave her face a severe look. She was reserved, cool, and more beautiful than I remembered. I had a strong sense Meg Kirkwood was hiding something.

We went through the preliminaries of hello and how are you and then a hostess led us to a booth overlooking the entrance to the mall. Meg Kirkwood slid neatly into the booth across from me. She ordered herb tea and dry toast. I ordered eggs over easy and sausage. She got right on to business before the food came.

"Mr. Murdock, you were recommended to me by Lieutenant Smith, who said you might be able to help me for a couple of days."

"Yes."

"Yesterday, you were unavailable."

"My client and I finished our business at five o'clock. I gave you a call."

"I got the message. So you are now free to work for me? Is that it?"

"That's it."

I was glad all I had to do was make simple responses, because her morning glow was distracting me. Her face was shining with that inner light painters try to capture on canvas. They know it will make them famous if they do. She looked at her placemat a lot, but when she raised her head to look at me, I got a thick, warm feeling. Six whiskeys would sometimes give me the same feeling, but Meg Kirkwood was instant health.

As she cross-examined me, she erected a careful fence between us. She was the manager-boss. I was the hired help. She had practiced this scene to perfection, probably because she was in business back in Fort Worth. She was a beautiful woman. Perfect teeth, straight nose, strong chin with a hint of stubbornness. And one artificial leg.

As she talked, I heard those lilting Texas sounds. "How much do you charge?"

"I get forty dollars an hour, plus expenses. If the job runs over six hours, I get two-fifty a day. If the job involves recovering money or property, and if recovery seems likely, I sometimes work for a piece of the action."

She whipped out a checkbook, a client action that never fails to give me pleasure.

"I'll be in town until tomorrow evening," she said. "Would a check for five hundred dollars be satisfactory?"

"Sure thing." She handed me the check. I toyed with the idea of telling her she had saved me from an alcoholic morning. That would have been unprofessional. "What's the job?"

Just then the waitress came with the food, so Meg Kirkwood paused, her eyes locked on the silverware in front of her. When the waitress had gone, she started back in with questions.

"Did you know my sister, Mr. Murdock?"

"No, ma'am."

"Then you were at the funeral services because of your client, Mr. Dean?"

"Yes."

"I'd like to talk to Mr. Dean. Can you arrange it?"

Before answering, I popped open the tiny jelly container. Today, it was strawberry jam. I spread the red stuff on my toast. "Mr. Dean is dead."

"What?"

"It will be on the news later today. The police think he was murdered." The strawberry jam was sweet, pungent.

"When?" There was shock in her voice.

"Last night. Around nine."

"But why?"

"They don't know. He was found dead in his car in a parking garage in South Coast Plaza." I didn't tell her about Webby's pitchfork theory.

Her face didn't change, but the glow faded. "Dead?" Her throat muscles were tight strands beneath smooth flesh.

"That's right."

"What is it you were doing for Mr. Dean?"

I shook my head again. "Sorry. That's privileged. I'd do the same for you, now that you're a client."

She stared at me with her blue eyes. Then she drank a sip of tea and bit into her toast. Her teeth belonged in a toothpaste ad.

"Very well. It probably doesn't matter. What I require from you is help in piecing together some information about my sister. She lived a—" Meg Kirkwood paused. "What I mean is that I am concerned about the kind of life she lived here. I paid a visit yesterday to her condominium at Lido Landing. Have you been there?"

"A couple of times."

Meg Kirkwood nodded, then went on. "It's lovely. The rent there is quite expensive—fifteen hundred dollars a month for a medium-sized place—and my sister was living in splendor, with two bedrooms, two baths, her own private sauna. The furnishings were lavish. She had installed one of those wall-sized video things. Her closets were full of clothes from Neimans, Saks, et cetera."

She pulled out a list, went down it, her voice controlled. "My sister had two furs—one mink, one fitch. Both are full length. She had four sets of skis, a built-in stereo, a king-size bed, at least ten thousand dollars' worth of clothes, and—" She stopped again to fish in her purse and came out with a set of car keys—"whatever little car goes with these."

I studied the keys. Foreign job, it looked like. Porsche, maybe, or MG or BMW.

Meg Kirkwood's voice had risen to a sharper pitch. She was trying to control herself by being ironic, but the picture of her sister's glitzy life-style was too bizarre. She leaned across the table to fix me with her sea blue eyes. They were hard, filled with pain. Tragic eyes. They got to me. She was quite a lady. "My sister had a job as a waitress. Even with huge tips, what she netted couldn't have paid the rent on that place. I'm in the word-processing business in Fort Worth, and I know exactly how much things cost."

"You're on the right track," I said.

She grasped my wrist. Her fingers were strong. "Someone was paying for it."

I nodded. "Probably."

"I want you to help me find out who."

"All right."

"Could it have been your Mr. Dean?"

"He gave her money. He told me."

"How much?"

"Seven grand, plus change. For Dean, that was a pile of money. His wife left him when she found out."

"The poor man." Meg Kirkwood computed the numbers quickly, then shook her head. "There has to be more. Twenty-five thousand. Perhaps more."

"She was a good-looking girl."

Meg sagged back against the booth. "I hate that idea, that men gave her things because she was pretty. That's what Billy Bob says. He's afraid to find out what she was up to, alone, on the beach. Billy Bob says I should leave well enough alone, let the dead die in peace. He rushed us out here. Then he turned tail and rushed back."

I figured it was Billy Bob who got going with the quick funeral. It was not the time to verify.

"But you don't agree."

Meg gave me a grateful look. "She was my sister, not his. And I feel responsible for what happened."

"Responsible" didn't cover it, but I try not to mince words with beautiful clients. Time enough for semantics after I ran down a few facts.

"Why?" I asked.

She swung the eyes at me again. Her voice was snappish. "That's my business, Mr. Murdock. It's my privileged information."

"Check," I said, and felt my cheeks get red. The lady could handle a barb. "Since I haven't seen the apartment, maybe we'd better start there, look around, check things out."

"That's our second stop. First, I need help collecting Gayla Jean's car. Perhaps you didn't notice, but my left leg is—" she paused, "—is artificial. A prosthesis."

87

She was waiting for my response, so I said: "No, I hadn't noticed."

She favored me with an almost-smile. "You see, my leg prohibits me from driving a stick shift." It was a practiced explanation, one she'd done a thousand times.

"Where's the car?" I asked, even though I had a good idea.

"At Mr. Waddell's. It's in Bluebird Canyon, in Laguna Beach, where the party was where she—"

"No problem." I finished my last bite of toast.

The lady paid the check, as part of my expenses. I decided to leave the Plymouth in Coco's parking lot. And then we drove together in Meg Kirkwood's rented Buick down along the coast to Laguna Beach. The sun was out. It was a beautiful day. You could smell spring in the air.

Meg Kirkwood drove with the same care and brittle precision that characterized her movements and her speech. Remembering the sexy night magic of Teresa Aiken, I wondered about Meg's sex life, or whether she ever had any fun, her and old Billy Bob. Behind the wheel of the Buick, she was stiff, mechanical, serene.

"Mind if I ask how you got the keys to her car?" I asked.

"No. They were given to me by Mr. Waddell. Yesterday evening." She gave me a sideways glance, then turned her attention back to the road. "I met him at the airport, after seeing Billy Bob off on his plane. We had a cocktail. He told me how sorry he was that something awful had happened as a result of two people meeting at one of his parties. He gave me the keys. He was pleasant. It seems he has an art gallery. When he discovered I was a fellow entrepreneur, he offered to show me around Laguna Beach."

Good old Philo, I thought. Meg Kirkwood was impressed by the fat man's money and manners.

"Did Waddell know Gayla Jean?"

"Only slightly. He thought he remembered her at another party, earlier in the year, or perhaps last year, at Christmas. He gave the impression there were scads of pretty girls at his parties. I believed him."

"Did Philo mention my client, Ellis Dean?"

"Yes. He said Gayla Jean had arrived with Mr. Dean. Mr. Waddell had no idea she left with someone else until he saw the paper, on Sunday morning. It was a terrible shock, he said."

"Did Philo know Modesto?"

"He didn't mention the name. Why do you ask?"

"Part of my training. Just being nosy."

She stopped at the light near Main Beach, where Laguna Canyon Road runs into PCH. "What a lovely spot," she said.

"Yes." The beach was starting to fill up with people. Four hefty regulars were warming up for some two-man, tapping a scuffed white volleyball back and forth across the net with iron hard fingertips. Sun seekers crossed in front of the car. A few were pale. Most of them had a good start on their summer tans.

"Everyone looks so healthy here."

"It's an illusion," I said. "Something we paint on for the tourist trade."

"You're quite a cynic, aren't you, Mr. Murdock?"

"Me? Heck no, I'm not a cynic. I just try to tell the truth."

It's a line that usually gets a laugh from a lady. Or at least it gets a wry grin. From Meg Kirkwood, it got nothing.

The light changed. She eased the Buick up the hill, to turn left into Bluebird Canyon and Philo's place. We didn't speak the rest of the way.

9

Philo Waddell's home was on Goldfinch Lane just off Bluebird Canyon Road. The big Spanish-style house sat on a small hill behind an ornamental iron fence that vanished on both sides into the local variety of underbrush. To get in, you talked into a little voicebox at the gate while you were scrutinized by one of those all-weather video cameras mounted on a swivel. Looking into the snout of a surveillance camera always made me want to blast it away with my .357. Too bad the piece was in the trunk of the Plymouth, back at Coco's. As Meg Kirkwood got entry clearance and drove in, I saw that Philo had himself a huge chunk of land—at least an acre—for that part of Laguna. The house was fifteen rooms or so, and worth at least two million. The land, if parceled up by developers, was worth ten times that.

She parked in the red-tiled driveway. Two doors of the five-car garage were up. In one stall was the big Mercedes I remembered from yesterday. In the other was a red

BMW, which I guessed was Gayla Jean's car. A Filipino butler wearing a white coat came out and ushered Meg Kirkwood inside. I decided to stay with the car.

I wandered around behind Philo's house to check out the tennis court where he and Ellis Dean had played their grudge matches. A doubles game was in progress, and the players were grunting and hustling as if they were playing on the circuit.

The tanned duo at my end were kids, young, lithe—a blond boy with hairy legs and a hefty blond girl in pink. The duo at the other end were older. The guy stroked cool, like a pro. He was dark, with a thin Mediterranean face that had to be French or Italian. His lady partner was lissome and sensual, and she uncoiled on her shots like a snake. Had Ellis Dean mentioned her being at the party? Watching her hit, you smelled money, a certain reckless who-gives-a-shit attitude, disdain for the world. She wore a yellow skirt that curled sexily around thin thighs and a striped yellow jersey that gave you the impression she wore no bra. She stroked the ball with contempt from the back court and got a charge out of killing shots at the net. Twice while I was watching she hit one of the blond kids with a body shot, like she enjoyed bruising, giving pain.

I was studying the foursome, admiring the balance of the match—the power of the kids versus the strategy of the Snake Lady and the cool pro—when a Land Rover with oversize tires roared into the parking area. A blond man was behind the wheel. He stared at me as if he knew me from somewhere. His face was round and beet red from too much sun. When he stepped down, I saw he was a muscle boy. Weight: at least 225, maybe 250. Height: six feet, an inch or so shorter than me. I figured him for thirty or so, but with weight-lifters you can't always tell. He had ten years on me, for sure. He wore a brief red bikini that showed off his manly equipment, and the top half of a black wet suit, unzipped, to show off his abdominals. His legs and feet were bare and crusted with golden sand.

"You got a problem, friend?" he said as he came toward me.

"Nope."

"What are you doing here, anyway?"

He didn't want an answer, so I didn't give him one. His legs bulged and contracted as he walked. The hairs on the back of my neck were telling me he wanted a fight, and I thought of my .357, back in the trunk of the Plymouth, ten miles from here. The way this case was shaping up, I was going to have to start carrying it every time I left my house. He moved across the asphalt toward me with the self-conscious gait of a pretty hunk, aware of every muscular ripple.

"This is private property, friend. Or can't you read?"

He kept coming and my adrenals started to pump. On the court, the players had stopped hitting to listen.

"I'm here with Ms. Kirkwood. To pick up a car."

Muscle Boy stopped when he was six feet away. A triumphant look crossed his beefy face. He grinned at me, like a witch doctor softening up the victim before the knife goes in.

"What car is that, friend?"

I decided to stay civil. "Her sister's car. Her name was Gayla Jean. She died Sunday morning, after attending a party right here. You probably saw her around."

He took another step. Behind me, I was aware of shuffling movement, as the foursome gathered behind the fence to watch.

"You've got fifteen seconds to shag out of here."

"I'm shagging." I moved two steps along the fence, toward Bluebird Canyon Road. Seeing that made him grin some more.

Then Muscle Boy signaled his plans by flexing his huge shoulders. Muscles contracted, sending telltale ripples to arms and neck and bare belly. He growled, giving me even more time to sidestep the charge when it came. Like a lot of weight-lifters, he was slow and clumsy, and admiring his biceps in the mirror had made him cocky about his fighting ability. He came for me, arms outstretched. I stepped aside, grabbed a hunk of wet suit, and slammed him into the cyclone fence. The fence shuddered on impact. The four spectators scattered and one of the ladies let out a yelp. Muscle Boy rebounded off the wire, snarling. I'd been lucky on the first rush. Now I wished again for the equalizing weight of the .357.

He decided to circle, which was as good a strategy as any if you weighed what he did. His forehead was bleeding where one eyebrow had caught the fence. The bad news was that he'd stopped talking, and telegraphing. The way he was built, it would take an hour or so to break him. By that time my hands would be so sore I wouldn't be able to drive a car or make a cup of coffee. Meanwhile, there was the chance that he'd get lucky, land a punch, and I'd be dead.

To make him think I was as dumb as he was, I shifted into a karate stance. When he saw that, he grinned, brushed the blood out of his eye socket, and came for me again. This time, instead of waiting for him, I took a couple of dance steps forward and kicked him in the left shin. His leg went out from under him. I was wearing my cowboy boots, because I'd wanted to impress Meg Kirkwood with my admiration for her home state, and the sharp toe got Muscle Boy's attention. But he was a slow learner, so when he made a grab for me as he fell I nailed his ankle. The sound of a small pop told me I'd hit pay dirt. His face turned white as he grabbed his ankle protectively with both big hands, and behind me I heard a woman's voice whispering, "Kill. Kill."

I turned and saw the lady in yellow, sharp face warped with excitement, eyes glazed. Her fingers dug deep into her upper arms. "Kill him!" she said again.

The foreign dude brushed past her to kneel beside Muscle Boy and make like a doctor who knew what he was doing, and Philo Waddell—wearing a blue blazer, white slacks, and a red scarf—was hurrying up from the house. Behind him were Meg and the Filipino in the white coat.

The foreign dude pronounced a broken bone and a need for immediate X rays. The Filipino brought the Land Rover up, we loaded Muscle Boy into the back, and the dude, whose name was Nicolo Something, drove off with the Filipino at the wheel.

Philo Waddell turned to me with hot anger in his eye. "You must be Murdock."

"That's right."

"What happened here?"

Before I could say anything, the lady in yellow walked over to me and grasped me by the arm. There was a bruise on her right shoulder, about the size of a quarter, and I could smell her perfume. "Butch was boorish, as usual," she said. "And Mr. Murdock was magnificent." She gave my arm a squeeze.

"That's right, Philo. Butch was acting crazy," said one of the blond kids.

"Acting crazy . . . again," said the other blond kid. "Oh. Oh. Oh." Both kids tittered through perfect California teeth.

"Let's go hit some, Buns," said the first blond kid.

"Oh, hey," said the other one. "Oh. Oh. Oh."

94

They shuffled back to the court, where they began hitting with the precision of mindless machinery.

Philo stared at me for a moment, as if he didn't believe a guy my age could take his prize bull. Then he held out his hand.

"My apologies, please, Mr. Murdock. Butch has been known to . . . ah . . . well . . ."

"Butch is a hunk of beach beef, Philo," the lady in yellow said. "We should keep Mr. Murdock around to teach him manners." She squeezed my arm again, and pressed a knee into my leg.

"Mr. Murdock is working for me," Meg said, coldly.

The ladies were already clawing like cats, and a grin creased Philo's ample face. He was heavy, like Orson Welles. His eyes didn't miss. "Stay for a cocktail, won't you? I'll do the honors, since Quan had to run his errand of mercy."

Quan must have been the name of the Filipino.

I wanted out of there, but Meg decided to stay. The three of us walked with Philo through a shaded overhang into a patio that overlooked a good-sized swimming pool. A glass-topped table glimmered against a backdrop of flowering shrubs and rich green vines. It was a picture right out of a magazine.

"Gin and tonic for me, dear," the lady in yellow said, and then introduced herself to Meg. "I'm Lucinda Smith-Travis. You must be Meg Kirkwood."

"Yes." The ladies had decided on a truce. They smiled, shook hands. Lucinda Smith-Travis was the lady in the rubber suit, the one who bet with Dean on the fighting cocks. She draped herself across a chair and then allowed her short yellow skirt to creep up so that I had a clear view of bright yellow panties. She saw me looking, flashed me a society smile, and rearranged herself. Good timing. Philo wheeled up a cart packed with ice and glasses and the best booze money could buy. Lucinda decided to angle her rich bitch charms at Meg. "May I call you Meg?"

"Of course." Meg looked relieved. Was she falling for this act?

"I was shocked when I heard about your sister. I hardly knew her, of course, but when someone so young dies, well, it leaves us all in a state. Doesn't it, Philo, dear?"

The fat man was busying himself with drinks. "Absolutely." When he talked, I could pick up the distant trace of a southern accent. Georgia. Alabama. Maybe Arkansas. He had ugly lips.

"Thank you," Meg said. "I'm still in shock, myself."

Philo handed drinks around. "My special mixture," he said.

I decided to use this relaxed moment in posh Bluebird Canyon to probe. "Did Gayla Jean come to a lot of parties here, Mr. Waddell?"

"Two, as I recall," Philo said. "Perhaps three."

"Did you remember who she came with Saturday?"

"No. She walked in with Ellis Dean, and a crush of others. It was only afterward that her car was discovered."

She'd ridden to the party with Dean. She'd walked out with Modesto. Dean followed because he was smitten. And jealous.

"Did you know she left with Modesto?"

The big man shrugged. "I had no idea she'd gone, until the car was found. There were almost three hundred guests. You can imagine the parking situation." He waved grandly at his canyon.

"She have any special friends that you know of?"

"These young people create their own social webs, as I'm sure you're aware. They live for a moment. They are out of one's reach."

"They're butterflies." Lucinda Smith-Travis crossed her society legs. "Oh. Sorry, dear," she said to Meg.

Meg took a sip of her drink, then looked at me, frowning.

Me, I was still working. This was my chance to pump Philo Baby. He was lying. I might trip him up. I didn't want to tell the group that Dean was dead. I hoped Meg Kirkwood hadn't told Philo. "You're friends with Ellis Dean, aren't you?"

"Where is this leading, Mr. Murdock?"

"I worked for Dean," I said. "As a bodyguard."

"Fascinating," Lucinda said, and leaned toward me, smirking.

"Until when?" Waddell asked.

"Until yesterday afternoon. He terminated my services after the funeral."

"Ah," Philo said, smiling. "If you remember your Hemingway, Jacob Barnes had what he called a 'tennis friend.' That was Ellis Dean to me."

At the mention of Hemingway, Meg perked up. "*The Sun Also Rises,*" she said. "Robert Cohn was Jake Barnes's tennis friend."

Waddell beamed at her. She smiled back. "Yes," he said, with energy.

"I was an English major," she said. "I used to love reading Hemingway." With the subject of literature on the table, Meg's face glowed.

"Philo kills Ellis Dean," Lucinda said, using her favorite verb.

Philo sipped his drink, set it down, and changed the subject. "Have you been in touch with your sister regularly?" he asked Meg.

"I got a card at Christmas. We haven't talked much since she left Fort Worth."

"Ah, and when was that?"

"Over a year ago. We'd had a terrible winter. Gayla Jean didn't leave the house for twenty-two days straight, and the cold was driving her crazy. Her New Year's present to herself was a bus ticket to California."

"They flock here by the thousands," Philo said, "these pretty, pretty birds. Like Icarus, they fly right into the sun. Most of them come to their senses and go back home."

Meg had tears in her eyes now, so she changed the subject.

"I love your flowers, Mr. Waddell. We won't have growth like that at home for another month, at least. And our summers are merciless."

"It is a garden spot, I admit."

"Philo is like Ferdinand, the Bull," Lucinda said, touching my knee with her tennis shoe. "Always sniffing the flowers."

Philo glared at her, but went on talking to Meg. Lucinda drained her drink, stood up, slithered to the drink cart, where she poured herself a fresh one.

"She was a lovely person, I'm sure," Waddell said, speaking to Meg in a low voice.

I was still working, so I decided to try again. "How did she meet Modesto, do you know?"

"Someone saw them dancing, I believe."

"Remember who?"

Philo waved a fat hand. "Alas, no. Such a crush."

"Then there were lots of young people?" Meg asked.

"Oh, goodness me, yes. Tons. Though I try not to limit my get-togethers to persons of a certain age."

"Three hundred guests, you said?" I was hanging in there.

"Correct. Two hundred plus were invited. They brought their friends. I assume that's how young Mister Modesto arrived."

"He wasn't invited, then?"

"How could he have been? I didn't know the man."

Philo was lying. Dean hears Philo talking on the phone in Spanish. Then Modesto shows up at the party.

I waded in. "There's a rumor around town you're running fighting cocks at your parties."

From the drink cart, Lucinda hooted. Smoothly, Waddell turned to me and said: "I beg your pardon?"

"Cockfights," I said. "Two trained roosters in a ring, with razors strapped to their feet. Spectators bet on their favorite bird. They try to kill each other." I grinned at Lucinda. "I bet Ms. Travis here would eat it up."

"Sounds ugly," she said.

"It's Smith-Travis," Philo corrected me, scowling. "And whoever started that rumor should have his head examined. It's against every law in the state."

"Ellis Dean was the one who told me."

"Then he's hallucinating."

I didn't say anything. Philo's face had sweat beads on it, but we had a long way to go before sweat would stand up in a California court. And now Meg was glaring at me as if I'd kicked sand in her ice cream. I decided to go back to Jaime Modesto.

"Did you recognize Modesto? From the movies?"

"No. My recreation comes from reading, writing, the arts."

He smiled at Meg. She smiled back. Any minute, they'd form their own great books club.

"There must be pretty tight security at your parties."

"Yes. There is."

"With all that security, I'm wondering how Modesto got in."

Lucinda had retaken her seat and was trying to distract me with her wicked legs. She was enjoying the question and answer session. She liked seeing old Philo squirm.

But Philo kept his cool. "You should have been a policeman, Mr. Murdock."

"Thanks. I was."

"Oh, really? Where?"

"Los Angeles. I was in the Hollenbeck Division for awhile."

"A policeman, here in our midst," Lucinda said. "They're so sexy."

"Have you tried to find out?" I kept on. "How Modesto got in, I mean?"

"I questioned my people, of course."

"And—?"

"That's none of your affair, Mr. Murdock. But I admire your persistence. So does Lucinda, don't you, dear?"

"I admire *everything* about Mr. Murdock."

The talk was making Meg nervous. She scrooched around in her garden chair, cutting her eyes at me.

"I might hire Murdock," Philo said, staring at Lucinda.

"I have a client," I said.

"When you're finished, of course. Have you a business card?"

"Never touch them," I said.

"Whatever would he do?" Lucinda asked.

"I was thinking of tightening security," Waddell said, "at our next little gathering."

They were putting me on, talking about me like I wasn't there. It was meant to piss me off, and it did.

"Sorry," I said, getting up. "Babysitting fat cat party guests is not my line of work." And then I said to Meg, "I'll wait for you by the garage, ma'am." I walked out.

I knew I had embarrassed her. I figured she would fire me. I didn't care. Philo's personal sweet boy had tried to maim me. Philo himself was making me angry with his Bluebird Canyon airs. They were a nasty crowd, smug, rich—and I was working for a lady who got high on literature and who needed smooth social gloss to make her feel okay.

She showed up a couple minutes later, looking flustered. Her face was back to marble statue. Goodbye glow.

"Did you actually say 'fat cat party guests'?" she asked.

"That's right."

"You don't even know him. He is a perfect stranger to you."

"True," I said.

"I have never in my life heard anything so rude, so—" Her voice rose in indecision. She stopped, waited for me to say I was sorry. I wasn't. One of my problems is I say what I mean, usually at the wrong time for society. It's why I quit high school early. She went on, in a fierce, controlled whisper. "You and I were guests. Mr. Waddell was trying to be pleasant. You come in here, beat up one of his friends, and then you spend the rest of what could have been a perfectly pleasant social visit making him feel awkward in his own home. I hope you know what you're doing, and I hope you can come up with some explanation for your behavior."

"You want it here?" I asked.

She looked around. "No," she said, handing me the keys to the red BMW. "I still need you to help me with the car. Would you follow me, please?"

"Sure thing." I watched her climb behind the wheel of the Buick, and then I got into the BMW, adjusted the seat for my legs, started up, and followed Meg Kirkwood down the hill and out of beautiful Bluebird Canyon.

10

The red BMW needed a tune-up. It stalled at the first stop sign on the way down to the Coast Highway, and then coughed its way through the city of Laguna. I take care of my vehicles, and it makes me sad to encounter a machine that needs work. It wasn't a surprise that Gayla Jean didn't keep her car up.

To my left, above the Pacific, storm clouds were building, and the weather report on the fancy Blaupunkt stereo said we were in for more rain. Meg Kirkwood led me across the Newport Bridge, then took a left at the first light and drove past the movie theater and the supermarket and then onto Lido Island.

You can get a better idea of Lido Island from the air. It's a thick finger of land sticking out into Newport Bay, with only one bridge connecting it to the mainland. The island is girded by a pair of roads, Via Lido Nord and Via Lido Soud, with a main drag slicing up the center. Lido

Landing, where Meg's sister had lived, was at the tip of the island, on Via Lido Soud, which faced south toward Bay Isle, Balboa Peninsula, and the sea.

Lido Landing wasn't more than a quarter-mile from Newport Pier, where my place was, but it was light years away in value per square foot. Meg used a keycard to open the automatic security gate, and once inside we were surrounded by Jags and Porsches and Mercedes 350SLs.

The lady was out of her car, waiting for me, when I parked the red BMW in a slot marked Visitor. Her arms were folded and her face was still stiff with anger. Her voice came out in a tense whisper.

"Before I fire you, Mr. Murdock, I'd like to have some explanation of just what was going on back there!"

Looking at her, I had the sudden urge to grin. Anger brought color to her cheeks and sparks to her beautiful blue eyes. I wasn't ready to tell her everything, but I had enough.

"Okay. The musclehead who jumped me was Butch Denning. He works for Philo. Guys like Butch always have some kind of record, but we can check that."

"So?"

"So Ellis Dean told me Butch knew your sister, that he acted the role of bouncer during some private photo sessions, and that means there's a good chance that Mr. Waddell is stretching the truth about not knowing her."

"Photo sessions?" Meg asked. "What do you mean?"

I sighed. I had wanted to keep the lady innocent, at least until I was sure of my facts, but it was too late for gallantry. "Ellis Dean and two other gentlemen each paid Gayla Jean $500 for the pleasure of photographing her for two hours. Butch probably took a cut." I gestured at the building. "Dean said the sessions took place here."

103

Her face showed outrage. "I don't believe it!"

"I haven't seen the photos myself, but Dean described a purple dress to me, and a pair of silver spike heels."

"He could have seen those anywhere. He could have made it up. Men do fantasize. Especially where my sister is concerned. They always have."

"Dean was desperate. His wife left him because she saw some of the photos. There was no reason for him to lay fantasies on me."

"All right," she said, with resolution. "We'll put that to the test, right now. We'll look for those items."

Going up in the elevator, I didn't say anything. Neither did Meg Kirkwood. The silence could have broken walls. Inside the apartment, Meg Kirkwood muttered something like, "Let's just see about that purple dress," and marched across a pure white shag through a door into the main bedroom. While she rustled among her sister's dresses, I poked around the living room.

It was a big room, with most of the southwest wall made of glass. On good days, the sun would hit the wall about two in the afternoon and walk across it, all the way to sundown. Today, all you could see was a new storm brewing. On a balcony outside I found a chaise longue, a small glass table with drink circles on it, a bottle of Bain du Soleil, and a stack of soggy magazines. Standing there, watching the dark sky, I had a clear vision of Gayla Jean Kirkwood sunbathing in the raw, opening herself to the heat of the sun. I shuffled through the first three or four magazines—*Cosmo, Playgirl, Glamour*—then went back inside.

The thing that bothered me about the big room was the bookshelf full of books. Gayla Jean was not coming across as a superscholar. Maybe she was storing them for somebody. I flipped through a couple of titles—*Justine*,

Balthazar, Moby-Dick, The Scarlet Letter—and was just putting them back onto the shelf when Meg Kirkwood came out. In one hand she carried the purple dress. In the other she carried a pair of silver spike heels.

"I found these," she said. "But that still doesn't mean Mr. Waddell was lying. Why would he lie?"

I started to say because he was a bad dude, but decided to button my lip.

"Mind if I poke around a little? That is, unless I'm still fired."

She shook her head distractedly. "No. No. Please do." She sat down, heavily, on the pale blue divan. "You're not fired. I think I should apologize. What are you looking for?"

"If I tell you, will you still have faith in the science of criminology?" Murdock the comedian.

"I suppose."

"I never know until I find it."

"That must make looking for it very difficult."

"Well, it's not that mysterious," I said. "A lady I once knew said I looked for patterns. She was a college teacher, and that's what she did when she taught poetry. She gave me the overview I needed for my work."

"What kind of patterns?"

"Patterns that make sense."

"Can you give me an example?"

"Sure." I indicated the bookshelf. "Was your sister into great books?"

"No. That puzzled me too." She looked at the bookshelf. "Back home, she hardly read anything. Now—" Meg Kirkwood shook her head. I didn't mention Philo and his love of reading.

I left her sitting there holding the purple dress and walked into Gayla Jean's main bedroom. The bed had

105

been made and the coverlet had the same silky, expensive look as the rest of the place. The clothes in the closets were colorful, plentiful, youthful, new. I hefted the mattress and checked between it and the box spring. Nothing. I was surprised she hadn't slept on a waterbed. In a portfolio behind the clothes I found some photographs. They were all of Gayla Jean, some in clothes, some in a bikini, some in a tank suit. No nudes there. Maybe Ellis Dean *had* been fantasizing. I left the portfolio on the bed and was going through the dresser drawers when Meg Kirkwood appeared at the door.

"Someone's been here," she said.

I stopped what I was doing. "When?"

"Last night, I guess. Or this morning."

"How do you know?"

"Things have been moved around. Billy Bob's a smoker, and I remember he left a silver lighter on the kitchen cabinet. Today it's been moved."

"How far?"

"Six inches or so."

Meg Kirkwood had either turned the bend, or she was a very precise lady.

"Anything else?"

"The bedclothes seemed out of place. I made the bed yesterday, because it was all rumpled. She was never one to clean up, poor dear. And today it was rumpled, but in a different way."

"Maybe it was the maid."

"No." She shook her head. Her eyes were troubled. "I don't think it was the maid."

I used Gayla Jean's phone to make a quick call to the manager's office. Today was Tuesday. The maid came on Thursday.

When I got off the phone, Meg Kirkwood was leafing

through the portfolio, looking at the pictures of her sister. "She was so beautiful," Meg said. "And so young."

I didn't say anything. I could have told her she was pretty beautiful herself, but the timing wasn't right. Meg looked up. A single tear brightened her right eye.

"Also," Meg Kirkwood said. "I found a file folder that might be of interest. It's in the other room." I followed her into the living room. All around me I could feel something, as if Gayla Jean was about to step through the mirrored bedroom door wearing the silver shoes and the purple dress. Maybe that's the way Ellis Dean had felt, lugging his camera in here, falling in love. That something was about to happen.

The file folder contained about fifty clippings from *Variety* and the *Hollywood Reporter* on movie stars that were too young to be interesting. Rodney Daniel, Megan Falange, Gitane Bellefontaine. The worst hairdo was on Megan Falange—a black and orange punker job that stuck up above her head in seven sharp spikes. I had seen their pictures on magazine covers, but refused, on principle, to pay five bucks to see them on the screen. Us adults have got to draw the line somewhere.

Most of the clippings were dated more than a year ago. Near the bottom of the stack I found two about Jaime Modesto's last movie, *Tijuana Rose*. The critics said it was a fine picture, moody, artful, tragic.

"Do you think they knew each other before the party?" Meg asked, when I came to the Modesto clippings.

"It's possible. How often do you think she went to L.A.?"

"She lived in Long Beach awhile, I think."

It was the first I'd heard about it. "She did? When?"

"When she first came out here. I think she met someone."

"Remember his name?"

"She called him her Long Beach Lover. She only wrote at Christmas."

Dead ends everywhere. "Would you like a drink? It's been a long day already, and I could use a beer."

"No, no. Nothing for me. If you're through in the bedroom, I think I'll stretch out for a minute and rest. Help yourself to anything you can find."

Meg Kirkwood was looking tired. Whatever had chewed on her to make her hire a private eye was still chewing on her. She went to lie down while I rustled up a Mexican Corona. Gayla Jean knew her beer, probably because she knew her men.

I spent four hours going through the books, hunting for something that would give me a lead. I flipped through every book on the shelf. Most of the books felt stiff, new, unread. I was on my third Corona when I put the last book back into the case. It had been many hours since breakfast, and my stomach was ready for food. There was no sound from the bedroom where Meg was napping, so I stood on the balcony where Gayla Jean had taken the sun and looked out to sea. The dark sky had moved closer and the wind was up and a wall of dark rain was slanting across the Lido. A raindrop tapped my face, and then one more, and without thinking I scooped up the soggy magazines and took them inside.

I was leafing through the magazines when the phone rang. Before I could answer, I heard Meg pick up the extension in the bedroom and say hello. It was her sister's apartment, so I let her handle it. The last two magazines were a *Playboy* and a *Penthouse*. I took a moment to check the centerfolds, found them both to my liking, and was about to put the magazines back at the bottom of the stack when I noticed a slip of paper marking a place. I opened the *Playboy* to the section on movies. The review was of an X-rated film called *Lady of the Black Masque*, and the reviewer had used words like "daring," "artful," and "penetrating" to describe the film. Someone had underlined the words with an orange ballpoint. There was a picture of the lady herself, presumably, sitting on a tall four-legged stool, holding a whip. Her costume—the mask, the leather vest, the long gloves, the hip-length buccaneer's boots—was all black, and displayed enough flashes of flesh to divert the attention of your average blue-movie goer. The *Penthouse* review used the same imaginative language as *Playboy* to describe the same film, but in the photo that accompanied the review, the masked lady had removed the black leather vest to display perky young breasts.

Both reviews made it a point to say *Lady of the Black Masque* was shot totally in black and white, to simulate a return to the art movies of the twenties. There was no way of telling what the lady's real hair color was. It could have been blonde. It could have been red.

From the bedroom, I heard Meg Kirkwood's voice rise in sudden anger, heard her slam down the phone. I dropped the magazines and went to check her out.

She saw me standing at the open door and said to come in. She was sitting on the edge of the big bed, brushing a strand of hair away from her face. The boots were on the floor near the bed. Her face when she glanced at me was filled with outrage.

"Do you know who that was? On the phone? Just now?"

"No."

"A man—some man—he must have thought I was Gayla Jean—he did a long song and dance about how much people liked my work and how so-and-so in Hollywood was dying to meet me and how would it be if I got into something slinky and came up for a party this evening?"

"Kind of short notice, I'd say. Where was the party?"

"All he said was 'the usual place,' wherever that is. He said the car would be in the area around eight."

"Maybe they don't read the papers, up in L.A."

I knew what the call meant, but I didn't say anything. Gayla Jean had been a party gal. The guys were probably small-time hustlers who needed pretty girls to trot out in front of investors from out of town. I wondered how much she made per night.

"How did you handle it?" I asked.

"Oh, I tried to play along, but he was so mealy-mouthed and obvious I'm afraid I got mad. He hung up when I told him she was dead."

"You don't usually get mad, do you?"

She gave me a shrewd look. "No. I don't."

I let the silence hang between us for a couple of minutes. "The books haven't been read," I said.

She shook her head. "I'm not surprised. Gayla hated school. I wonder what she was doing with all those books."

"Maybe somebody loaned them to her. Somebody literary."

"That's quite a loan." She turned to look out the window. "It's going to storm again, isn't it?"

"It just started up," I said.

She shivered, hugged herself. "Are you finished? I'd like to get out of here."

"Sure thing. I'm hungry. How about you?"

She shook her head. "I suppose."

"I know a cozy spot that serves a great seafood linguini."

I could see her hesitate, the gaze turning inward, to

110

probe some private pocket in the mind. Again she shivered, then brought her attention back to the room. Her probing look could have detected metal for airport security. "All right. I'd like to leave her car here. Would you mind driving?"

"Be happy to."

It was raining steadily when we reached the ground level. I ran through the rain to get the Buick, and then I pulled up close to the front door of Lido Landing, so she wouldn't get wet. For a lady with only one good leg, she maneuvered nicely. I admired that. It took discipline, training, guts. As she got in, her skirt slid up above her knee, and I saw the outlines of a slender strap, which must have been part of her leg harness. She saw me out of the corner of her eye.

"Where are you taking me?" she asked.

"Dale's Harborside. I know the folks who run it. It's a nice place for a rainy night."

"That's good," she said, and settled back against the seat. As I drove through the rain, I thought how good it felt having her there in the seat beside me.

11

It was after seven when we arrived. Dale's Harborside was packed to the walls with beach people and local tourists from inland middle-class strongholds like Irvine, Tustin, and Anaheim Hills. The place smelled of wet wool, french fries, seafood cooking. Jane, the frisky blonde waitress, took less than two minutes to find us a table. I was surprised when Meg Kirkwood ordered beer.

"We might as well get a pitcher," she said. "It's been a thirsty day."

"I'll drink to that."

We ordered clam linguini.

As we drank, I was aware of people staring our way, and I assumed it was not my particular pulchritude they were ogling. "Pulchritude" is a fifty-dollar word I picked up while I was an English major for the CIA. It means "beautiful," but it carries a plump and bounteous sound.

The hungry eyes watching made me realize how attractive Meg was, as if I needed any help when the glow started up. Across the room, against a set of chipped Victorian mirrors, an old party in an ascot and blue blazer raised his glass and smiled our way. The clam linguini came, steaming, and we dug in.

"This is marvelous," she said, between mouthfuls. "And I love this little place."

"Thanks. They're good people, the folks who own it. If they opened earlier, I'd eat breakfast here."

"You live nearby?"

"Across the street."

"Really?"

"Yeah. Above the Surf Shop."

"Right on the water," she said.

"Yes."

She didn't say anything after that, but just went on chewing. And then a quiet smile drifted across her features, a rare happening for this lady. "It's good."

"What's good?"

"You," she said. "Living on the beach. It just seems— very appropriate. Very you."

"Also," I said, "I have etchings. Crude. Simple. Primitive."

The smile broadened, turning her from paying client into desirable woman. "I'll just bet you do," she said.

Across the room, the old party raised his glass again. His toothy smile made me hurt.

"He's been watching us since we came in," Meg said.

"I'll drink to his good taste."

My comment made Meg blush. To change the subject, she asked me how long I'd lived in California.

"Since the late sixties," I said. "I landed here when I got my discharge."

"Oh? What branch of the service were you in?"

"Army. I was in for the whole nine yards, ran into some imported Russian shrapnel. All the way from Krasnoyarsk to me."

"Ugh," she said. "Was it bad?"

"Bad enough," I said. "But compared to some guys, who lost eyes, arms, legs, I got off easy."

"Where was it?" she asked, her voice a low murmur.

"Viet Nam," I said. "The Tet Offensive of 1968."

"No. I meant, where were you hit?"

"Inside thigh," I said. "On the right. Way high up."

"The leg," she said, looking at me with sympathy. I decided not to ask about her leg. She would tell me, soon enough.

"It makes me sweat to talk about it."

"Sorry." She studied her beer mug. "I didn't mean to pry."

"You're not prying. It's good for me to sweat. Cleans out the pores."

A smart woman can always tell when a man is avoiding his emotions. She put her hand over mine, left it there for a half-second. I liked the warmth. "You're a nice man, Matt Murdock," she said, using my name for the first time.

"Thanks. Ready to see those etchings?"

She took her hand away, shook her head, stared at the patrons of Dale's Harborside. She was a thousand miles away, playing a videotape of her past. "Do you have a few minutes?" she asked. "To listen?"

"Sure thing."

"I want to tell you about Gayla Jean," Meg Kirkwood said, "and also about me."

"Okay."

"I didn't always have this——" She indicated her leg, beneath the table. "When I talk to myself, I call it The Leg.

114

It's changed my life, and I don't think I'll ever get used to it. We were together when it happened, Gayla Jean and I, in a car that belonged to someone else, a boy named Fred Malik, and Gayla Jean was driving. Have you been to Austin?"

"Several times," I said, remembering trips from my childhood. "I remember it as a nice town. Lots of trees."

"It's the best town in Texas," Meg said, with some emotion in her voice. "When I got to the university there as a freshman I was sure I'd made it to heaven without having to die. I grew up in Mexia, a stifling little place near Waco, and my parents wanted me to go either to Baylor, which is pretty churchy, or to a nice school for young ladies. So I'd keep my chastity."

"But you went to the big university instead?" I said.

"Yes. I had dreams of being a writer, so I went to UT to major in journalism, and then I drifted to the English department, where I had some fabulous teachers, and that experience made me want to earn a graduate degree and teach. And that's what I was doing when—" she stopped again and stared out across the room until her eyes met the eyes of the old party in the blazer, "—when the accident happened."

"How old were you then?"

She looked back at me, then stared at the empty beer pitcher.

"I was twenty-three, and in my second year of graduate work. I had just passed the qualifying exam for the doctorate in English. I was practically engaged to a third-year law student named Jerry Jacobs, who came from a wealthy River Oaks family, down in Houston. My mother could hardly wait until the wedding. I was the model child in our family. Back home in Mexia, Gayla Jean was acting wild, skipping classes at high school, staying out late. She was just sixteen, but she looked older, and according to my mother, one of the fellows she was dating was in his thirties and Gayla Jean was threatening to move in with him. So they sent her down to Austin for a lesson from her model sister. I introduced her to Jerry, who got her a date with a law school friend, Freddy Malik. The thing I remember about Freddy was that he had a heavy beard, what they used to call a five o'clock shadow. We went out on a Saturday. They had tickets for a football game. I never cared for football, but Jerry and Freddy were avid Longhorn boosters, and they said it would be nice for Gayla Jean, so we went. After the game, we drove out to Bull Creek, for a fraternity party. Gayla Jean was the belle of the ball."

"How did you feel about that?"

"It stung, Mr. Murdock, and you are very perceptive. I was jealous of the way she magnetized men. They started staring at her when she was ten. They started putting their hands on her when she was twelve. And the real problem was, she let them."

"And you wouldn't have."

She stared straight at me. X-ray vision.

"They came after me, too. Not as many. But certainly enough to let me know how men act, what they want. And the answer is, no, I didn't let them."

I had the sudden urge to take her in my arms and comfort her. Bad timing, Murdock. Real bad. She went on with her story.

"Freddy and Jerry had too many drinks, and Jerry even got himself thrown into the river, so someone else had to drive. I assumed I would be the driver, but Gayla Jean put her hands into Freddy's pocket—it was his car, a lovely blue Pontiac—got her hands on the keys, and by the time I made it out to the car she was behind the

116

wheel. While I was arguing with her, Freddy hopped into the front, with Gayla. Jerry and I rode in back. The accident happened at a crossroads when Gayla Jean ran through a stop sign. A loaded farm truck crashed into us, killing Freddy. The accident jammed a piece of the door frame down on my left leg, and by the time help arrived, well—they had to take it off."

She stopped, lowered her eyes again, shifted in her chair. Talking about her stay in the hospital had made her sad. When she looked up from the table, her eyes were bright with tears. Jane, the waitress, came over to see if we needed more beer, but went away when she got a look at Meg's face.

The seconds ticked by while I waited for her to go on.

"I was in the hospital for weeks. The therapy took more than a year. I didn't have the heart to continue my graduate work, even though the people in the department were very nice. I was a romantic, and I wanted them to remember me whole, with two good legs. I blamed myself for letting Gayla Jean take control, and the moment my head was clear, I vowed never to let anyone take control over me again."

"You must have been pissed at her. Sorry. I meant angry."

"No. That's the right word. Pissed. It describes everything perfectly. She wasn't hurt at all, by the way, except for a scratch and a black eye that made her even more glamorous. Didn't Brenda Starr have a black eye?"

"I don't remember." I thought of Teresa Aiken, reporter.

"I used to want to be like Brenda Starr. She seemed so mysterious, so tragic." Meg Kirkwood gave me a hopeless little smile and then went on with her story. She was blushing now, probably a result of saying "pissed" out loud. "I hated the therapy, all those exercises, the pain, being trapped in a hospital, those terrible antiseptic smells. When I finally got home, my parents tried to be helpful. Both of them waited on me, doted on me. And I began to punish my sister. She had ruined my life. I decided to ruin hers."

I could remember feeling that way about a couple of people I'd known. "How?" I asked.

"I shut her out, refused to forgive her. I cursed her every move, never letting up. I froze my sister out."

"How long did this go on?"

"Six years, if you count the time she was out here."

"Long time for a curse. Six years."

"Yes. And curses take their toll, on the curser. I remember she'd try to get close to me and I'd look straight through her as if she wasn't there. At the dinner table, I pretended to answer her questions, for our parents' sake, but carefully maintained the chill."

"You think that's why she came to California?"

"Part of it. Oh, she was wild, but she might not have stayed if she'd had a place to run back to. I fixed that, all right. I closed those doors after her and bolted them shut, and now she's dead."

"And now you're here, blaming yourself, trying to find out what happened?"

"Yes. Silly, isn't it?"

"It's like those medieval knights," I said, trying to make her feel better about herself. "They went off hunting for dragons and stuff."

"True," she said. "They were seeking redemption. But I don't feel anything like a medieval knight. And redemption seems—so very far out of reach."

"You'll dig out," I said.

The silence hung there, like a thick plastic wall. To break it, I asked: "Are your folks still living in Mexia?"

"No. They died three years ago in an automobile accident. They were on their way to Longview, to visit relatives. It was raining and wintry, like today."

Her folks were gone. Her sister was gone. That meant she was all alone. Like me.

She excused herself to make a trip to the Ladies, and when she got back, I excused myself. On my way back I stopped to pay the check. It didn't take but a couple of minutes, but when I got back to the table, there was the old party from across the room. He was sitting next to Meg, warming my spot, leaning close to her face to whisper something. Meg had pulled away and had shoved her back tight against the cushion. The old party's hands were tanned dark, and a diamond ring winked off one finger. As I came into view, she saw me over his shoulder. He saw her looking, and turned around, startled.

There are hundreds of these old guys on the beach. They either have money or they look like they have money. Most of them made it somewhere else—Iowa, Chicago, Dallas, New York—and they've ditched their wives and taken up residence on the beach to capture a piece of lost youth by attaching their old claws to young beach flesh. Half of them are in Florida. The other half roost in my part of California. Studying them, you hope you'll never belly down that low. They dress real sharp and drive expensive cars and this one was trying to hustle my client.

"Ready to leave?" I asked.

"Yes!" she almost shouted. "Oh, yes!"

"Oh!" said the old party, as if he was surprised to see me. "So sorry. I thought the lady was, well—"

119

"She isn't," I said.

He was up out of his chair quick, and I knew from his tanned face and the tanned hands that he spent his afternoons on the tennis courts, or maybe a yacht or the golf course, making deals with his California broker and dreaming of tight girl flesh. If he had made one bad move, I would have nailed him, but he was a quarter of a century older and beneath the deep tan he was as frail as a little old lady.

No choice. I let the bastard walk.

He vanished into the night and Meg was digging in her purse for money. "How much is it?"

"I already paid. Let's split."

She stood up, shakily. "I'll reimburse you."

"No sweat. This one's on me."

"Thank you."

We walked out into the wet night. Streetlights gleamed off the slick sidewalks. My place above the Surf Shop was dark. Meg hugged herself as she walked along, trying to shut out the chill ocean breeze.

"Your car," she suddenly remembered. "It's at the breakfast place."

"Coco's," I said.

"Can you drive me back?" she said. "And take a taxi to Coco's? I don't want to—"

"Sure thing."

The rented Buick took several tries before it kicked over, and for a minute there I thought it was time to trot out the jumper cables. The ignition caught, finally, and we started for Meg's hotel.

We were heading north on Coast Highway when she told me about the old party. "Do you know what that awful man wanted?"

"Nope."

120

"He offered me money—a thousand dollars—if I would meet him later."

"I knew I should have popped him one," I said.

She went on as if she hadn't heard me. "He wanted me—because of the leg." She put a hand on her maimed left leg. "He even said as much. 'I saw you when you walked in,' he said. 'And I just want you to know I have a special thing for women like you.' Can you imagine? 'A special thing!' What kind of world are we living in? Tell me that! What kind of world?"

"Sick," I said. Sick was the way I was feeling.

"I hated his whispery little voice," she said. "It was creepy."

I didn't say anything, but just kept the car pointed north.

"Men react to the leg in different ways," she said. "It made Jerry Jacobs sick. For awhile, I thought Jerry had died in the accident because he hadn't come to visit me, but then a friend said she'd seen him at a fraternity party, and I realized things weren't going to work out between us, so I called him from the hospital and he came for a visit and just the idea of the leg almost made him pass out."

"Tough on you."

"He let me keep the engagement ring. I suppose he didn't have the heart to ask for it back. I mailed it to him. The older gentleman back there was different. He has a taste for para-amps, which is what I am. My therapist called it monopede mania."

They were ugly words, but I didn't say anything. Meg Kirkwood was in pain, and there wasn't anything I could do about it, so I just kept driving. I was hoping she wouldn't ask me how I felt about her leg.

12

The little red light on the phone in Meg's room was blinking when she opened the motel door. "Come in," she said, "while I call you a taxi." She had regained her composure on the ride through the wet shining streets along the Southern California beach and now she wore her mask of correct precision again.

Me, I still felt sick about what had happened at Dale's. Everywhere she went, there would be old parties clawing at her for their own sick reasons.

"It's probably Billy Bob," she said, "calling to check on me, find out when I'm coming back home."

I was interested in that, too. Her vulnerability was digging into me, making me want to protect her. I usually draw a line between me and a client. With Meg Kirkwood, I was going over the line. I couldn't help myself.

"I'll wait outside if you like. There's an idea I want to talk over. About your sister."

"All right."

I stepped outside while she phoned Fort Worth. I wondered what her connection was with Billy Bob. Was it business? Or was it more than business? Was Meg Kirkwood close to becoming Mrs. Billy Bob? I wondered how Billy Bob felt about the leg. Through the door I could hear her voice murmuring, but I couldn't make out the message. She talked for five minutes, hung up, then came to the door and asked me in.

"How's old Billy Bob?" I asked.

"He wants me to come home. Tomorrow. He's got me on a flight out of John Wayne Airport in the afternoon. American."

"What did you say?"

"I told him I wasn't ready to come home. Not just yet. Would you like to sit down?"

"Okay."

We sat on the motel furniture while I thought about my next move. I wanted to undress her and hold her close and make love to her, but I knew it wasn't the time. So I stuck to business.

"I have a hunch," I began. "I want to follow it up."

"Spoken like a true detective."

It was time she knew. "Ellis Dean told me he took some photos of the accident on Coast Highway. He says Modesto and your sister were murdered."

The shock registered on her lip first. The lip trembled. She tried to keep her head rigid, but her eyes rolled back in her head. She closed her eyes, then they snapped back open. The right hand trembled as she gripped the material of her skirt. The left hand covered the right hand, fighting for control.

"Photos? Where are they?" Her voice was tight.

"I haven't seen them. They might be at Dean's place. They might be with Dean's killer."

She shook her head. Tears welled up in her eyes. "I don't understand. Why haven't you told me this before?"

I shrugged. "Without the photos, it's just a hunch."

"But you've had it all along?"

"It's been growing as a possibility."

"Is there more?"

I looked straight at her. "If Dean was right, it was premeditated. Someone planned the killing. As I see it, we've got three possibilities. They were after Modesto. They were after your sister. Or they were after them both."

"Who would want to do a thing like that?"

"Whoever killed Ellis Dean, I imagine."

"You're going in circles. Is there proof?"

"No proof." My argument was going badly. How could I explain Murdock's famous hunches? "Maybe it's at Dean's. Maybe it's up in L.A., at Modesto's. That's where I want to go. Tomorrow."

"Where?" Meg Kirkwood wasn't listening.

"Los Angeles. To check out Modesto."

"No. Not tomorrow."

"How come?"

"I don't want you to."

"That's where the case leads. You can come with me."

"What for? What will I do while you're . . . investigating?"

"Come with me. You're in this far. My hunch tells me your sister knew Modesto. From before the party."

She hugged herself. "I don't want to go up there. Why should I?"

I tried to smile reassuringly. Should I lie and tell her Murdock's hunches always paid off? In a good year, my average with hunches was barely fifty-fifty. Should I tell her I wanted her with me? It was a primitive urge, and she was a civilized lady. "For the ride. And also because I'd like to have you along."

She blinked, like she didn't understand, didn't know the meaning of sex appeal. "I beg your pardon?"

"I like having you next to me," I said, and my voice cracked like a teenage kid with a crush. "Goddam it, Meg, you're a beautiful woman, a very special one, and I—"

It was a good thing I said that much, because she didn't give me a chance to say more. I had scared her. She stood, jerkily, and said, "No!"

I didn't move. She needed help. I still felt like the great protector.

"Get out! Get out right now!"

"Hey!" I said. "Wait a minute. I only—"

"You're fired!" she said, pointing at the door. She reminded me of some high priestess out of a misty legend, stern, cold, unforgiving, with the mist turning to chill sleet.

"Okay," I said. "Okay. Only—"

Her face was frozen, her eyes were like arctic rim ice. Now I knew how the dead sister felt, getting the freeze. I followed her directions to the door and walked out into the night. A wind blew in from the sea, slicing through my jacket, making me shiver. The door slammed behind me, and I was alone with closed motel doors and row after row of pale orange nightlights.

I walked to the lobby, where they called me a cab. The cab took me to Coco's parking lot, where the Plymouth started without a single cough. I drove back to my place, above the Surf Shop. I paused long enough to grab my set of hand-tooled lock picks and the big five-cell flash. Staring at my face in the mirror, I strapped on the .357 Magnum. I changed from boots into running shoes, and then I cranked up the Plymouth and drove south to Ellis Dean's house in Laguna:

Surprise. I expected the house on the hill to be dark, but when I came around the corner I saw lights. There was a big Ford LTD parked in front, and a Volvo wagon in the drive. As I drove past I thought I saw a shadow pass behind the living room drapes. I parked the Plymouth up the road about thirty yards, then walked back down the hill to Dean's. I figured Mrs. Dean might be back, now that her husband was dead. Or it could have been a relative or friend, checking out the house. Or it could have been the person who killed Dean.

Before knocking at the front door, I needed to know. I stood next to the side door, didn't hear anything. No voices. No footsteps. No TV. I moved to the rear of the house. The drapes were open back here, and I looked into the kitchen where Dean had served me coffee only yesterday morning. Then someone turned on the lights and came into the room. It was a heavyset guy in a purple jogging suit and matching purple shoes. His shirttail was hanging out in back, and he gave the general appearance of being one sloppy dude. Sloppy Dude began opening cabinets, closing the doors with a bang when he didn't find what he was looking for. I waited a couple more minutes, to make sure he was alone. If there were two guys, I wanted to know about it ahead of time, before I tackled them.

Sloppy Dude left the kitchen without turning off the lights. I had the lock open in twenty-seven seconds, not my fastest time ever, and I was inside. The .357 was in my left hand, the five-cell flash in my right. I can shoot with either hand, but I swing best with my right. I went through the kitchen, stepped into the living room with the cathedral ceiling. A fire smoldered in Dean's fireplace. There was no sign of old Sloppy, but I heard some-one banging around in the garage. The door connecting the garage to the living room was open a crack. I looked through and saw him going through some storage cabi-nets. He was pulling out empty ceramic plant pots and small garden tools and cans of weed-killer. The work was making him grunt and I could see sweat circles soaking the purple material under his armpits. I let him keep on searching. In a couple of minutes, he whoofed, a trium-phant sound for him, and the noises stopped. I opened the door and stood there, looking down into the garage.

Old Sloppy was opening a medium-sized portfolio that contained a stack of enlarged photographs. The light was bad, so I couldn't make out the subject of the photos, but I guessed they were shots of Gayla Jean. There was a work table in the garage, and Sloppy had spread the portfolio out so he could examine the pictures. I let him lick his lips a minute or so before I cocked the .357. The sharp, metallic sound brought his head up fast. His eyes were small and furtive. He looked like an animal. He zeroed in on the piece. "What the fuck?"

"Philo sent me," I said.

"What the fuck for? Didn't he think I could handle it?"

"Philo thinks you're a screw-up," I said.

Sloppy started moving toward me with a shrewd look on his face. "Why the hardware?"

"Philo wants you dead," I said.

He stopped. Fear covered his face. He was clean-shaven, and he must have weighed two-seventy. Sweat ran down his fat cheeks.

"You don't work for Philo," he said.

I grinned at him. "Come up the stairs real slow, Clyde, or you'll be using your medical insurance for a new kneecap."

When he got up into the house, I had him assume the position against the wall and frisked him. He carried a leather sap weighted with a chunk of lead, and a switch-blade sharp as a razor. No gun anywhere. His eyes got mean when I stood on the blade and snapped his toy off at the hilt. Then I spread eagled him on the floor and hog-tied him with some string I found in the kitchen drawer. My best hog-tie jobs are with baling wire or coat hangers, but string was enough to hold old Sloppy. All the time I worked, he cursed me. "You're dead, mother-fucker. If Philo doesn't kill you, I will."

They all say that. It's a reflex action, like flinching when you get hit.

With Sloppy safe on the floor, I went back to the garage to gather the pictures in the portfolio. They were of Gayla Jean, complete with the see-through purple dress and silver heels of Ellis Dean's deadly fantasy. About half of them were nudes. About half of the nudes were beaver shots. In all of the pictures, Gayla Jean looked sexy, sensual, devilish.

I left the pictures behind the divan near the front door and went upstairs to check the rest of the house. Even though I was no longer working for Meg Kirkwood, I was ready to show her the pictures. Just for old times. As I walked upstairs, I realized I was angry with Meg, partly for being so prissy and literary, partly for rejecting me. She was a powerful lady. I wanted her.

I found Mrs. Ellis Dean bound and gagged and cov-ered with a heap of clothes in the walk-in closet in the master bedroom. She was a pale, frail woman in her late thirties, but she was strong enough not to faint when I cut her loose. She wore pink panties decorated with a prim rim of lace and a pink matching bra, and it looked like Sloppy Dude had either caught her dressing or forced her to undress. The first thing Mrs. Dean did was to grab a robe. Then she glared at me and said, "He took Melissa! He took Melissa!"

Melissa turned out to be the teenage daughter, and I found her, also in her skivvies, on the floor of another closet. The daughter had pale skin, like her mother, and she had Dean's features and shy, hesitant manner. I got the mother's permission to cut the daughter loose. There was one bruise on her right shoulder, and another couple on her thighs. "Don't hurt me any more," she said, and then she realized I wasn't old Sloppy, and bit her bruised lip. "Where is he?" she asked.

"Downstairs," I said. "You okay?"

"Now I am." She looked away.

While the ladies got dressed, I called my pal Webby Smith, at the Laguna Beach PD. He said he'd send a patrol car. Mrs. Dean and I sat in the kitchen to wait for the cops, drinking coffee. Mine was laced with some of Dean's Courvoisier. Between sips, we tried to make conversation. I told her I'd been working for her husband, as a security consultant, and that he'd let me go with the understanding that I was to check on the house.

"Then he knew we were coming back?" Mrs. Dean asked.

"I think so, ma'am." Matt Murdock, Mr. Nice Guy.

"Poor Ellis. How did he die?"

Her question brought up the image of Ellis Dean, dead in his Saab Turbo, with a pitchfork sticking out of his gut.

"I'm not sure, ma'am. You can ask Lieutenant Smith, down at the station."

Mrs. Dean poured us more coffee. Melissa, dressed in jeans and a pale yellow sweater, came down and sat at the table. Mrs. Dean wouldn't allow her to have brandy in her coffee. The girl had a bookish look. She kept staring up at me over her cup, smiling faintly. I had seen that look before, in girls her age. California kids hide behind it when they hit the teenage years. To them, it's sexy.

"And who is that awful man?" Mrs. Dean finally asked.

"Just a thief, I guess. Crime's up two hundred percent along the coast. A house like this, isolated, on a dark road in an upscale neighborhood, it's a sitting duck."

"Upscale? I never thought of this neighborhood as particularly upscale."

"That's because you're not a crook, Mrs. Dean."

At that, Melissa Dean laughed. She had a pretty laugh, and a good set of sharp teeth, like a chipmunk. I figured her for fifteen or sixteen.

"Not a crook, mother," she said. "That's very funny."

"He was here when we arrived," Mrs. Dean said. "The garage door opener wouldn't work, so we parked and came to the door. He took one look at us, slapped Melissa when she tried to run to the phone. He made us both undress. I will never forget those hands, touching my skin. He tied us up. I am certain he planned to have his way with—both of us."

"Don't be so corny, mother."

Mrs. Dean's hand shook. She stared over at her daughter, who left the table and walked away from us into the living room, where Sloppy Dude was still hog-tied. I could see her, but I couldn't see him. She stood there watching him for a minute, then about-faced and vanished into the garage.

"Poor Melissa," Mrs. Dean said. "She's terribly shy—perhaps you noticed—and a thing like this, well, it could cripple her forever, emotionally, I mean."

I nodded, even though I didn't agree with her assessment. The daughter was a tough cookie with a sexy chipmunk overbite. Mrs. Dean's coffee was not as good as

Ellis Dean's had been, and neither one of them could hold a candle to me, a thought that made me know for sure I was getting old and set in my ways.

The door to the garage opened and Melissa Dean stepped back inside. Her arms were rigid and she was moving like a person in a straitjacket. Then I saw something in her right hand as she raised it above her head and ran out of sight.

"Hey!" Sloppy Dude yelled. "Hey, baby! No!" And then he screamed, and I was out of my chair, bolting for the living room. The girl was digging at Sloppy's behind with a bright wood chisel. He tried to roll away from her, out of the path of the chisel, and before I could get there she drove the blade down into his fat rear end and he screamed again. The chisel didn't stand up straight from his butt, but fell over onto the carpet, which showed how bad her aim had been. Too bad, because his big butt made one sweet target. I grabbed the girl, who was huffing and sweaty from her deed. She was stronger than she looked.

"Bastard!" she said. Her voice rattled in her throat. "Filthy bastard scum!"

Then Mrs. Dean made the scene and did some shrill screaming of her own. "Oh, Melissa! My God. My God! What have you done?" At times like these I try to accomplish one thing at a time.

First, I shoved the girl into her mother's arms and ordered them to cool it upstairs.

Second, I checked the wound in Sloppy's butt. It was halfway between a scratch and a laceration. There was blood oozing out, but not gushing. The chisel was razor-sharp, with no sign of rust. It made me think of Ellis Dean, surgical steel, things that were cared for. The sharp blade had torn loose a flap of Sloppy's purple jogging suit. Fear made him stink. "You need a bath, Clyde."

He kept on moaning.

I found a clean dish towel in a kitchen drawer. I packed the towel against the wound and popped the warmups back in place to hold it. Then I grinned at Sloppy.

"You're gonna die, Clyde," I said. "This here is Gangrene City." I poked his butt, making him grunt.

"Christ!" he moaned. "Do something! It hurts like hell!"

"Don't mess with the quiet ones," I said. "They'll fry you and eat you for breakfast. Better tell me everything you know before the cops get here."

"Fuck you!" he said.

The third thing I did was to tote the portfolio of Gayla Jean out to my Plymouth, where I locked it in the trunk. Then I went back inside and doctored Sloppy's lacerated butt with some of Ellis Dean's whiskey. I untied his hands, to let him know I was a good guy. He shifted to one side, to ease the pain from the chisel. When I saw how he drank, tonguing the bottle opening, I stepped into the kitchen and got myself a beer.

Two long slugs of whiskey loosened him up. His name was Bert Freed. He was from Pueblo, Colorado. He had lived off and on in Vegas. He was out here doing a search and recover job for Mr. Philo Waddell, an art dealer who wanted his portfolio back. Sloppy was making $500 bucks for the night.

"His portfolio?" I asked.

"I could use a chaser, myself," Sloppy said, indicating the beer.

I handed him my beer and watched him guzzle most of

it down. Guzzling had got him where he was today. There was no going back when you were a guzzler.

"He told you it was his?" I asked again.

"Yeah, sure he did," Sloppy said, eyeing me. "Who the hell are you, anyway?"

"Friend of the family," I said, nudging his thigh with my boot toe. "This your usual line of work, B and E?"

"Some of this," he said. "Some of that."

"Small time mob stuff?" I asked. I had stepped off a bus in Pueblo once, back in the early seventies. You could smell mob everywhere. The head mob guys probably liked it for their health, asthma, emphysema, lead poisoning, that kind of thing.

"Stuff it," Sloppy said.

I showed him the chisel. In the light from Dean's living room lamp, it glinted wickedly. "I could finish what the girl started," I said. "This baby would shave whiskers off a hog."

Sloppy hunched there, against the wall, sweat running down his jowls. In another time, in another country, if he had been green-skinned and VC, I could have executed him in the name of freedom and earned myself a decoration from the president.

"Mr. Murdock?" called Mrs. Dean from the top of the stairs. "Are you still there?"

"Yes, I'm here, ma'am," I called back.

And just then I saw the blue and red roof lights cycling their way through the plate glass window into Ellis Dean's upper-middle-class living room. The doorbell rang, and I handed a sweating Sloppy over to the law.

13

Once you hit the San Diego Freeway, it's about an hour from my place on the Newport Pier to the heart of Los Angeles. There's no reason to roll out early, because you just fight the folks with real jobs who have a daily commute of over 100 miles, so I usually leave at eight, which puts me in Los Angeles the Fair around nine.

It's an ugly city, with pretty parts like Bel Air and Beverly Hills, and some choice spots along the water, like Santa Monica and Venice and Marina Del Rey.

Marina Del Rey was where Jaime Modesto had lived.

The address on Marquesas Way was a gift from my pal Webby Smith. The place where Jaime Modesto had lived was a condo complex about ten years old, white stucco, red roofs, expensive-looking, with palm trees, the requisite peanut-shaped pool, a couple of oversized bougainvillea about to burst into bloom, and a parking lot that needed a new topping of asphalt slurry.

You can usually tell about the upkeep of a complex

from the parking lot. This one needed work. I drove in, parked the Plymouth, double-checked the address, double-checked the cars. I counted five Porsches, seven BMWs, five Cadillacs, four Toyotas, two new Chrysler convertibles, a handful of other iron like Mazdas and Datsuns, two Jeeps, and one of those VWs they call the Thing. There was a telephone service truck parked in one slot, and against the far wall sat a red pickup.

The pickup was parked down at the end of the lot, angled in backward for a fast getaway. Before I got out to reconnoiter, I opened the glove box and pulled out the .357. I didn't take the time to strap on the shoulder holster, but stuffed the gun in my belt, in back. Having a piece stuffed in your pants, anywhere in your pants, makes you think about wearing a holster to bed.

It took a couple of minutes to find the bullet hole, which somebody had filled with solder and then painted over. The hole was in the frame, between the cab and the engine compartment. The paint was still mushy. The last time I'd seen the red pickup had been Sunday night, late, on Coast Highway outside a condo complex at the edge of Corona Del Mar. It had sailed off through a stand of palm trees after taking a bullet from my .357. If the driver of this red job was here to check out Modesto's condo, the connections were getting too messy.

Also—he could be casing me right now.

I wrote down the license number and went inside. An elevator whisked me to the third floor, where one end of a corridor opened out on the blue water of a marina, with boats riding at anchor. Modesto's place was 313, a number I did not like. I stood at the door, listening. Somebody was inside, bumping against the furniture. I got the sense whoever was doing the bumping was in a hurry. The door was locked. The picks were the best way, but my hands were sweaty. It took me a good two minutes before the knob turned and the door opened.

I shoved the picks in my pocket, took a deep breath, held the .357 muzzle up the way I'd taught so many guys to do at the academy, and slammed into the room. When I was inside, I rolled to one side, expecting a bullet from the dark corners, and came up behind a heavy divan, which is good for stopping bullets.

The burglar didn't disappoint me.

He fired three shots, squeezed off with a professional hand. I counted to three, then fired back, using a triangle pattern. Two of my slugs hit the wall. You can tell because they slap against construction stucco with a soft splat. The third one hit something that sounded like burglar. I heard a soft grunt, a curse, and then he was into the room, a cowboy with regulation hat, leather vest, tight shirt with pearl buttons, faded jeans, and the biggest hogleg I'd seen since I was tracking Commie opium smugglers on the Ho Chi Minh Trail.

He emptied the gun at me, splattering the lamp behind my head. Hot flame seared my right shoulder. Hit, I thought, and fired back. The knowledge that you are not immortal always seems to throw you off the track, and my next shot went wild. The cowboy was weaving and bobbing like a halfback on his way to a touchdown. When he was almost out the door, I slammed two more slugs at him, but they didn't slow him down. The burning sensation was spreading from my shoulder to my right ear now. I saw movement off to my left, and, crazy with fear and adrenaline, turned and fired at it. When a hanging wall mirror shattered into a thousand pieces, I knew I had blasted my own reflection.

Getting old, Murdock.

A leg cramp hobbled me as I got up, heading for the hallway. Outside the apartment, I ran into an old boy in baggy golf knickers. His face was red, as if he had been drinking his breakfast. His eyes were wide with excitement, and he waved a golf iron at me.

"Where's the goddam war?" he asked. "Whoo-boy!"

I pushed past him. A trail of blood led to a door marked Stairs. I stopped to reload. My mind was churning, I felt sick to my stomach, and the fire was spreading, spreading. Going to burn my brain up. Not good.

"Where's the goddam war?" the old party asked again. He was coming toward me, his knickers bloated against the light from the window.

I pushed the door to the stairs open because I wanted the cowboy dead. I needed backup, but there wasn't time. I didn't know how bad I was hit. Twice now he had slipped by me. I didn't know his name, which made it a lot like war. The trail of blood led down. He was fast, faster than me. From one quick glimpse, I was sure he was the same dude who had followed Ellis Dean to the Ancient Mariner last Sunday night. I was also sure he had killed Dean. The knowledge wasn't doing me much good. He had almost killed me back there.

The trail of blood drops led to a tan metal door that opened only from the inside. The metal was clammy to the touch, and when I swung it open I dropped awkwardly to one knee, holding the .357 with both hands, just in time to see the rear of the red pickup leaving the parking lot. No time for a shot. I took a couple of steps, felt the first raindrops on my face. Christ, I was alive.

The shakes started as I was climbing the stairs, back to Modesto's. My leg cramped twice before I got there.

Inside 313 I found Mr. Knickers and a dark-skinned man in a telephone service worker's uniform. His name tag said Trevino. He was bruised and groggy.

"I called the cops," Mr. Knickers said. "Think I oughta

call the National Guard? SAC, maybe? Or what about the goddam Coast Guard? Whoo-ee!"

"What happened to you?" I asked Trevino.

"Come to take out the phone," he said. "Got beat up by a cowboy pendejo."

"Where were you?"

"The bedroom," he said.

"How long ago?" I asked.

"Twenty minutes. Maybe thirty. I don't know, man."

"Get a look at him?" I asked.

"For two seconds." He held up two fingers. "Solamente dos," he said. "Madre mia, it hurts, this head of mine."

"You're bleeding, there," Mr. Knickers said to me.

Since I'd wasted the mirror in the living room, I went into the bathroom to take a look at my wound. The door was closed, the shower curtain was pulled shut, and behind the curtain, in a tub full of water, was a dead girl. The murderer hadn't bothered to undress her. He had just held her head under water until she gave up on breathing. Her long black hair trailed out in swirls in the water. She wore an orange dress with soggy white flowers, and her eyes were wide open.

"I got him into the bedroom," Mr. Knickers said, from the doorway. "Who the hell are you?"

"Private detective," I said, without turning. "Who are you?"

"I'm a neighbor, goddamit. Name's Kincaid." He took a step inside, saw the dead girl. "Judas H. Priest. Who the hell is that?"

I didn't bother answering. People in crisis say things that sound dumb because they're in crisis. To sound smart again, they need to exit crisis. Exiting sometimes takes awhile. I took off my jacket and started unbuttoning the shirt. My fingers felt numb and cold. Let the cops handle the stiff. They get paid for it.

"You know Modesto? The guy who lives here?"

"Sure, I know him. The hot Mex movie star, right? With the fancy set of teeth and the Trans Am with the racing stripes and the honeys coming in here in the dark. Cats, what I say. They're all cats."

"Ever talk to him?"

"No spikka da Espanish," Mr. Knickers said, giving me his best WASP grin.

"Ever see her before?" I indicated the dead girl in the tub.

Knickers bent down so he could peer at her. "Maybe. Nah, I don't think. Nice set of puppies on her, though." He stared at the girl with a look of fascination. He would be crowing about this day for a long time. "Think we should pull her out?"

"Leave it for the cops," I said.

I stripped off my shirt, checked the wound in the mirror. A long bloody gash tore along the top of my right shoulder. Couple inches to the left and it would have penetrated my ear. It hurt worse than it looked. The shirt was torn up and bloody. "Locate me a shirt, would you, Kincaid?"

Mr. Knickers said sure thing and tromped out. For the first time, I saw he was wearing hiking boots with red shoelaces. Welcome to Marina Del Rey. I found some isopropyl alcohol in the medicine cabinet. Dabbing it on with a Kleenex brought tears to my eyes. I had some painkiller in the car, but first there was mop-up at Modesto's.

"Here's a couple of shirts." Kincaid stood in the doorway with two of Modesto's shirts. One was Mexican, the frilly kind 300-pound bar bouncers wear outside their pants. The other was a faded blue workshirt. I chose the workshirt.

"Thanks."

The shoulder gash was making my head hurt, and as I walked out of the bathroom, I got the whirlies.

"What you need is a drink, fella."

"Yeah." And what he needed was a morning drinking buddy.

"Hey, in there?" the phone guy called, from the bedroom. "What's going down, anyway?"

"A dead girl!" Kincaid raced in to tell him the latest, while I hunted for the girl's I.D.

I found it under a chair in the living room, near the entry way, where it had probably slid when the murderer had waylaid her. I heard a siren wail, then stop, so I took the purse into the kitchen. It was black and small and cheap, with a busted zipper. Inside was an alien's green card, a set of keys, three singles, two fives, and a twenty. There was the usual female stuff—small hairbrush, lipstick, spare bobby pins—and a red address book. The name on the green card was Esmerelda Rincon. The entry date said December 22, last year. I thumbed through the address book. It was all names and numbers, most of them with a 213 area code. 213 is the greater Los Angeles dialing area. Along in the W's, I hit pay dirt. Philo Waddell's name was there, spelled Wadel, and a number with a 714 area code. That's the area code for my part of California, mine and Philo's. On the inside front cover were the initials, J.M.

"The cops are here!" Mr. Knickers yelled from the other room. I slid the address book into my boot. It hurt to bend, to walk, to smile. I was withholding evidence. I walked into the living room to meet the law.

There were two of them, in black uniforms, rain beaded up on their police visors. The older one, according to his plastic I.D., was named Luciano. He had a weary smile that put him about a year from retirement.

The younger one was blond, husky, with a good tan

and mean yellow eyes. His name tag said Rakovich. He was ambitious, this Rakovich. You can spot them in any squad room. They're in the top of their class at the academy. They're ex-jocks who look sharp in the uniform. They fantasize about getting a law degree and making Captain by the time they hit thirty. They're hot to transfer to Vice or Homicide or Narcotics, where the action is. And until they get the transfer, they hassle everyone on the beat.

Rakovich tossed the purse to his partner, then tapped me with his stick. "Spread 'em, pal," he said. He whistled when he found the .357, which distracted him from finding the red address book. "Hey. Looka here. Lookit what he's packing."

"Has he got a carry permit?" the big cop asked.

"Hey!" Rakovich said. "I never thought to ask."

"Well," the old cop said. "Ask."

Rakovich tapped me on the right shoulder, sending a stab of pain burning through my ear. "You got a permit, pal?"

"In the jacket," I said. "On the sofa, there."

"There's a dead girl in the bathroom," Kincaid said.

"What?"

"A dead girl. In the bathroom. Ask him."

"Watch him, Gino." Rakovich pulled his piece, started for the bathroom. "I'll check it out."

As Rakovich left the room, the big cop turned his weary smile on me. "Gung ho rookie," he said to me. And then: "Don't I know you from somewhere?"

"I taught small arms at the academy."

"Yeah." He stuck out his hand. "I remember. Back six, seven years. Murdock, right?"

"Right. Only it was ten years back."

"Ten years. Jesus." Shaking hands hurt the shoulder. Luciano noticed. "You take one?"

"Almost," I said.

"Paramedics should be along any minute."

"Good."

"What went down here, anyway?"

"I'm on a case down in Orange County," I told him. "I had a lead on the guy who used to live here, a Latino movie actor named Modesto. When I got here, some crazy cowboy threw down on me with a horse pistol."

The old cop was a pro. He had his book out now. "How long ago?"

"Twenty minutes. Maybe a half hour."

"Description?"

"Six-four. Weight about two-twenty. Cowboy uniform. Jeans, western shirt, black leather vest, brown Stetson. I saw a belt buckle glint, and I'm guessing it was big and shiny. He was driving a red Chevy pickup." I paused. "And here's the license number."

Luciano's weary smile turned into a smile of professional appreciation. "You're kidding," he said.

"Nope."

I read him the license number. He was on the phone, putting out an All Points, when hotshot Rakovich came back. The kid's face was green. He glared at me.

"Book him, Gino," he whispered.

A chief homicide dick arrived, to take over. His name was Coltrane. He had gray hair and a matching silver mustache and a gray tweed jacket that must have set him back five bills. Coltrane was shaved, barbered, polite, attentive. He wore a pair of dark gray slacks with a military crease. His tie was tied carefully, and I had the feeling he was on the road to promotion. While a junior dick wrote down my answers, Coltrane asked me questions. I told him everything I knew, except about Philo Waddell and the red address book.

That was mine.

"So, Mr. Murdock. Let me see if I've got everything straight. You were hired by a citizen named Dean as bodyguard. A half-hour after you were hired, a red pickup tried to run your client off the road. You fired at the pickup. In a late-night confession, Dean tells you he knows who murdered Modesto and this girl, Gayla Kirkwood. You accompany Dean to her funeral, where you meet the sister, from Fort Worth. That evening, your client releases you—"

"No," I said. "He fired me."

Coltrane smiled. It was the smile of a man on the way up the ladder. "Your services were no longer needed. This was—" he paused to check the notebook the junior dick had been writing in "—this was on Monday. Monday night, your client was murdered, his body found in a parking garage in South Coast Plaza, so on Tuesday you make contact with Ms. Kirkwood, the sister, offering your services. Ms. Kirkwood hires you. You search the girl's apartment, find nothing connecting her to Modesto, and later that evening you are released by Ms. Kirkwood."

I didn't say anything. I didn't like the word "released." It made me feel like a carrier pigeon in wartime, or maybe a bird in a gilded cage.

"On a hunch, you return to the Dean house, where you surprise one—" Coltrane motioned for the notebook again. I wondered when in his career to the top of the Great Pyramid he had stopped taking his own notes. It was a handy symbol of power, having someone else take your notes. "—One Bertram Freed. We're checking that now with the Laguna Beach P.D. Today, Wednesday, you drive up to Los Angeles, where you surprise the man in the pickup. Your bullet hole is still there. You come up to the apartment, exchange shots, break up the place generally, and find a dead girl in the bathtub and a telephone repairman on the floor."

"Not in that order," I said.

"The phone man is here," Coltrane went on, "because Modesto is three months behind on his bill. The dead girl, Esmerelda Rincon, is here because she was a friend of Modesto's. We can assume she didn't know he was dead, came here to tell him something, or to get something from the apartment. She had her own key. Mr. Kincaid is here because he pays rent on an apartment down the hall. He thinks he remembers seeing Miss Rincon." Coltrane leaned forward and smiled his gray smile. "What I still can't figure out, Murdock, is why you're here."

Times like these, you wish you had stayed in construction work. Mr. Knickers had changed his story about the girl. I put that down to old age and excitement, something that would affect us all, in time.

"Like I said, I had a hunch Modesto and Gayla Kirkwood were connected."

"A hunch," Coltrane said.

"Yes, sir."

"How long were you in the army, Murdock?"

"Eleven years, lieutenant. 1957 to 1968."

"And how long in the PI game?"

"Since the late seventies."

"A hunch, you say?"

"Yes, sir. A hunch."

"How's that shoulder?"

"The painkiller helped," I said.

"Like to look at some mug books? We may turn up this cowboy creep." It might have been phrased as a question, but from Coltrane it was an order. If Coltrane had been in the army, he would have enlisted as a major.

"Sure, lieutenant," I said. "No problem."

As we went out, the old cop, Luciano, came up, carrying a stack of girlie magazines. *Playboy. Penthouse. Hustler.*

144

On top of the magazines was a stack of envelopes, unopened. The top envelope was from MasterCard, the credit people.

"Kid owed some money," the old cop said. "Want me to hang onto this stuff?"

"Go through it," Coltrane said. "You know why?"

"Because you say so, lieutenant." Luciano was smiling. He had a good connection with Coltrane.

"No," Coltrane said. "It's because Murdock here has a hunch. Tell him, Murdock."

I waited a minute. I didn't want to piss Coltrane off. But I wanted to show them I wasn't working here any more. "I don't think he had time to find what he was looking for."

"Who?" the junior dick said. It was the first time he'd said anything.

"The phantom cowboy," Coltrane said. "Tell him what the cowboy was after."

I shook my head. "Pictures. Videos. Academy Awards."

Coltrane turned back to Luciano. "Dry hunch," he said.

Luciano laughed. In a year or so he would be sitting on a pier somewhere, fishing, while he drew down retirement pay. I liked him. Maybe he'd fish off my pier, down in Newport.

I walked out of Modesto's with Coltrane and the junior dick. The old cop followed, carrying the magazines and the unpaid bills. The junior dick had my .357 and my license. It was going to be a long afternoon.

14

An afternoon with the police mug books at the L.A.P.D. is not my idea of pleasant time spent. A woman cop sat with me. Her name tag said Divelacchio. She told me her name was Susan, and I was to call her Susie, like the rest of the guys. Susie had a nice smile. She also smelled terrific. I wondered how it would be for a civilian to ask a lady cop what perfume she used.

Susie plied me with strong departmental coffee. About one o'clock, the junior dick dropped in to see how I was doing. About two, Luciano came in with a paper sack of sandwiches, and the three of us had a picnic. I was an ex-Catholic and they weren't, so we had common ground for lunchtime talk.

I found the cowboy's picture at 3:57 P.M. I remember because my shoulder was starting to burn, which meant the painkiller was wearing off, which meant it lasted exactly five hours and thirty-two minutes. Where pain is concerned, I make careful mental notes.

The cowboy's name was Fred J. Johnson. Alias Fred T. Thomas. Alias Fred J. Nelson. Alias Fred T. Jones. Nothing very original about this cowboy. He had done a year in Idaho as a juvenile, and then two years in the navy, as a frogman and demolitions guy. He had received a dishonorable discharge four years back. There was nothing in the folder to tell you why. My guess was dope or prostitution. After the service, Freddie had done two years at the Texas State Pen at Huntsville, for armed assault. His last known address was in Las Vegas, which was where our sloppy burglar, Bert Freed, had worked. Geographic connections weren't everything, but they certainly gave you a place to start from. And Vegas was the home of the mob.

After I showed the mug book to Coltrane, he gave me back my pistol and license and even got Susie Divelacchio to drive me back to Marina Del Rey, where the Plymouth was parked. By then, it was almost five o'clock. The rain had stopped, but there was a cold wind coming in from the sea. "Watch the lieutenant," Susie said.

"How come?" I asked.

"Just before he strikes," she said, "he makes you think he likes you. Watch him."

"Okay," I said. It was good advice.

I stood in the wind for a minute after she drove off, studying the building where Jaime Modesto had lived. There was no use going back up, because Coltrane would have it sealed. There was no reason to fight the five o'clock traffic all the way back to Newport, either, so I found a motel in Venice, a couple of blocks from the beach. And I settled down with the red book to make some calls.

About half the voices I located during the next two hours were Latino. Using what Spanish I had, I told them I was a lawyer (abogado) representing the estate of Jaime Modesto. I told them their name had turned up in his last will and testament. Most of them were happy to give me their addresses, or arrange a meeting somewhere close. Since they didn't hide anything, I figured them for dead ends.

I could have called Philo Waddell, but I didn't.

In the S section of the little red book I found the name Earl Schwartz. There were two numbers. The first one didn't answer, but on the second one I hit pay dirt. Schwartz had been Modesto's talent agent. The best way to get through to most guys is to tell them you're a cop. That's why it's against the law to impersonate an officer. The next best way is to play insurance agent, because insurance companies have money and dead people have a funny way of throwing it around before they die. Throwing money around makes some people feel immortal, like there's more around the corner.

"Mr. Schwartz, my name is O'Brien, Tommy O'Brien. I'm from Lincoln Mutual, out of Phoenix, and I have reason to believe you're in line for a chunk of Mr. Modesto's insurance money."

Schwartz was a careful guy with a voice like a cement mixer. He asked me to repeat everything. So I did. Finally, smelling money, Schwartz softened up.

"I didn't even know the little schmuck knew about insurance."

"It's a good policy, Mr. Schwartz. It pays double on any death ruled accidental by the police."

"This one sure was. Accident, I mean. Dead of night. Fire. Whew. What an awful way to go."

"I was wondering, Mr. Schwartz, I need your signature on a couple of forms, before we go ahead with processing. Would it be possible to get together for five minutes?"

He paused. I had the hook out, stacked with bait. Also, the guy was curious.

"How much did you say?"

"There are two policies. The face amount of the one with you as beneficiary is ten thousand dollars."

"The little schmuck," Schwartz said. And then he gave me the address of his office, on Sunset Boulevard.

It was a dark four-story building on East Sunset, about a block from Doheny which is a thousand light-years away from Beverly Hills. The Earl Schwartz Agency, Talent and Bookings, was on the fourth floor. The elevator smelled like fresh paint. I got off at four. At 404, I knocked and went in.

Earl Schwartz was sitting behind his desk, studying a picture portfolio. He was taller than he'd sounded on the phone, a guy in his mid-fifties balancing overtime with the fork against a 48 suit size. He had a full head of gray hair and quick, black eyes that sized you up. His glance let me know I was not suited for the silver screen. Another teenage hope shattered.

"You the insurance guy?"

"That's right."

"What company was it, again?"

"Lincoln Mutual." I flashed an old business card at him.

"Sit. Show me the forms I got to sign."

I sat. The walls of the office were covered with photos

of Pretty People. There were pretty girls in every form of dress and undress. There were pretty guys trying to look tough, sexy, and with it. About a third of the wall behind the Earl was devoted to Jaime Modesto, and I wondered what would have happened to Gayla Jean if she had made it this far, to Earl Schwartz, Talent and Bookings.

"First, a couple of questions."

Schwartz leaned back in his swivel chair, put his feet on the desk. He needed a cigar and a straw boater, just to make the picture complete. "Shoot. O'Brien, is it?"

"That's right." I brought out my notebook. "Just to clear up our records, you understand?"

"Gotcha."

"Ah, how long were you and Mr. Modesto associated?"

"The kid worked for me maybe three years."

"And he made how many films during that time?"

"Three. The first two were for the tamale market. Pardon my French. I meant Latino. Did okay, for that market, anyway. His best B.O. was *Tijuana Rose*. It was nominated at fucking Cannes."

"Really?" I frowned at his foul use of language.

"No fucking joke," he said, trying to shock me.

"I'm sorry. You said B.O.?"

"Yeah. Box Office."

I smiled, gratefully. "And what was the last contract you negotiated for Mr. Modesto?"

"What's that got to do with insurance?"

"It's on the form, Mr. Schwartz. Sorry, just a couple more. The head office, you know."

"Ah, fuck it. His last picture was a dog. *City of Bikinis*. Can you imagine charging five biscuits to see a title like that? Art film, my sweet ass. Would you pay money to see a flick called *City of Bikinis*?"

"Sorry. I don't go to many films."

"Where you from, O'Brien?"

"I work out of Phoenix. Tell me, Mr. Schwartz, was Mr. Modesto in trouble with the law?"

"He would have been. You know Selma Vardoulis? Lives in Scottsdale?"

"Sorry, can't say I do. What did you mean—he would have been?"

Schwartz sighed. Something was coming. You could feel it. "Would you believe the little schmuck was getting ready to do some X-rateds?"

I frowned, always a good gesture to show you don't quite get the message. I scribbled in the notebook. "Sorry. X-rateds?"

"You know. T and A. Skin. Sex. What they used to call stags."

"Oh."

"Hollywood suicide, pal. The kid wanted to break his contract."

The key had been there, all the time. "Are you sure? Do you have proof?"

Schwartz leaned over at me. "Why do you need to know? The schmuck's dead and gone in a fire, ain't he? So why do you come nosing around? Who the hell are you, anyway? Show me that I.D., again, why dontcha!"

"Sure thing, Earl," I said, and pulled the .357.

"Huh!" His eyes stared at the gun. The color drained from his oily face.

I dropped off the Tommy O'Brien insurance mask. "Just one more question, Earl, and then I'll leave you to your memoirs."

"Whuuu—" He was red in the face, like a man about to bust a blood vessel.

"Give me the name of the outfit Modesto was going to make the films for."

"The name . . . whu . . . whu . . ."

"The name," I repeated.

"Sizzle," he stammered. "Sizzle Productions, over on Western."

"Address?" I asked. "Phone?"

"Gotta card," he said, tearing open his top desk drawer. "Somewhere, I gotta card. Goddam. Goddam."

It took him a couple of minutes of frantic searching, but he got it. Sizzle Productions, it read. Jay Frame and Joy Tumble, Props. There was an address on Western, as Schwartz had said, and two phone numbers. Frame and Tumble were aliases. I wanted to know more, but I figured Schwartz would go into cardiac arrest if I didn't get out of there. Besides, it only got you bad karma when you pushed guys like him around. They weren't really bad. Just real sorry.

I holstered the piece and got out. Behind me, I heard him dialing someone on the phone, but I was in the elevator going down before he made any connection.

The elevator still smelled like fresh paint.

15

My wounded shoulder woke me in the night as I dreamed of Meg Kirkwood. The dream had given Meg two good legs, both finely turned on God's lathe, and in the dream we had passed beyond our client/detective relationship to a chummy walk along a deserted beach, backdrop of blue sky and palm trees, and down the beach a striped and multicolored umbrella shading a table for two from the sun. I couldn't see what I was wearing for our slow motion walk, but Meg had on khaki shorts, the kind models wear in magazine ads, and a white shirt. Her red hair was bronze in the sunlight. She was barefoot, beautiful, locked in time, smiling. Both legs were fantastic.

I woke up, shoulder burning, sweaty with desire. I washed down two pain pills, checked the wound in the bathroom mirror. It still didn't look as bad as it felt.

After a breakfast of coffee, sausage, whole wheat toast,

and scrambled eggs, I dug into the trunk of the Plymouth until I found my box of fake I.D.'s. There were over a hundred or so that I had gathered down through the years. I chose a name tag that said J. D. Strang, a printed I.D. that said City Inspector, an Eisenhower jacket, and a yellow hard hat, a relic from my construction days. To complete the picture, I dug out my clipboard. Nothing looks more official than a clipboard.

Armed, I drove across town to Western, and the offices of Sizzle Productions.

The folks at Sizzle had their own building, a two-story job, painted pale blue. A blood red awning stretched from the building's doorway to a couple of brass poles at the edge of the sidewalk. Beneath the awning was a blood red carpet. A tasteful brass nameplate on the wall near the door said simply: Sizzle Productions. I felt as if someone was watching me, looked up, saw the metal snout of a closed circuit TV camera. There was a buzzer for folks who wanted inside, and a sign above it asking you to ring, please. I did.

"Yes, please?" The voice was musical, female, friendly. It came from a tiny speaker mounted beneath the TV snout.

"Inspector, ma'am," I said.

"Do you have some identification, please?"

I showed my City Inspector nameplate to the camera, then held up my fake I.D. with the same hand that held the clipboard.

"Please state your business."

"Just routine, ma'am. The office got a report on a methyl oxide leak in the area. We've checked the buildings on both sides, and they're okay. But our equipment shows a pressure drop."

"What did you say? Ethyl what?"

"Methyl," I said. "Methyl oxide. It's a byproduct of the regular distillation process. It's odorless, ma'am, only when it mixes with certain kinds of paint, it just explodes."

"Oh, dear. You'd better come in."

She buzzed, I pushed, the door opened, and then I was inside the lobby at Sizzle. A blonde about twenty sat behind a desk. She wore a yellow dress, spike heels, and cat-eye glasses. The desk was glass on chrome pedestals and your eye was drawn to the spectacular legs of the blonde, to linger as the legs crossed, then recrossed, beneath smoked glass. The yellow skirt rode high above her knees, flash of shin, smoked stockings to match the smoked glass.

The part of the floor where I was standing was laid out like a chess board, with brown and white squares alternating. I saw two doors off to my right, one more behind the blonde. A red light was flashing above the second door to my right, along with a bright white sign that said Shooting in Progress.

The part of the floor where the blonde sat behind the desk was surrounded with white shag carpet, chrome furniture, green plants, and more shag carpet.

"How long will it take, Mr., ah, Inspector?"

"Five minutes," I said. "Can you show me the gas meter?"

"Oh, I'm not allowed to leave my post, as it were," she said, imitating her idea of a college grad. "But someone will, I'm sure."

The yellow dress was equipped with a strategic scoop neck that made her eligible for a *Playboy* centerfold. As I walked toward her, she leaned forward, to make sure she had my attention. Up close, she wasn't as pretty as I'd hoped, but her skin had the enviable flawlessness of

155

youth, and mindless sex radiated off her like beach sunshine off a bright mirror. The nameplate on the see-
through glass desktop read Hester Prynne.

"You're pretty cute," she said. "For an inspector."

"Thanks," I said. And then I used some of that valu-
able liberal arts scoop I picked up being an English major
for the CIA. "How's Reverend Dimmesdale?"

"Who?" Hester asked.

Before I had a chance to explain, the door behind the
blonde swung open, and the Sizzle bouncer appeared,
wearing tight black pants and a black shirt with a white
bow tie. His shoulders told me he was a weight-lifter. His
waxed handlebar mustache told me he was a jerk. "Jarvis,"
the blonde said. "Will you show Mr. Inspector the gas
meter, please?"

Jarvis grinned as if he would love to break my bones
and suck their marrow for his lunch. I followed him
through the door. The red In Progress light was still
flashing.

With Jarvis close by, I poked around inside the Sizzle
building, flashing my light into dark corners, checking
gas lines, tapping walls. I had watched inspectors work.
They just stand around, chew tobacco, tell dirty jokes,
and eyeball things. But when you're in the PI business,
you give people what they want to see. So I kept on tapping walls, for Jarvis.

I found the room I wanted on the second floor in the
far corner, away from the street. The room was full of
shelves. A third of the shelves were full of those round
metal canisters that films come in. The others were filled
with stacks of videotapes. The room had no windows.

I poked around, tapped a couple of walls, then turned
to Jarvis.

"Are you the owner of this building?"

He shook his head.

"You'd better get him up here, on the double."

He shook his head and stood his ground. I got the message. Jarvis wasn't leaving me.

"See this?" I held up a boxed videotape. The label on it was in Spanish. The gaudy picture showed a masked dude wearing a black outfit. The title of the film was *El Bandido de la Noche*. Night Bandit was my translation.

He nodded. His frown told me I wasn't supposed to handle the merchandise.

"When you mix this magnesium ARS with methyl oxide gas, you get a big explosion. That's what film is made of, pal. Magnesium ARS." It was bullshit, but I was betting Jarvis wouldn't know that. He didn't look to me like a chemistry major.

Jarvis shook his head again. He grabbed the videotape out of my hand, shoved me aside, put the tape on the shelf, then shoved me out the door.

"I'm warning you, pal. This place could go up, poof, just like that."

Jarvis wasn't listening. He was hustling me along the pale carpet toward the front stairs. Just as we reached the top of the stairs, an office door opened and a dude in a blue business suit stepped out. He was toting a briefcase. His hair was cropped short. He regarded me through a pair of European-style eyeglasses.

"Jarvis? What's all this?"

Jarvis shook his head. Maybe the deaf mute stuff was no act.

"City inspector, sir," I said. "Just checking for gas leaks."

"Find any?" the suit asked.

"Not yet," I said.

"Be sure and let us know when you do," he said. "Jarvis will show you out."

"I'm not through."

"Don't be long."

When Jarvis got me downstairs, the red In Progress light was off above the door, so I went in there. It was a studio. They had just finished a scene, and you could smell the pungent mixture of unreal sex and real money. A circular bed dominated center stage. Two camera guys were arguing about lighting and effect. And the star of the show, a brunette who didn't look old enough to vote, was sitting in a director's chair munching a croissant. The star wore a pale pink dressing gown with ruffles around the neck. Her dark hair was mussed. Her eyes were bored.

"Que pasa," I said.

She replied in lightning fast Spanish.

With Jarvis right behind me, I tapped a couple of walls, and found what I was looking for behind a dusty curtain. A metal fire door.

Then Jarvis led me out of there and back to Hester.

"Find any gas?" she asked, sweetly.

"You've got trouble upstairs," I said. "In that storage area. This afternoon, I'm bringing a crew back. If I have to, I'll bring a cop and a court order."

"Jarvis," she said. "Show the inspector out."

"Just one more question," I said.

"Just one? Promise?"

"Who was the guy in the suit?"

"Oh. That was Mr. Frame," Hester said.

My charade had run its course. Jarvis showed me out.

I spent my lunch hour in a hamburger joint on Melrose, drinking too much draft beer and asking myself, between sips, why I was doing this. No money. No glory.

No loyal woman to tell you you did good. Yet here I was, doing it.

After lunch, I went back to my motel, paid for one more night, and spent three hours diving down into a groggy and dreamless sleep. I woke up feeling a hundred and two, showered, edged the beard, went out, filled the travel thermos with weak commercial coffee, paid seven dollars for a pepperoni pizza. I brought the pizza and coffee back to the room, where I watched two hours of news that told me the world creaked on, despite greed, war, corruption, stupidity, and forgetting to oil the machinery. Just after eight, I left the motel and drove back to the Sizzle building.

I parked about a half-block away. There were lights on in two of the upstairs windows. I checked my gear: small flash, jimmy bar, lock picks, smoke bomb, rucksack. I made sure the .357 was loaded, and then I jimmied the metal door leading onto the soundstage behind the dusty curtain. I was sweating hard by the time I got the door open. The room was dark, and the dust from the curtain made me come close to sneezing.

I hugged the wall leading to the hallway for half a minute while I listened for voices. When I didn't hear anything, I looked out the door and across the expanse of chessboard floor and white shag to Hester's glass desk. Without Hester, Sizzle had no sizzle. Holding the .357 in my right hand, I went up the carpeted stairs. If thickness of carpet was any indication, Sizzle Productions was in the black.

A quick inventory of films and videotapes indicated the same thing. It looked as if Mr. Jay Frame was making money. I played the flash along the shelves until I found *Bandido de la Noche*.

Three Night Bandit films were stacked together on one

shelf. From the cartoon-type picture on the box, you couldn't tell whether the bandit was Jaime Modesto or not, but I followed my hunch and dumped the three likely candidates in the rucksack. It took me eight minutes to find a print of *Lady of the Black Masque*. There were only three copies, and they were on a shelf labeled "Club Shipment." The film outfit that had made *Lady* was called Butterfly Productions. Were they talking about the insect with the pretty wings or a certain kind of kiss? With pornographers, you never knew.

I took a minute to plant a smoke bomb against the wall near the door. I set the timer for two minutes. It would go off with a nice loud pop, and then fill the building with enough smoke to bring the fire department. Also, you never knew when you would need a diversion. I was halfway down the stairs when the front door opened and a night watchman stepped in. I hustled back upstairs. He was a young dude, lanky and lean. He wore a brown uniform and a police cap. In his right hand he carried a weighty blue and yellow flashlight, a four-battery job, and when he felt me above him, he hauled a six-shooter out of his holster.

"Who's there?" he called.

I edged backward, into the office Frame had come out of this morning. I was through the door and into the room when I noticed a sliver of light. It came from under a door inside Frame's office. Now that I was inside, I heard water running. Executive shower, probably.

"Come the fuck out!" the guard yelled. "Jarvis? You playing games again?"

Just then, the water was turned off, and I heard a foot squeak against porcelain, the kind of sound you make when you're climbing in or out of a tub, and since I was

160

trapped, probably between a lanky kid and Jarvis, I chose the easy way out.

The kid was three-quarters of the way up the stairs when I moved out of Frame's fancy office and kicked him in the chest. The gun went off, alerting Jarvis, and the kid went backward, ass over heels, and landed in a heap on the chessboard floor. I was halfway down the stairs myself when Jarvis dropped on me like a beached whale. Going down, I smelled soap, shampoo, acrid L.A. water. I kicked out at Jarvis, where I hoped his privates would be, and connected with a band of muscle that felt like the steel fire door. Jarvis clubbed me across the back, and then across the right shoulder, where the wound was. Red pain zigzagged across my back, and I tried to roll away so I could get a hold on my .357. He caught me and clubbed me again, and I kicked out at him, blindly, half seeing his bare and gleaming chest in the light from Hester's lamp, smelling his damp flesh, knowing that if he clubbed me once more this dizzy feeling would turn to eternal darkness.

I knew I was on the floor because my nose was full of Hester's white shag. Jarvis was above me, grinning. I got a full view of him, naked, hairless except for his head and mustache, wearing a purple terry cloth robe that hung down like a curtain from his weight-lifter's shoulders.

Still grinning, he took a swipe at me with a huge fist. I rolled away, and at the same time kicked at his shinbone. The shinbone is brittle on a lot of guys, and there are nerve ends all over it. I was groggy so the kick grazed his knee just enough to irritate him some more. He came after me, the purple robe flaring open, and kicked me in the kidney. Pain roared up to my ears, and I had just enough sense left to make a grab for the .357. As I did,

161

an explosion went off upstairs—Murdock's smoke bomb to the rescue—and that made old Jarvis look up, and by the time he looked back I had the piece leveled at his gut.

He saw it, but he must have figured he was close enough to outrun a bullet, so he came for me anyway, silently, when there should have been a roar. I shot him low, in the leg just above the knee. For a minute, I didn't think he'd stop, but then the leg gave out and he crashed to the floor. It was like the wreck of a concrete blimp.

I kept the gun on Jarvis long enough to make sure the fight had gone out of him. When I tried to stand, the whirlies hit me, and then the smoke made me cough. While I was still trying to stand, the kid in the uniform woke up, saying, "What the bloody fuck? What the bloody fuck?" I stumbled over to him. He was groggy and pale from his quick trip down the stairs, and his piece was across the room. I took his keys and the piece. He watched me for a minute through pale eyes, then lay down again on the chessboard floor, out of it.

By the time I made it to the Plymouth, smoke was pouring out the door of the Sizzle building. Across the street, people had gathered in a tight little circle to watch the excitement, and I heard someone ask: "Has anybody called the fire department?"

I tossed the rucksack and the kid's piece into the back seat, got behind the wheel, closed the door, took a deep breath. Two ladder trucks passed me as I headed east on Melrose. In less than a minute, I was on the Hollywood Freeway, Highway 101, heading southeast and out of town.

16

Driving down through the dark coastal night to Newport Beach, I had the feeling there was something wrong
with my car. It kept crossing the lines separating my part
of the freeway from everybody else's. I could tell because
first I would hear angry horns blaring at me, and then
people would drive up behind me and blink their brights
on and off, on and off, and the last thing would be the
little reflector bumps they put on the roads out here in
California.

I would hear those reflectors bump-bump-bumping
against my tires.

I stopped twice for coffee, once in Gardena, which
showed me I hadn't got very far out of L.A. The second
time I stopped at Bob's Big Boy in San Clemente, which
was a good ten to twelve miles south of the Newport Pier.
I had missed my turnoff to Newport Beach.

A face kept sliding across my windshield as I drove. It

had waxed mustaches and a mean mouth. It was the face of a bad dude named Jarvis. And he was trying to kill me. And I still didn't know why I had gone to so much trouble for some X-rated tapes.

One of the reasons was sitting outside my second-story beach bungalow when I rolled in. Her name was Meg Kirkwood and she was parked in front of the Surf Shop in her rented Buick. The only reason my headlights picked her up was because I decided not to negotiate the one-way streets to get to my garage and drove in the front way. Meg was sitting behind the wheel, looking out at the ocean. I was glad to see her. But I was also very tired. I wanted a bath, a beer, and a pain pill. My car clock said 11:02. I didn't know what time I had left the Sizzle building.

Carrying the rucksack full of X-rated loot, I walked over to tap on Meg's window. After a minute, she rolled the window down. I smelled sweet perfume mixed with alcohol. She was wearing an orange jacket, pulled tight against the beach chill. The jacket had no buttons, and I guessed she wore a party dress underneath. In the street light, Meg's eyes were shining.

"I came to beg forgiveness," she said. "And to tell you how sorry I am. For our tiff, and all."

I had to grin at "tiff." "Come on up," I said.

She indicated the rucksack. "Etchings?"

"Catch of the day," I said. It had been a long day and a rough night. Meg didn't notice.

"I'm a little drunk," she said. "Help me with the door."

I helped her with the door. Going up the stairs, she held onto me as if she needed help with more than going up stairs.

"I was here last night, too," she said. "Did you ever come home?"

"I was in L.A.," I said.

"Fishing, right?" she asked.

"Right."

"Catch anything?"

"Maybe."

She stood close to me while I unlocked, so that I could feel the long warmth of her body. The wind made her shiver, and she tightened her grip on my arm.

"Cold," she said. "Brrr."

"Welcome to Murdock's castle," I said.

We came inside together, brushing hips. It was a good feeling, friendly, alive. "Oh, I like it," she said. "It's cozy."

"It always needs cleaning up," I said. "Want a beer?"

"Um," she said, and found her way to the bathroom.

She was in a dreamy mood, and I figured she was here to tell me what had made her dreamy. In a way, I didn't want to know. I got us both a beer, and then I took a pain pill, and by the time she came back, looking beautiful and wistful, the pain had receded fifty percent. The rucksack with the X-rated tapes was in the corner. Ellis Dean's portfolio of Gayla Jean was in a secret hidey-hole behind the fridge, where I had stashed it before going off on my pilgrimage to Los Angeles.

"Thank you," she said, taking the beer. "And what did you find in the beautiful city?"

"Dirt," I said.

"Something about Gayla Jean?"

"Maybe. I'm not sure."

She leaned close so I could smell her. Her eyes were like huge crown jewels, liquid, gorgeous, eternal. She nodded, bringing her hair close. In this light, it was darker, with flashes of brightness when she turned. I remembered my dream, where she had had two good legs. Matt Murdock, perfectionist.

"Aren't we being mysterious, though?"

I drank some beer. "I'm not being mysterious. I'm just not sure."

"Oh, yes," she said. "You're always mysterious. Mysterious Matt, that's your name, isn't it? Matt Mysterious. Or perhaps, Mysterious Matt Murdock. M.M.M. You should put that on your business card, only you don't believe in them, do you?"

"Not much."

She leaned close again to give me a soft kiss on the cheek. It was halfway between a sister's kiss and a lover's kiss and I was sure that was the way Meg Kirkwood wanted it. Ambiguous. She was a planner, this lady. "I almost went back home," she said. "To Fort Worth."

"I thought you'd already gone."

"Billy Bob is furious. He says he'll be out to fetch me this weekend."

"How is old Billy Bob?"

"The same. He loves me. Or thinks he does. The truth is, he doesn't know the real me."

"Who does?"

"No one."

"You want someone to know the real you?"

"You." She paused to stare at me. Women do that. They try to look through you, all the way through. "At least, I think I do."

"I'm willing," I said.

"Yes," she said. "I think you are. That's nice." She put the beer down and stretched her arms above her head. The orange jacket without the buttons opened up to show a black dress with some frilly lace across the neckline. As she stretched, throwing her head back and thrusting out her breasts, her slender wrists shoved up out of the sleeves of the short jacket and I thought again

166

how vulnerable she was. I shoved back an urge to take down her hair. "Mr. Waddell thinks I can open an office here," she said. "There's a niche for my kind of word processing. He's offered to help me."

"Great. Have you told Billy Bob?" The news hit me harder than it was going to hit Billy Bob because I knew more about Philo.

"Not yet. Of course, things aren't settled yet, either. They are—still in motion."

"Great," I said.

"You don't sound happy."

"Sorry. I'm tired. And Philo is a bad dude."

"I know you think that. He respects you. Tremendously."

"I'll bet."

"He does. He says he wishes you were working for him, full time. He says good men are hard to find."

"That's because I kicked his hired hand around."

"He's going to let Butch go."

"Oh, yeah? When?"

"Soon," she said. "As soon as he's found a suitable replacement."

"Don't tell me that's why you're here. To bring job tidings from Philo?"

"No. I came to ask a favor. But the way this conversation is going, I'm not sure that I did the right thing, after all."

"Sorry." I leaned forward, took her by the hand. "What's the favor?"

"Philo—I mean, Mr. Waddell—has located a fabulous piece of property. It's in foreclosure, or will be soon. I told him you were an expert in construction, and he suggested you take a look at it. Before I do anything, I mean."

"Where is it?"

"There are two pieces, actually. One is in town, and it would be for the business. The other one, in foreclosure, is in Laguna Canyon, a couple of miles inland. We went out to see it today. A man named Burgoyne built it. There's a small stone house, a place for a garden. The road needs work. But Philo—Mr. Waddell—says that it would be better for you to give it a good going over first."

I wondered what Philo Baby was up to. I also wondered what had happened to Meg Kirkwood's guilt trip about her dead baby sister. "Sure thing," I said. "When would be good?"

"Tomorrow," she said.

"How early?"

"Afternoon, I think. I'll be meeting a banker at lunch—one of Mr. Waddell's contacts—to discuss a credit line. You need more money out here. Things are higher."

"You sound like a native."

"It's the California life-style," she said, turning on the glow.

"What about Gayla Jean?" I asked.

"What about her?"

"I thought you wanted to dig into her past, find out what really happened."

"I still do. Nothing's changed." She gave me another ambiguous look. "It's just that, well, I feel so free here, so unfettered. It only took a day—as soon as Billy Bob left. And Mr. Waddell assures me there is room for an experienced person in word processing. And I made this wonderful discovery, all by myself."

The lady was playing detective. "What discovery?"

"The rent on Gayla Jean's apartment. It's paid up through July."

"Who paid it?"

168

"She did, according to the management over there. I can live there while I'm setting up the business. It's a lovely place, and it's rent free. You can come calling." She winked at me.

"I don't see why you'd want to stay there."

"And why not?"

"Because," I said.

"Nothing went on there," she said, clenching her fists. "Don't you understand? She had everything! And this time, this is for me!"

It was time to put an end to the half-truths, so I marched over to the fridge, swung it out from the wall, pressed the hidden panel I had built in five years back, opened the door to my hidey-hole, and brought out Ellis Dean's portfolio.

"This went on," I said, and handed it to Meg Kirkwood.

It was the wrong thing to do. But I was tired. And I hurt. And I wanted to swing her away from Philo Waddell. So I sat there, across from her, while she slowly went through the photos of her dead sister. When she finished, she said: "She was very beautiful, my sister."

"Yes."

She stood up, smoothed her dress, tugged the short orange party jacket around her body. The glow had left her face, and her eyes when she looked at me were stone cold.

"How long have you had those in your possession?" she asked.

"Tuesday night," I said. "After I dropped you at your motel."

"Why did you wait so long to show them to me?"

"I was in L.A. Remember?"

"I've been here almost an hour. We've been discussing things almost an hour."

I didn't answer.

"Who took them?"

"Ellis Dean," I said.

"Then they have nothing to do with Mr. Waddell, do they?"

"His boy Butch was the bouncer at the photo sessions."

"That doesn't implicate Mr. Waddell. You were my employee, and you went off on *your* own. Remember?"

"Bullshit."

She walked to the door. In the long dress, moving smoothly through life and across my emotions, she didn't look like a lady with an artificial leg. "I came here tonight with passion on my mind," she said. Her hand was on the knob. My stomach was hurting.

"I know."

"I tried with you, Matt. I tried harder than I've tried with a man in years."

"Thanks."

"Yet you keep bringing up darkness."

"That's my job."

She indicated the photos of her dead sister. "She excites you, doesn't she? Even when she's dead?"

I shook my head. "No. You excite me."

"I reached out to you. And you don't seem to care."

"I care," I said.

"You're like all the rest of them," she said. "They all wanted her. And now she's dead."

She walked out. I moved to the door to watch her approach her rented Buick. She opened the door and got behind the wheel. The car started with a cough and a puff of white exhaust. After she drove off, I stood there for a couple of minutes, feeling sick and tired and used up. I went back inside, closed the door, opened another Bud, and spent a couple of hours studying the four X-rated tapes I'd brought from the Sizzle storage room up in L.A.

One of my ex-lady friends, a professor of psychology over at Saddleback Community College, in Irvine, says that when you've seen one blue-movie you've seen them all. She's right. They are grim comedies without plot or laughter or forgiveness, where acres of flesh parade across the screen. The flesh is real. The action is pure fantasy, where males dominate, where females submit. There is no motivation. There is only sex, flesh, more sex, flesh, dim fantasy.

But I was after information, not academic theory, and maybe a connection between Modesto and Gayla Jean. The phone guy had come to Marina Del Rey to take out Modesto's phone, which meant Modesto was out of cash, and he hadn't joined the rush to own his own phone. The cops had found unpaid bills all over Modesto's apartment. Modesto had made some X-rated flicks, for cash. Modesto had come to Bluebird Canyon, to Philo's party, for a reason. Philo had money. So maybe Modesto was leaning on Philo, for cash. It was mostly conjecture, flimsy, with a shudder of truth.

The Bandido cassettes were all in Spanish, targeted for a growing Latino market. The Bandido himself was masked, but there wasn't any doubt it was Jaime Modesto. He was a good looking kid with an unforgettable Latin lover smile. To make these flicks, you'd have to be at the far edge.

The other blue-movie made me sweat. The star was a young girl who vibrated that marketable super-quality, virginal sexuality. She had red hair, a gorgeous shape, and a wicked mouth. She wore a mask all during the movie, but during the close ups, if you put the machine on freeze frame and then held up a photo from Ellis Dean's portfolio, you could see that *Lady of the Black Masque* was Gayla Jean Kirkwood, Meg's baby sister.

One of the porno studs was the blond tennis jock I'd seen on Philo's private court, late Tuesday morning. His eyes looked stoned.

The film had been made by Butterfly Productions. There was no address on the box, and it was probably a dummy corporation with funds shoveled through three other dummies before they got whisked to an offshore operation in the Bahamas.

Tomorrow, I would take the tapes over to UC Irvine for some more analysis. Tonight, I would have to rest.

It was long after midnight, and my body ached from the beating from old Jarvis. Before turning in, I put the Dean portfolio and the Sizzle videotapes in the hidey-hole, closed it up, and swung the fridge back into place.

I fell asleep fast because of the Bud and the pain pills, and when I woke in the night I thought of Meg Kirkwood, leaving me in a huff, her back straight, her walk, and I knew, without a doubt, that she was still jealous of her beautiful sister.

Bitten by jealousy, from beyond the grave. Sad.

17

The phone woke me before I was ready to get up. It was Terry Aiken, girl reporter. Her voice had the dulcet tones of a lady who wanted information.

"Murdock?"

"Yo."

"Terry Aiken here, from the OC *Trib*."

"I remember you." In the background, I could hear the hum of voices and what sounded like soft keys clicking. Newsrooms in the days of my youth sounded like a thousand typewriters. These days, it's all electronic, word processing, images on a green screen, secret keys.

"I was just lying here in bed," she lied, "thinking of us."

"Terrific," I said. "What time is it?"

"It's seven-forty," she said. "What about meeting for breakfast? On me?"

"How about lunch?" I said.

"At lunchtime, I'll be in L.A. County."

I rolled over and looked out at the sky. White clouds,

scudding, streaks of cold sunlight. A good day to stay in bed, nursing your hurts. "How about tomorrow?"

"Got a date," she said. "To go whale watching."

"Good luck. It's past their season."

"Actually," she said, "I think I'll get engaged instead."

"Congratulations," I said.

She changed subjects, and almost told me what she really wanted.

"How are you coming on your end of the Modesto murder?"

"One client died, if you remember. The next one fired me."

"Oh. Too bad. Maybe my editor could put you on retainer."

"I'd like that in writing," I said.

"Anyone ever tell you you're a great lover?" Terry Aiken said.

"Not lately. Thanks."

"You're hiding something. I can hear it in your voice."

"Wish I knew what it was."

"Don't go Zen on me, Murdock."

"I wouldn't know how to start."

"I spent the last two nights at Grogan's Grogerie, hoping you'd show. You didn't."

"It's not one of my usual watering holes. What were you doing there?"

"Working, what else?"

"Find anything out?"

"Uh-uh. Not on your life. This is an even trade, understand?"

"Okay, kid. I'll trade you. Modesto was into X-rated flicks. He made three that I know of, dressed up as the bandit of the night. The name of the production company is Sizzle Productions, up in L.A. somewhere."

The news delighted her. "Hey, wow! Are you sure?"

"Pretty sure. Now it's your turn."

"Okay. A waitress at Grogan's is also pretty sure Philo Waddell got Gayla Jean that waitressing job." She paused, to let that sink in.

"Why would he do that?"

"Murdock, you surprise me. Why does a dirty old man do a favor for a sweet young thing?"

"He's overcome with generosity and purity of heart."

She laughed, scornfully. "You're too much. Listen, dear, I have to go or my editor will replace me with a robot. Give me a call, hear?"

I knew she was off to Los Angeles to check on my hot Sizzle lead. I was wondering how I could use her information to persuade Meg Kirkwood about Philo.

"Will do."

The morning began slowly, grinding through its gears. I had breakfast, drank a Bud, took another pain pill, and made an appointment with Professor Jeremy Gordon, over at UC Irvine.

Walking into Jeremy Gordon's office always makes me feel better about myself. It is a mess, papers everywhere, books stacked on top of each other, memo pads, computer printouts, diskettes scattered around. You see a guy like Jeremy Gordon, and you feel hope for the elite of society. He's making fifty grand a year, with time off for research. He's got tenure, which means a secure berth in a far-out department called Social Ecology. Every summer, he goes to Europe. The guy reads three languages, teaches a couple classes a quarter, doesn't worry about how his clothes look, has a great time. Jeremy Gordon makes you believe in democracy.

The reason I wanted to talk to him was because for the last couple of years he'd been writing a book, and he'd hired me to dig around in the dirt for him. The book was called *Churches and Dirty Minds: An Analytical History of American Pornography,* and to write it he'd looked at every corner of the pornography business, logically and analytically, and then he'd catalogued everything until he had a picture of what went on, worldwide. He'd even interviewed porno patrons coming out of movie houses. That had stopped, he told me, because of the videocassette revolution, which had put a virtual end to porno movie houses.

He got up from an IBM PC when he saw me at the door. "Well, well, if it isn't the Nero Wolfe of Newport Beach. Come in, come in. Don't you ever get any older?"

"Thanks, doc. You're looking good yourself."

We shook hands. His blue eyes gleamed. He was a guy in his early fifties, mustache, not much hair on top. He wore a baggy sweater, tweeds, an oxford shirt, and penny loafers he'd owned as a graduate student back east.

"Sit. Honestly, it must be the life you lead, but I think you've discovered the elixir of youth."

"Fast women and Budweiser chasers."

"Ah, God. Let me write it down. I should interview you. You're a veritable mineshaft of underworld myth."

"You already did. You were going to send me a copy."

"Would you believe my publisher is late? I've seen galleys, and now I'm waiting for page proofs. What have you got for me?" He indicated the rucksack containing the X-rated videocassettes.

"I need anything you can get me on who made these films," I said, handing them over.

"Um. Um. Um." He studied the labels. "*El Bandido de la Noche.* Sounds new. Obvious Latino market. Is it in Spanish?"

"Yes."

"They'll export it to South America. Argentina. Bolivia.

176

Chile. They'll do a dubbed translation for Brazil. It will go to the clubs."

"What kind of clubs?"

"Blue-movie clubs. They're all the rage."

"I haven't heard anything about them."

"You won't, either. Only the best people go, and that includes newspaper publishers. This other one I've heard of. *Lady of the Black Masque,* I mean. It's practically a contemporary classic. Haven't seen it, though, because it's been circulated privately."

"In the VC clubs?" VC was short for videocassette.

"Exactly. I was a guest at one, up in the glorious City of Angels, last October. All the talk was about this *Masque* picture. My reception was cordial until they found I was working on a book."

"Where was the meeting place?"

"One of your better homes in Bel Air. I wasn't invited back, and my contact has since been incarcerated."

"Vice conviction?"

"Alas, no. Drugs." He dug some reading glasses out of his pocket and studied the label on the cassette. "Where did you find this, if I might ask?"

"Made a deal with some blue-movie folk."

"What sort of deal?"

"I promised not to blow up their building if they would lend me a tape."

"Ah, Murdock as Robin Hood. The role fits, you know?"

"Thanks. Can you help me out here?"

"Something undercoverish, I hope?"

"Info first. The undercover comes later."

"Agreed."

"What do you know about Butterfly Productions?"

He closed his eyes, rocked back in his swivel chair.

"Butterfly. Butterfly. New York, I think. An address in upper Manhattan, doubtless a blind drop. I can make some calls. What else?"

"What's the grift in blue flickers these days?" Grift was a fifty-dollar word, out of date, meaning swindle. I used it to make him smile, which he did.

"Snuffs are back," he said. "I've plotted them on a three-year cycle."

"Ugh," I said.

"Yes." He punched the glasses higher on his nose. "In the old days, snuffs were the pièce de résistance, at the end of a night of blues, as a sort of icing. Everyone was inebriated, or coked to the gills. Lately, snuff clubs are cropping up, in all the major cities."

"Which cities?"

"New York, Chicago, Los Angeles, St. Louis, Dallas. The list is endless."

"Supply and demand," I said.

"Precisely."

"I thought the law came down on those bozos four or five years back."

"It's the three-year cycle," Gordon said. "I explain it all in chapter eleven. The book will be landmark, I'm sure." He rubbed his hands, like a scholar hunched over a candle, then got back to the subject. "There were several snuff convictions, two of them right here in Orange County. But the people convicted were low-level operators, amateurs, if you will."

"You think there's a mob tie-in?"

The professor smiled. Whenever a teacher smiles, I always remember why I dropped out of high school, back when I was a green kid in El Paso. Teachers always make you think they know a lot.

"I was unable to prove it, in the book."

"But you think so, right?"

"Yes. I do."

He looked at his watch, said he had a class to teach. I got up, shook hands, thanked him. He said to give him a call later in the afternoon. He might have something on Butterfly Productions. He also said he was looking forward to "viewing" the films.

I was halfway down the hall when he called to me. I stopped to wait for him. He shuffled down toward me, a brainy guy carrying a briefcase, eyes gleaming with books yet to be written.

He was panting as if he'd been running a marathon. "Something I remembered. About the snuffs."

"What?"

"They're killing cripples," he said, the frown creasing his scholar's forehead. "There was a story about a beggar down in Mexico. She was an Indio, young, early twenties, and quite pretty. She'd lost a leg in an industrial accident. They used her in a snuff film. At the climax of the film, they stabbed her to death, onscreen, with the cameras running."

"Jesus," I said.

"Awful, isn't it? The film is called *La Muerta de la Punalada*—death by stabbing. It's sweeping the clubs now. My information is spotty. I hope my book does something to stop it."

"Yeah." There was a cold knot in my stomach. "Any more? About Mexico, I mean?" I could sense Jaime Modesto, hovering.

"No. Sorry. It's a dark world, of myth and rumor. I must run. Ring me later. All right?"

I nodded and then he was past me, hurrying to class.

18

With fear freezing my heart, I started a cold-sweat hunt for Meg Kirkwood. She'd said something about a meeting, with a banker, probably a connection of Philo's. But Orange County was fat with bankers, so that tip was no help.

I left messages for her at the Newporter, where she was still registered. I called Philo's place, but Quan, the Filipino servant, assured me no one was there. Not believing him, I drove to Bluebird Canyon, pushed inside Philo's house after getting permission from Quan to use the phone, and took a good look around. It was an expensive layout, artsy, with sleek modern furniture and high-class paintings on the walls and Persian carpets neatly displayed on shining parquet floors. Standing in Philo's high-tech kitchen, I called Meg's motel again. No message. She still hadn't checked out. The kitchen was spotless, as if no one cooked there.

I wanted to search Philo's house from one end to the other, especially the basement, but Quan stuck with me. "Finish now?" he kept asking. "Finish now?"

After leaving Bluebird Canyon, I stopped off at Waddell's Gallery, on Forest Avenue, the fancy pants main drag of Laguna Beach. It was a handsome building, aged brick, dark wood, good lighting. I know zip about art, but a quick glance showed me Philo was into promoting the local talent. Each work, whether painting or sculpture, had a tag that told you the price, the artist, and the artist's place of residence. More than half the painters were local—Laguna Beach, South Laguna, Laguna Hills, Laguna Niguel.

Philo wasn't there, but the cute beach chick who answered my questions assured me he was due back around two, two thirty and if I would leave my name, she would make sure he returned my call. Everybody but me seemed to know where Philo was. As I turned to leave, I spotted a staircase leading up to a second floor.

"Is there other art stuff up there?" I asked.

"Oh, no, sir. That's Mr. Waddell's private office. And a conference room, of course, for his business meetings."

"Of course."

"Thank you," she said.

Meg was a book lover, so I took a chance and went by Fahrenheit 415, the bookstore on Coast Highway. Yes, a pretty lady from Texas had been there yesterday, or the day before. Not today.

It was past lunchtime, but I wasn't hungry. I walked over to the beach, thinking I might get a lead if I hammered on Butch boy, Philo's weight-lifter sidekick. Today was Friday, clouds scudding, a stiff breeze, bleak coastal sun. On the basketball court, jocks with ripply muscles played shirts versus skins. No sign of Butch, anywhere. In an attempt to calm myself, I drank a couple of beers at a local pub. Then I took another swing by Philo's citadel in Bluebird Canyon. The electric gate was open, just the way I had left it. The place still looked deserted.

On my way back to my place, I stopped by Grogan's Grogerie, inside Le Club. I drank another beer, and asked if the waitress had seen Mr. Waddell lately. She knew Mr. Waddell, but he hadn't been in for several days now. I tipped her just the same. In desperation, I stopped by Lido Landing, used my lock picks to get through the security gate and then into Gayla Jean's up-scale third floor pad.

One look at the apartment told me where Meg Kirkwood had been spending her days while I was chasing bad guys up in L.A. The first thing you saw, walking in, was a neat stack of packing boxes. The top box had two pairs of Gayla Jean's ski boots in it. The box underneath it was filled with the kind of ladies' underwear you can find at Frederick's of Hollywood. The next three boxes I looked into were loaded with Gayla Jean's collection of magazines—*Cosmo, Glamour, Playgirl, Playboy.* It was clear Meg Kirkwood was going to exercise her brain on the more demanding reading in Gayla Jean's bookshelf. The living room smelled fresh, as if the steam cleaning people had just been here. The bedroom windows were open, and a fresh sea breeze ruffled the drapes. The bathroom and kitchen were spotless.

When a woman cleans house, you can smell symbolism at work. Meg Kirkwood was making Lido Landing her own.

It was almost four by then, so I put in a couple of calls. One to Jeremy Gordon, over at the university. His line was busy. Then I called Meg's motel.

"Mr. Murdock?" It was a man's voice, soft, singsong.

"That's me," I said.

"Just a moment, sir. Something just came in, a few moments ago. It's from Ms. Kirkwood."

I waited. In the background, I heard a shrill voice talking about reservations, a phone ringing, the rustling of papers. There was a click, and the singsong voice came back on.

"Sorry to keep you waiting, sir. Here it is. Have you a pencil?"

"Shoot," I said.

"The message reads, and I quote, 'Matt. Meet me at the old Burgoyne place, seven P.M., Laguna Canyon Road. Friday.' It's signed, 'Meg.' That's Ms. Kirkwood's first name."

"Thanks," I said. My hand was shaking. Was it relief? Or added anxiety? "Did you talk to the lady?"

"Yes. I took the message. Why?"

"Did she have a Texas accent?"

"Yes, as a matter of fact. Why do you ask?"

"Just making sure it's not a snipe hunt," I said.

"Ms. Kirkwood is a guest here, Mr. Murdock. We do know our guests. I can assure you, it was she."

"Thanks," I said, and hung up.

The time was 4:12, three hours before meeting Meg. I knew the Burgoyne property from my construction days. It was prime California canyon land, a stone house, some acreage up above the stables. She was proving how much she loved Laguna.

Well, it was her life, her money.

Now that I had a message from her, I felt a little easier. I took one last look around. The feeling of dread was heavy. In this apartment, Meg's sister had paraded her pretty flesh in front of anonymous camera eyes for money. I didn't want Meg living here. It was a place with a curse. From the Burgoyne property, she could at least start fresh.

Jeremy Gordon's line was still busy. "Wordy academic bastard!" I growled. And then I drove back to my place on the pier.

Time hung heavily as I waited. I hate things being out of my control, which is the reason I became a top kick in the army, and later on, against everything my old man stood for, an officer. I like to think I make fewer mistakes than the next guy, and if I can take the high ground, I can hold it forever. It's not altogether true, of course. But thinking that way gives you confidence.

To kill time, I opened a fresh beer. I hadn't been counting, but this one made me fuzzy in the head, so I brewed some coffee, which I laced with brandy, to keep away the cold sea wind. I was readying a second cup when a visitor climbed the stairs to my second-story castle. The Channel 4 news was on from L.A., predicting rain and mud slides. The footsteps paused halfway up, started again, came onto the landing. Through the kitchen window, I saw a brunette lady in a snazzy fur coat. Earrings. Dark hair pulled back from a sharp face.

Lucinda Smith-Travis, slumming.

She rapped, lightly. I opened the door to find her smirking at me.

"Mr. Murdock, I presume."

She took a step forward, to come inside, but I blocked her entry. Her eyes were glazed, like she was stoned. Her face was made up for a cocktail party. Standing there, looking rich and bitchy, she clutched the fur close to her neck with a gloved hand. Around the wrist was an expensive diamond bracelet. Below the coat, I saw slick black leather boots.

"Well, aren't you inviting me in?"

184

"Nope." I grinned at her. Money gave her dark sex appeal an extra vibration, a thrumming electrical pulse. But there was something else, something snaky and evil and bruised, that you could almost smell.

She smiled then. "Really?"

I nodded. "Really."

"The subject is money. For services rendered."

"I'm listening."

She clutched the fur closer around her throat and shivered. "Please. May I come in?"

I didn't need to leave for my meeting with Meg until 6:30, so I had more than an hour to kill. I don't like society ladies, but that wasn't a reason to make Lucinda-baby catch cold. I stepped aside, waved her in. She gave me a smoky look and walked into my house.

"What a lair," she said, taking in the empty beer cans.

"Maid's day off. Want a beer?"

"I smell coffee. Is there some?"

"Black or otherwise?"

"Black, please."

While I got the coffee, Lucinda prowled around. She checked the TV, the week-old newspapers, the single shelf of paperback books. When I came back with her coffee mug, she was admiring my gun rack. She took a sip of coffee, sighed, tried to look grateful. When you have money, looking grateful is an act.

"What marvelous coffee."

"French brew. From Viet Nam."

"Oh, were you there?"

"I was there."

"I'll get right to the point," she said. "I'd like to hire you."

"I've got a client."

"Yes. Meg Kirkwood, I know. I meant, after you're finished with her case. Is that what you call it? A case?"

"That's what we call it."

Carrying her mug of steaming coffee, Lucinda moved
from the gun rack to a director's chair. As she sat down,
the fur coat fell open, revealing a slinky dress, beige, with
a V neck. The beige material reminded me of curtains,
lamp shades. Light winked off her leather boots as she
crossed her legs.

"My case involves an errant husband."

"Mr. Smith-Travis."

"Yes. He spends time in Los Angeles. Too much time.
I'd like you to find out who with. You do work out of the
beach area?"

I thought about my recent journey to L.A. "Sometimes."

"Excellent."

"How urgent is it?"

"Reasonably." She sipped her coffee. "I've been a long
time coming to the decision. It's time to strike."

"I'll think about it."

"I'd hoped you would. What do you charge, by the
way?"

I didn't know why she was here, but the wandering
husband story was crap. For Lucinda, I upped the money
to high society rates. "For you, four hundred a day, plus
expenses."

"Is that the going rate for private investigators?"

"You're free to shop around."

"No." She flashed me a neon smile, right off the society
page. "I like your style. How are things going with Meg?"

"Right on track."

"What are you searching for?"

"We're digging into Gayla Jean's past."

186

"Hoping to find what?"

"Whatever turns up."

She switched subjects. "Dear Meg. There were Texas girls at school, toothy, leggy animals. That accent fools you on southern women. They talk with a mouth full of honey, but they are so—" she paused, to hunt for the right word, "—so tartly intuitive."

"Yeah."

"So warm and relaxed."

"Yeah."

"Philo is totally captivated."

"He probably felt the same way about her sister."

There was a long pause while Lucinda thought how she would handle that. "I wouldn't know," she said.

"How long have you known Philo, Mrs. Smith?"

"Smith-Travis. You can call me Lucinda."

"Okay, Lucinda, how long have you known Philo?"

"A year. No. More than that. Two years."

"Where did you meet?"

"At a Memorial Day party at Le Club."

"What do you think of him?"

She paused to recross her legs and rearrange the beige skirt. Gray light filtered in from the ocean. The right half of her narrow, rich girl face was in shadow. She reminded me of a she-wolf circling its wounded prey. "In what way?"

"How do you read him? What makes him go? What's he want out of life now that he's got a big house in Laguna with a pool and a tennis court?"

"That's only the surface Philo," she purred. "Only what he lets the world see."

"What's down deep?"

"He's frustrated, basically."

"How do you mean?"

"It's the arts," she said. "He's dying to be a famous writer, or a famous painter. Something creative. He wants someone to write a book about him, make him immortal."

"So that's why he runs an art gallery?"

"Of course."

"Did Philo study art at college?"

"I don't think he ever went to college."

Lucinda, however, operated like a college girl. "Where'd you go?"

"Bryn Mawr. With a major in political science."

"Is that where you met Mr. Smith-Travis?"

She flashed me a look of heavy irony, owner to dumb slave. "Bryn Mawr was all girls." Then she added: "We met in Acapulco."

The beers and brandy helped buffer her careful put-down. "He do business down there?"

"Sometimes. Not so much lately, with the devaluations and all this talk of unprotected exports."

I had her going, so I shifted topics.

"How well did you know Ellis Dean?"

"That poor little man. Not well. We saw each other once or twice."

"He called you Lucinda. Like he knew you."

"A lot of people call me Lucinda. You, for instance."

"He and Philo had a weekly tennis match. I thought maybe you'd played in a foursome."

"Philo hates doubles. He has no patience with someone else's mistakes. No. I didn't play tennis with Mr. Dean. And the match was biweekly, sometimes monthly."

"He told me you bet on fighting cocks. What about that?"

She glanced up, a hard look in her eye. "Absurd. Not worth refuting."

"Okay. What do you remember about the party the night Meg's sister went off with Jaime Modesto?"

She half turned to drape the fur over the back of the chair. As she turned, the hem of the beige skirt crept up over her knees. She didn't bother to pull it down. "Very little, I'm afraid. I had quite a lot to drink. There were oodles of young people."

"How well did you know Gayla Jean Kirkwood?"

Lucinda Smith-Travis stood up, swayed, grabbed the chair to steady herself. "What is this? The Inquisition?"

Dragging the fur coat, she headed for the door.

"Leaving already?" I grabbed her arm. She tried to pull away.

"Let go!"

"What's Philo up to?" I was angry now. She'd come here to bait me, or to stall for time.

"If you don't let go, I'll scream."

"Let's call the cops. You can tell them what went down at Philo's party."

I was close. You could see the fear in her face. Her wolf smile brought out hard lines at each corner of her mouth. "Forget my job offer, Mr. Detective. I wouldn't hire you in a million years."

"What went down at Philo's party?"

"I'm leaving." She tried to break free. I held on. Her arm felt soft. I remembered the bruise on her shoulder, from the other day, at Philo's.

"What's this shit about the Burgoyne place?"

"I wouldn't know!"

"What does Philo want with Meg?"

She glared at me. "You should know!"

"Me? What should I know?"

"Men! You all want the same thing! The little crippled girl!"

189

I let her go. She had trouble getting the door open. She tugged with both hands. The fur coat fell onto the floor. I helped her with the door. She snatched up the coat and marched out. I stood there, leaning against the edge of the door, listening to her boots on the stairs. I stepped onto the deck, into the wind. She had the fur slung over her shoulder as she rounded the corner and went out of sight. Out in the Pacific, dark clouds swirled. You could smell rain on the way, and soon.

Back inside, I rinsed Lucinda's coffee mug in boiling water and made fresh coffee. I called Jeremy Gordon, over at UC Irvine. Busy. The time was 6:02 at the latest before I got through.

"Gordon? This is Murdock. Goddam you, I've been calling since three!"

"It's the modem and my dean," he said. "The electronic age meets nineteenth century academia. Together, they tie up the line. Sorry."

"That's okay. Have you got anything?"

"It's not digested, you understand."

"Give!" I yelled.

"Well, Butterfly is a new company, and they have an address in New York. The phone has been disconnected. One informant thought they might be moving west, toward the Sun Belt."

"Give me the number, anyway," I said.

Gordon gave me the number. My hand shook as I wrote it down. 212 area code. Seven dirty digits.

"They've only done three films," Gordon went on. "The first was *Sex on the Beach*. The second was *The Lady of the Black Masque*, which I screened this afternoon. Beautiful girl, even if you couldn't see her face. The third is called *Golden Boy*, a spin-off of the King Midas fable. Each woman he loves turns to gold. News from the business says it will top the other two in sales. It's not finished, so this is mere rumor."

"Lady X. She in *Golden Boy?*"

"Lady X is the new sensation of the porn world. She's hotter than the star of *Deep Throat*, which had the best gross sales of any blue film ever. Of course, hot stars burn out. A year of fame, at the most, and then . . ."

"What if something happened to Lady X?"

"Loss of revenue, while she's hot."

"Since she's masked," I said, "they could use replacements."

"True."

Insights tore at my brain. Replacements. Philo could replace Gayla Jean with a girl with the same hair, the same—

Philo could replace her with Meg.

I heard papers rustling on his desk. "I think that's all. Let me see. Just checking my notes here. Um, ah, yes, here it is. Just a rumor. A highlight of *Golden Boy,* which is, as I'm sure you have already gathered, about a Midas creature with a phallus made of gold, is a real, honest-to-goodness cockfight."

"Cockfight." The pencil point snapped as I wrote it down.

"Yes. And I'm told that they put humans in with the fighting cocks."

"Who wins?" I asked, feeling the chill closing in.

"My informant didn't say."

"Where do you get this dirt, Gordon?" I was getting angry with him now. It was crazy. So was I. I wanted to kill Philo Waddell and Lucinda Smith-Travis and smash everything connected with both of them. I should have killed Lucinda while she was here, on my turf.

"I renewed a few contacts, dear boy. From my days in

researching smut. Hope this helps you, wherever you are. Must rush now. Dinner date and all. I'll send you a copy of the book when it's out."

"Thanks," I said, and I was alone with the problem.

The clock read 6:08. I had to act, had to get out of there. When you don't have enough to go on, you go on what you have. I knew Philo was in it. But I didn't have proof. Not enough to phone the cops. For the next couple of hours, I would shift to Automatic Pilot. First, I would meet Meg at the Burgoyne place, put her somewhere safe. Second, I would go after Philo. He had bothered me long enough. I would establish a rhythm, one-two, one-two. The clock said 6:10 as I took down the Colt Commando from the gun rack. One, meet Meg. Two, get Philo.

One-two. One-two.

Rhythm.

One, the coffee was cold. Two, I opened another beer. One, some black clouds were rolling in from a storm out in the Pacific, and in less than an hour it would be too dark to see anything in Laguna Canyon. Two, the clock said 6:15. Question: What toys would I need for Philo? Answer: .357 Magnum; 12-gauge pump loader. Humming now, ready to rescue, destroy, save, kill. One. Two.

Simple rhythm, like a dance.

I thought about the Burgoyne place.

Five, six years back, on a hot summer day, I'd been up the narrow arroyo that Harry had turned into a driveway. I remembered it as a terrific place for an ambush. I didn't really figure Meg would be there, but I couldn't be sure.

I checked the magazine on the Commando, sighted through the night scope, packed three extra clips in the ammo bag, and took that load down to my pickup. On the next trip, I carried down a sawed-off shotgun, along with a duck hunter's belt of thirty extra shells. On the next trip, I carried down two extra handguns—an army issue .45 and a target .22 that I had used to try out for the Olympic Pistol Squad.

I hummed as I made the trips. The clock said 6:23 when I made the last trip. I could have used a grenade launcher, a bazooka, maybe even a baby flamethrower. But they were illegal.

I heated what was left of the coffee and filled my thermos. The last thing I did before driving out was strip down to my T-shirt and strap on some body armor. There is cheap body armor and expensive body armor. I get mine wholesale, and it still costs over $600. When the lead flies, the best body armor is worth every nickel.

A flurry of raindrops sprayed my windshield as I turned off the 55 bridge onto PCH. I sipped coffee as I drove, and I could feel the adrenaline start to build. It was 6:42 P.M. when I stopped at the light next to Main Beach in Laguna. I turned inland, on Laguna Canyon Road.

19

The stables below the Burgoyne place were three miles into the canyon. Inside a white rain-slick fence, a kid in a yellow slicker rode a palomino horse. The kid knew her stuff. She stood up in the stirrups so her butt didn't touch the saddle.

I turned right, drove past the stables. Lights glowed from one of the buildings over to my right. I drove on, turned left, and parked at the bottom of Harry Burgoyne's curved stone driveway. A fancy sign with the letters worn off pointed crookedly up the hill. The first three letters were gone, leaving only GOYNE. Through the field glasses, I could see one corner of the Burgoyne place. Perfect spot for an ambush, just the way I remembered. If you started up that curved driveway, you'd be exposed for seventy-five yards.

Was Meg up there?

I swung the glasses to my right, where a small stand of

trees and California scrub overlooked the house. Plenty of cover for a sniper. My bones told me Philo was out to stomp me. I had beaten up his boy. He wanted something from Meg. If I was dead, he could deal with her. I had the bad feeling Philo had something special in mind for her because Meg herself was special. He had a sick mind. To dig Lucinda and Butch, he would need a sick mind.

Don't think about it, I told myself.

I got out of the pickup, pulled on a green poncho to shed rain, and then buckled the ammo bag around my waist. I took the time to double-check the Colt Commando. It wasn't quite dark enough yet for the full power of the night scope. I took a deep breath, said "one-two" to myself, and then double-timed back toward the exercise ring, where I met the kid in the yellow slicker. She was a thin-faced girl about fourteen, and she was leading the palomino to the stables.

"Hi," I said.

She saw the Commando and stopped. It is a wicked-looking piece of equipment.

"Hello."

"I need a favor," I said.

"What kind of favor?"

"I'd like you to call the Laguna Beach Police, and tell them Mr. Murdock needs some backup. Give them the address of the stables. Could you do that?"

"Come on," she said, grinning. Mention the police, and you have a good chance of making honest folks relax. Crooks tighten up. It's Murdock's instant honesty test.

"What's your name?" I asked.

"Cindy," she said.

"Okay, Cindy. Here it is. There are a couple of bad guys up there, and they're holding a friend of mine against her will. I need you to call the cops. I also need you to show me a way up behind the Burgoyne place."

Her eyes probed mine. It took her a minute to digest the information. "You're not kidding, are you?"

"No. Is there a trail up?"

"Sure. Which side?"

"That way," I said, pointing. "Over to the right."

"Are you going to shoot them?"

"Only in self-defense," I said.

"What's your name?" she asked.

"Murdock," I said. "I'm a private investigator. You want to see some I.D.?"

Cindy was a savvy kid. "Yes," she said. "I do."

I showed her my PI license.

"I saw them come in, earlier." Cindy peered at me in the dim light, comparing me with the mug shot. "This is a terrible picture. It could be anyone." She handed the I.D. back.

"Thanks." I put the I.D. back in my pocket. "How many were there."

"Two cars. Or, I mean, one car and a pickup."

"Was the pickup red?" I asked.

"Sort of. Dark red, I think."

That was my cowboy, Fred J. Johnson, circling back for revenge.

"It's getting dark," she said.

"Yeah."

"Do you want me to call the police first? Or show you the way first?"

Good girl! "Show me the way."

As we started up the hill, I felt the wind quicken, and a fine spray of mist drifted across my face. Cindy climbed with the sure-footed confidence of youth. Keeping up with her took extra effort, and my leg muscles reminded me I wasn't a kid any more. Tomorrow, if I was still alive, my muscles would be shouting at me.

We were almost on a level with the scraggly stand of trees I had spotted through the binoculars.

"Okay, Cindy," I said. "Thanks. This is as far as you go. Now I need you to zip back down and call the cops."

"Can't I stay?"

"No."

"Ahh," she said, and stuffed her hands into the pockets of her yellow slicker. "I want to watch."

Kids these days are raised on too many movies. "Please. Go on down."

"Oh, all right. Murdock, right?"

"Right."

I waited until she was 100 feet or so below me, and then I eased up behind the stand of trees. A guy was there, all right, hatless, dressed in a dark jacket. He was cradling a Winchester pump against his body. I had the advantage, so I decided to take a prisoner. Not a smart move. But civilized.

He was facing down the hill, peering through the trees toward Laguna Canyon Road. From where he sat, he had a good command of about twenty yards of paved stone driveway. Guys on the Maginot Line were controlling what was in front of them, too.

I was on him before he knew it, the muzzle of the Commando up against his neck, right under the jawbone. It is a very vulnerable spot. Makes you feel as if you are about to lose half your face.

"Okay, Clyde," I said. "Drop the piece and then spread-eagle on the dirt."

In the last flicker of twilight, I saw his pocked face turn pale. His eyes were too close together around the bony nose, and made him seem like a guy who bites the heads off chickens. Geek. The geek dropped the Winchester and hit the ground. As he fell, he tried to kick me and I stepped out of the path of his swinging foot and then stepped back in and laid the toe of my boot into his kidney. He stopped trying to kick me and doubled up, groaning. I gave him a quick body search. One .38 Special and a switchblade knife. I tossed them both down the hill, and then started to tie him up.

I was down on top of him with one knee in his back tying his hands with some cotton twine when I heard a noise behind me, up the hill, to my left. The knots weren't tight, so I took an extra instant to cinch the last knot, and that gave the other guy a good shot at me.

Like I said, sometimes you get too old for investigative work.

I felt the lead tear into me before I heard the shots, three of them, in close and professional succession, and to escape the pain in my left shoulder I rolled sideways, putting the geek between me and the shooter, seeing the muzzle flash bloom out of the gathering darkness. That gave me something to shoot at, so I pumped a couple of rounds over that way.

By then the geek figured out what was happening, and as he tried to roll aside, the shooter let go with three more shots, and one of them put the geek over the edge, into afterlife. I fired one more shot before I scurried backward, into the trees. The shooter answered with three rounds, timed and neatly spaced, and I knew that I had to keep firing and moving, or he'd shoot me dead right through my own muzzle flash.

He was going to keep firing and moving, too. I had a worthy opponent.

"We got your lady friend," he called. "The carrot-top."

I fired three bursts in the direction of his voice. Then I

rolled to my left a split second before the bullets rattled through the branches above my head. The rain was coming down harder now. I sighted through the night scope on the Commando, but saw only short trees and scraggly bushes.

"She's got a body on her, that one does. And hot? Whoo-ee!"

This time I didn't fire, but started crawling forward with my Commando cradled across my forearms. It's a tough way to cover much distance, but the cowboy's voice didn't sound far away.

"Your ass is grass, Shamus. You're tough, but Fred J. Johnson is tougher."

The voice made the cowboy sound older than he looked. I had seen him twice now. Once in the Ancient Mariner, the night I'd been hired by Ellis Dean. Again in Modesto's apartment, in Marina Del Rey. Both times, he had appeared to be in his late twenties. Now, in the dark of Laguna Canyon, his voice floating out through the softly falling rain, he seemed more of a man, and therefore more of an enemy.

I had closed what I thought was half the distance. I stopped crawling and sighted through the night scope. I thought I saw his head and shoulders sticking out from behind a rock. When I blinked and looked again, he wasn't there.

"You're getting old!" he called again. "Time to hang it up and find yourself a wheelchair!" He followed that sage advice with a laugh that was supposed to make me angry. It did.

I started crawling again, toward the voice, but I hadn't gone five yards when I heard the sound of a body dragging itself across moist earth. I stopped, swung the Commando into position, and sighted. What I saw was a man crawling toward me from the left, holding an automatic pistol in his right hand. Looking through a night scope turns the world a fuzzy red. The crawling man did not look like the cowboy.

Counting the geek, there were three of them.

You can tell when you've shifted over from being a soldier to being a civilian again because you lose your killing reflex. I had the second guy in my sights, and I decided not to kill him. Instead, I put a round into his leg, and he fired a wild shot that whistled close to my ear, and the next thing I knew someone had dropped on me from above, out of the dark, knocking my breath away, and I smelled sweat and hair oil and bad body odor and sensed a knife blade coming and kicked out, blindly. My kick landed home. Someone said "Ooof!" The Colt Commando was out of my hands, so I clawed underneath the poncho for the .45, and then he was on me again, the sweat, the hair oil strong in my nose. I grabbed both his wrists. I could tell he was stronger. We rolled across the mountain.

"Your lady friend's a stuck pig." He grinned in the darkness. "I fucked her, this afternoon. Ass. Mouth. Everywhere."

"Scumbag." My muscles were weakening fast and my head was jammed out beyond a rough rocky overhang as we paused in the middle of our dogfight to exchange opinions on what we thought of each other, and then I shoved him away and he resisted, out of reflex, and I jerked him toward me and let go of both wrists, throwing him slightly off balance and giving him an extra boost with my knees as he slid over me, his belt buckle scraping my lip and nose, slamming into a dip in the mountain somewhere below us.

I waited for half a minute, to catch my breath, and

then I pulled the .45 and turned the flashlight on him. He was trying to crawl out, but one of his legs wasn't giving him any help. In the distance, just before I spoke, I heard sirens. Maybe the police. Maybe an ambulance.

"Johnson." My voice shook, which was not a confidence-builder.

"Fuck you!" he said.

I aimed carefully and laid a slug six inches from his ear.

"This is a forty-five, Johnson. The next one goes to your kneecap."

"Fuck you!"

Hot tears stung my eyes as I shot him in the leg. The pain drove him back down to the bottom of the dip. He was a tough guy, but he moaned.

I was sick to my stomach from my own bullet wound, but my intent was clear. If he didn't open up about Meg, I would kill him where he lay.

"Where are they, Johnson? Where did they take her?"

This time he didn't hesitate. "Waddell's," he moaned.

"The gallery?" I snarled. "Or the house?"

"House," he said.

"Where in the house?"

"Basement," he said. "There's a room where he makes films. Don't leave me here."

I found the Commando in the mud, picked it up, sighted through it until I located the middle man. He was lying where I had shot him, out. I holstered the .45 and slung the Commando over my right shoulder, leaving the right hand free for the flashlight.

My left arm was numb as I started back down the trail. When I was halfway down, I heard movement, someone coming up, so I stopped. The feet had a light and youthful sound to them. I paused, breathing hard, to try and gather my energies for the twisting drive to Bluebird Canyon. Before the footsteps got to me, I saw a flashlight beam playing against the walls of the trail, and then a scared little voice called my name: "Mr. Murdock?"

It was the kid in the yellow slicker. "Cindy? That you?"

"Are you all right?"

"Almost, kid. Almost. What the hell are you doing here?"

"I called the police. At first, they thought I was kidding. They knew your name."

She came up close and held the light in my eyes. "Move the light away, Cindy." I was close to tears again.

"What happened up there?"

"My friend's not there." I had a sudden thought. "Can you drive?"

"Sure," she answered, proudly.

"A stick?"

"Sure. My brother has a Camaro. It's a stick."

"I need another favor." I reached out, put a hand on her shoulder.

"What?" She was eager for life, this kid, in her bright yellow slicker. Eager for adventure.

"My shoulder got hurt. I need you to drive me to Bluebird Canyon."

"Hey! I live near there."

"Great," I said. "We'll kill two birds."

"My mom always says that," Cindy said.

"Great," I said, and we started down the slippery hill in the rain toward the pickup.

20

With brave Cindy behind the wheel and me propped against the door of the death seat, we started back down Laguna Canyon Road, toward Bluebird Canyon. The drive normally takes twelve to fifteen minutes. That night, it seemed forever.

Cindy was a good little driver. She sensed I was in a rush, so she zipped along the slick and shining curves grinning, her tongue between her teeth while she concentrated, gums showing pale pink in the glare of the oncoming headlights.

We passed two cop cars, roof lights flashing, and then one more. One of the reasons I stopped being a cop was that you seldom arrive in time for the action. It gets tiresome, all that mopping up. The streets of Laguna Beach were already deserted. Woozy from the gunshot wound, I swallowed another pain pill.

"Punch it, kid," I said.

"We're speeding now, Mr. Murdock."

"Call me Matt. And punch it. Okay?"

"Okay!"

She almost lost control of the pickup as we charged up Shadow Lane, past the small park, and slid onto Bluebird Canyon Drive. I leaned over and helped her steady the wheel with my one good arm, and she muttered "Sorry," and then "Thanks," and a couple minutes later we were on Goldfinch Lane, where Philo Waddell lived. The house behind the fence was dark. As the headlights swung by, I saw Butch's Land Rover in the drive. Next to it was a black limo, which suggested visitors. The gate was closed, and probably locked.

"Pull up over there, kid. I'll take over."

She stopped, looked at me. Her voice trembled. "What is it? I can do it." My shoulder burned. The pain pill was just starting to work. "Crash the gate," I said. "Gotta crash the gate."

"I can do it. Please!"

My head swam. Someone else was going to have to make the decisions from now on. Might as well be Cindy. If I had been thinking straight, I would have sent some police units up here. No, I thought. That wouldn't work, because there's still nothing solid on Philo Baby and by the time anyone gathered evidence Meg Kirkwood would be—

"Go into first," I said. "Take a deep breath. Then rev the motor a couple times, to get the feel for it. When you've got the feel, lay some rubber on this track and aim the nose at the center of the gate. If you get above 40, shift into second."

I didn't tell her about tachometers and red-lining. Sometimes you can give people too much information. They stall out, just like machines.

"Is that it?" Her voice trembled. For all I knew, she'd been waiting all her life for a chance to bust something up with a 400-horse pickup.

"That's it."

"Then what?"

"Then go home."

She didn't answer. With a determined look on her face, Cindy backed up to get a running start. She shifted into first, revved the motor, and we were hurtling straight for the center of Philo's electric gate.

"Goddam!" I yelled. There was the sound of tearing metal and the shriek of tires clawing at concrete and hard rock. A gash appeared in the windshield of my pickup and I heard Cindy yelling at me and then we were through. She had enough momentum to keep going until we smacked into the rear of the Land Rover. As I was climbing out, the front door to Philo's house opened and a guy with a gun opened up on us. I fired at his muzzle blast, and he tumbled off the porch into the rain.

"Oh, no," Cindy said.

"Help me unpack the shotgun." I pulled at the corner of the tarp. My arm burned, and I was dizzy. "And then go home."

"What about you?"

"Got work to do."

"I'm staying."

"You'll be in the way."

Just then the Filipino came out, wearing a raincoat and carrying an umbrella and a small valise. I swung the shotgun to cover him. The movement sent pain jabbing through my arm. "Lie down. Lock your hands over your head."

He went into a prone position, locked his hands.

I turned to Cindy. "Go home. Call the cops. Tell them—"

"I know." Her voice was disappointed. "Mr. Murdock needs help."

"You got this address?"

"Um. Bluebird Canyon."

"The street is Goldfinch."

"Goldfinch. I got it."

"Okay. And thanks."

"Be careful, Mr. Murdock. I mean Matt."

Cindy climbed into the pickup, closed the door. The engine started on the first turn. I moved toward Quan, who lay with his nose touching Philo's tile porch. Cindy backed away from the Land Rover, and I noticed for the first time the limo had Nevada plates. She wheeled around the driveway, drove through the gate. I waited until the tail-lights of the pickup were out of sight. Then I tried the door of the limo. It was locked, so I busted a window. No keys in the ignition. I put a pistol bullet into the works, shattering the keyhole. If they could hot-wire it, they might drive it out of here.

"Get up," I said to Quan.

He got to his feet, shivering.

"Where are they?"

"Down some those stairs." He waved vaguely at the interior of the house.

"How many?"

"Plenty fella, four mebbe five."

I prodded him with the shotgun barrel. "Show me."

Hands on his head, Quan led me through Philo's lavish living room and down a wide flight of stairs. One room of the basement was fitted out like a gentlemen's club from the nineteenth century. Leather chairs. Four tables for billiards. Over against a wall, a polished bar with a shiny brass footrail. We went through a wide door, around a corner, then down a hallway paved with red Mexican tile. A room to the right held fish tanks. A room to the left said Games. Thanks to that last pill, the pain in my arm was down to a low buzz. By the time we reached a metal door with no label I figured the basement could hold 300 whooping party goers. My brain danced a slow, dead waltz.

"In there," Quan said.

"Open it." I listened, didn't hear a sound. The room was probably soundproofed. "Open it." I bumped him with the shotgun.

"Got no key."

I shoved the shotgun under his chin. "Three seconds, hotdog. One," I counted. "Two."

Sweat poured down his face, putting out a sweet odor, like over-ripe papaya. "Then I go, okay?"

"Maybe. First the door."

Sweating, the Filipino opened a panel in the wall next to the door and pressed some buttons on a gizmo that looked like a touch tone telephone. I heard a sequence of beeps, and then the metal door slid open on well oiled wheels and I looked past a potted palm tree into a scene that was pure infernal hell.

Meg Kirkwood was on her hands and knees inside a ring made by a brick wall about eighteen inches high. She wore what was left of a long white gown. The gown was in shreds. Random patches of blood spotted the white material. Blood streaked her arms, legs, neck. Sweat matted the red hair around her pale forehead. Someone had removed her prosthesis. She circled slowly, awkwardly. On her right foot, she wore a shoe, spike heel, silver color. The mate to that shoe was out of sight. Beyond

Meg lay a dead rooster, with bloody feathers. Because of the palm, I couldn't see what Meg stared at.

Over to the right, outside the barrier of the ring, Philo Waddell was talking to Lucinda Smith-Travis, a man in a blue business suit, and a gray-haired fellow in gray. Blue Suit was Mister Jay Frame, honcho of Sizzle Productions. The man in gray had on a sport shirt open at the collar. I figured him for Vegas. The scene made my blood boil. While Meg struggled for her life, they held a business conference.

Philo had on a black cloak and a green, shiny mask that seemed to be made out of alligator hide. In his right hand, he held a whip and some handcuffs with a long silver chain attached. The mask made the scene crazier.

Lucinda wore black, a floor-length dress with long sleeves and a big diamond-shaped opening in front that bared her tanned belly. Draped around Lucinda's neck was a snake, about five feet long. In her right hand, its handle resting on the floor, was a pitchfork.

Butch was the nearest one to me. With a walking cast on his left foot, his eyeball up against a regulation movie camera, he was shooting footage of Meg on her knees. The dirty bastards. Rage made me hot. Inside the poncho, my body steamed.

Lucinda caught sight of me just as I stepped into the rat's nest, swinging the shotgun over to line up on Butch. She opened her mouth to cry the alarm, and the look on her face made Philo and Blue Suit turn around. At the same time, the man in gray signaled to someone I couldn't see.

"Murdock?" Philo said.

Meg stayed focused on whatever it was in the ring, and then I saw what it was—another fighting cock, pure white

feathers, razors buckled onto his yellow feet, preening for the attack.

Then everything happened at once. Butch roared and came for me with a battle-ax right out of the middle ages. He was moving good, despite the walking cast, and had hate and madness in his eye. I ached to fight him man to man and hand to hand, but fatigue had pushed away my civilian reflexes and brought back my soldier training, and now Frame had pulled a small silver pistol—a Baretta, it looked like—and was pinging away. Bullets slapped into the metal door as it slid closed. Two bullets lodged in the body armor. I crouched, swinging the shotgun into position, and fired. The blast forced Blue Suit backwards six feet before he fell. He crashed into the man in gray, who had a gun out. Off to the right, a guy in a three-piece black suit was shooting. I pumped in another round as I dropped to the floor and shot the man in black.

"He's mine!" Butch screamed, and swung the battle-ax. I rolled, felt the breeze created by the ax. Butch's round-house swing missed me and connected with the bottom part of the metal door, which was now closed. Philo's house shuddered. I came up in firing position. The shotgun kicked, heavily, as I fired. Butch slammed against the camera, knocking it down.

Moving quickly, Philo grabbed Lady Lucinda by the arm and shoved her toward me. Lucinda stumbled, and the snake fell off her neck and slithered into the ring with Meg.

"Matt!" Meg screamed.

The snake was five feet away from Meg, and closing.

I swung the barrel to cover the snake. Meg was in my line of fire. Too close. Might hit her.

"Don't kill him!" Lucinda came for me with the pitchfork.

"Christ!" I took three steps toward Lucinda until Meg was out of the line of fire and chugged a round at the snake. It exploded in a spray of blood.

Lucinda yelled "I'll kill you!" and stabbed one tine of her pitchfork through the upper part of my poncho, where it lodged in the body armor. The other tines stopped a half inch from my face. Wanting more than anything to kill her, I clipped Lucinda on the jaw with the butt of the shotgun. She sank to the floor. I saw Philo and the man in gray as they disappeared around a corner. Meg still needed help.

"Matt!" Meg jabbed at the fighting cock with a short-bladed kitchen knife. The cock must have been trained to slash people. Meg landed a good one, but the cock used his razors to lay open a gash on her arm.

Head buzzing with fatigue, I stumbled into the ring. The cock took a run at me. I tried a kick, missed, felt a sharp sting as one of his razors slashed my trousers. He hovered in the air. Using the shotgun like a club, I belted him in the mid-section. He squawked. Feathers exploded, in slow motion.

I grabbed Meg, hauled her out of the ring. You could smell cordite, sweat, human excrement. There was no sign of Philo. At the far end of the big room, I saw a half-open door.

"You okay?"

She shook her head. She was still in shock, her eyes dilated, and there were ugly little cuts on her arms and body. "They took it!" she whispered. "They took the leg!" In her hand, she still held the knife, a dull piece of kitchen flatware with no blade, no point.

I gave her a pain pill and went looking for the leg. It

was on a table equipped with little straps for arms and wrists. Near the table the same kind of straps were attached to the wall by chains. At the end of the leg was the mate to the silver shoe Meg wore.

"Philo's gone," she said, dully.

"Yeah." I indicated the door. "Through there."

"Kill him, Matt."

"He's gone," I said. My mind was through computing for awhile. I wanted Philo, too, but I wasn't going to leave Meg. She was strapping on her prosthesis. Her knees were raised. The bastards had removed her underwear.

"I know where he's gone," she said.

"Where?"

"The Gallery."

"Why? What for?"

"He's got something there. Films, I think. Something. I heard them talking, earlier."

"Think we can catch him?"

"We must!" She clutched my arm. "We have to!"

"Let's go."

Together, helping each other, we limped across the room to the door Philo had taken. It opened out into a small garden on the side of the house away from the garage and the parking area. The rain had stopped. A fresh breeze blew. The earth smelled damp, ripe, clean. Meg shivered. I stripped off the poncho, helped her into it.

As we made our way around the house, she told me part of what happened.

"I called the motel, about four. They said you'd call back. I left a message. I was supposed to meet him— Philo—around five. We had an appointment with the trustee who handles the Burgoyne place. I couldn't believe it was listed so cheaply, but Philo kept reassuring me. Things would work out, he said. I went to the gallery. There was a closed sign on the door, but it was unlocked, so I went in to wait. It was getting chilly, and I'd worn a summer dress. The little shopgirl wasn't there, but I heard voices upstairs, so I started up. The room was dark, and I recognized their voices—Mr. Waddell's and Lucinda's—but not the others.

"I stood in the doorway for a minute, so that my eyes got used to the light. They were watching some clips from a dirty movie. It's not my style. I was shocked, so I started to leave. He either heard me or sensed I was there and insisted that I stay and watch. It was awful. And do you know what?"

"What?"

Meg dug her fingers into my arm. We were almost to the garage. The Land Rover loomed large against the moonlight.

"Gayla Jean was in the film!" Meg shuddered. "Philo and the two men went crazy, watching the film. I tried to leave, telling him I was meeting you. That man held me while Philo took Lucinda aside. She left. They brought me here, to that room, and—"

She burst into sobs. I held her for a couple of minutes. The wind was chilly. We needed to get out of there.

The first door of the five-car garage was open and the stall for Philo's Mercedes was empty. Meg climbed into the back seat of the Land Rover while I slid under the dash. It had been a long time since I'd hotwired a car. The exercise did not go well. Foggy brain. Hands wouldn't work. Too dark to see. From the back seat, Meg whimpered. How long could she hold on?

"Goddam!" Sparks snapped at me, then died.

"Someone's coming," Meg said. "A car."

Thinking it might be Philo, coming back, I got out

from under the dash. My head whirled as I stood straight. I blinked, grabbed the door of the Land Rover to steady myself. Bright headlights turned into Philo's drive. It was a pickup. Mine. It rolled to a stop. In the lights from the pickup, I saw a body lying by the limo.

"Matt?" Cindy called.

"Cindy!" I walked over. "I told you to go home."

"I was worried. I came back."

"Did you call the cops?"

"Yes. And I heard sirens down in the Canyon."

I brought Meg over from the Land Rover, helped her into the pickup. Cindy stared at Meg, then moved the Colt Commando aside. Meg's teeth were chattering. I got a flashlight from behind the seat and checked the body. It was the man in gray, the one who'd left with Philo.

"Where to, folks?" she said, trying to keep her voice from shaking.

"Waddell's Gallery," I said. "It's on Forest."

"I know where it is," Cindy said. "A friend of my parents is a painter. He hangs paintings in there."

"Great," I said, and hugged Meg tighter.

We were halfway to town when a police cruiser whipped past, roof lights cranking. Late again. Cindy turned right on Glenneyre, headed for Forest, the high rent district.

The streets of Laguna Beach were slick from the rain. I spotted a few cars on Forest Avenue, but no Mercedes. I told Cindy to drive around back. The big Mercedes was parked behind the building, angled up close to the brick wall. Lights burned upstairs. Cindy stopped the pickup and I got out for a recon. I walked through the puddles of the parking lot until I stood underneath the window of the gallery. The .357 was no longer in my shoulder holster. I didn't remember losing it.

Upstairs, the hulking figure of Philo Waddell moved across the window, once, then back again.

Back at the pickup, I checked behind the seat for the .357 and the .22 target pistol, but couldn't find either one in the dark.

"What are you hunting for?" Meg asked.

"Ammunition," I said.

Slumping against the pickup, I checked the magazine of the .45. When I was ready, I looked Meg and Cindy in the eye. "Stay here," I ordered the women. Huddled in the poncho, Meg looked small, wistful.

"No!" Meg said. "I'm going with you!"

"You're crazy," I said.

"I'm the one who got herself raped and degraded," she said, her voice a harsh whisper. "Not you!"

"What will you do when you get there?"

"Watch," she said, "while you kill him."

I wasn't planning on killing him, but I didn't tell Meg. She was hurt, stunned, angry. And besides, I wanted Philo to stand trial and live a long and dirty life behind bars. He would be a juicy morsel for the flesh hunters in prison.

With the poncho hiding her nakedness, Meg supported herself against the damp stucco wall while I tried to pick the lock into Philo's gallery. I could have blown the lock with the .45, but my brain would not stand any more noise. My hands betrayed me at that point, and the lock picks kept shaking, slipping loose. Finally, the lock gave, and we opened the door and entered. In the dark, the gallery was spooky. I could hear Philo moving around upstairs, bumping against furniture, closing doors and drawers. He sounded clumsy, and in a hurry.

Helping Meg upstairs took my last thimble of energy. The adrenaline stream was over for the night. I could feel the aftereffects starting, hitting me in sonic waves, boom, boom, boom. Then we stood at the door that looked into Philo's conference room, and Meg indicated the videocassette player with tears in her eyes. Most of one wall was taken up with a giant video screen.

I should have gone in after him alone, but Meg was with me, shivering now, and I didn't want to leave her alone. I was trapped between her raging need and the force of Philo's evil. We walked across the soft carpeting to his office. The door was half open, and we caught Philo halfway between an open wall safe and a huge walnut desk. He carried a polished leather valise. On the desktop was a pile of a dozen videocassettes. I guessed they were master copies of his X-rated output. He looked hassled, but he'd taken the time to change out of his cloak and alligator mask and was now wearing a blue business suit. Dressed for the getaway. He looked up and frowned when we came to the door.

I leveled the .45 at him. He looked at me, then at Meg. "So?" he said.

I left Meg leaning on the door frame and moved inside a couple of steps. "Lean on the desk there, Philo. Spread your feet."

"You think she'll testify?" He put his hands on the edge of the desk. I started toward him. His small eyes gleamed. Sweat popped out on his forehead. "Without her, there's no case. Nothing."

I kicked his legs apart and patted him down. On the desk was an airline ticket. In the valise I found six packets of hundred-dollar bills, a leather-bound diary, a passport, and a black Mauser automatic, HSC, just right for your vest pocket.

Keeping the .45 on him, I moved to the open safe. Inside were some manila envelopes.

"More than a hundred thousand. Take it and let me out of here."

Without answering, I moved away from the safe. From the door, Meg stared at Philo. Her face looked dead. Still watching Philo, I turned away from Meg, picked up the phone, dialed 911, the emergency number.

"Chilly arrogant bitch," Philo said. "Just like her sister. Greedy for life. Blind untutored twins. They wink and simper. They wag their hips to inflame, to enrage, to trick you. They dream platinum dreams. But they are 'nice' girls and before they deliver sweet pleasure there's a steep payment. It gets steeper, ever steeper, and when you force them, finally, to face up to the absurd reality of their sexual bitchery, they . . ."

A recorded voice on the phone said someone would be with me in a minute. I heard Meg move, behind me, to my left. Philo stopped talking, threw up his hands, palms out, to shield his face, and I knew why Meg had come upstairs. I yelled, "No, Meg!" and turned to see her as she fired the first shot from the .22. Three shots, two close together, and then a third, echoing. I watched the holes appear in Philo, one in his chest, a second to the right of his big nose, the last one centered in his right palm. He was four feet away from me. The surprised look stayed on his face as he crashed down, scattering videotapes, and then sagged to the floor.

Meg staggered over to him, holding the pistol in both hands. "Damn! Damn! Damn!" She aimed the pistol at Philo, setting up for the fourth shot, but then she dropped the .22 onto the carpet.

I checked Philo's pulse. Zero. He was dead.

The recorded voice was still telling me someone would be with me in a minute. I hung up.

Meg watched me from a chair as I wadded up papers

216

from Philo's wastebasket. When I had a good pile, I leaned the porno tapes against the pile of paper, making the sides of a teepee. Except for a choked sob, Meg was quiet. I moved the leather valise to the door, and then I struck a match to the paper. Blue bonfire.

We watched them smolder, then catch. Film makes a nice quick fire, but the plastic cassettes stink. Meg stared into the fire. I took the Mauser out of the valise, put it into Philo's hand, pressed his fingers around the butt, then let the gun drop.

The desk caught, and you could smell varnish, hot and sweet.

"Are we leaving?" Meg asked. "Should we call the police?"

I picked up the phone again, dialed 911. A male voice came on, asking how he could help. I told him to send firemen and police to Waddell's Gallery, on Forest, in Laguna Beach. I hung up when he asked for my name. I walked to Meg's chair, helped her to her feet.

As we moved together toward the door, the automatic sprinklers came on, bathing us in a misty spray. We stopped, turned our faces upward, into the spray. Meg was crying. I probably was too.

21

I was sitting in a chair by the window when Doctor Murchison came in to check on Meg. He was a large round man with a Burl Ives beard and a jolly smile. In his white coat and brown Levis, the doc was all hope and medical jargon and stability. Meg was asleep. My left arm was in a sling, but Meg was the one in trouble. The doctor told me she'd be under sedation for another week, at the least. His eyes told me she might be under sedation for the rest of her days.

"How was your night?" the doc asked me.

"I made it through. How's Ms. Kirkwood?"

He gave me a worried look that erased the smile from his face. "She's crippled inside now, as well as out. Those flesh wounds are superficial, but what worries me is what's happened to her psyche."

Doctors use words like "psyche" and expect you to understand what they're talking about. I figured he meant Meg's spirit was busted up.

"When can she get out of here?" I don't like hospitals. They remind me of the jungle, and what happens to you when you get hit and the medics are not around.

"A week. Possibly ten days. She is one battered lady."

We talked some more, and then the doc left and I sat there staring at Meg under the sheet until it was clear I couldn't do any good.

Around one o'clock, I slipped out to Denny's, where I ate scrambled eggs and sausage. When I got back, Billy Bob Marshall from Fort Worth was at the nurses' station on Meg's floor, surrounded by three reporters while he tried to browbeat the floor supervisor. Talking in his loud Texas twang, Billy Bob kept telling the nurse he wanted Meg flown back to Texas.

"I know a specialist," Billy Bob said. "I want my darlin' to have the best."

One of the reporters was Teresa Aiken, of the Orange County *Trib*.

"Murdock!" She took me by the coat sleeve and stepped up close. Her eyes were excited. She smelled fresh and alive. "I've been calling you, every half hour. I need an exclusive."

"Trade you," I said. "For everything you know. Just keep my name out of it."

"It's a deal!" The light of ambition shone brightly in her brown eyes. We made a date for later, at my place. She went away to do her research, and I called a cop to come and hustle the reporters back downstairs.

To take the heat off the floor supervisor, I introduced myself and led Billy Bob aside for a brief summary of what had happened. We sat in purple plastic chairs in a fourth-floor lounge.

"Ms. Kirkwood made some shocking discoveries about her sister, Mr. Marshall. She found out these people were using her sister to make stag films, and when she got in too close, they decided to substitute Meg for Gayla Jean."

"I read about it some in the goldang paper. Couldn't believe it. You folks got a crazy world out here. Where do you figure in this, Mr. Murdock?" Billy Bob was scowling, blaming me, blaming anyone.

"Ms. Kirkwood hired me for some background investigations."

"And where were you when she was almost murdered?"

"Los Angeles," I said, lying. "It was lucky I made it back in time."

I didn't know why I was shaving the truth for Billy Bob. He would read about Meg Kirkwood in the papers, because he'd have to sit around for a week, while she mended, and Teresa Aiken was going to have herself a hot story. Maybe I thought it would help if Billy Bob didn't know exactly what Philo did to Meg.

That's one trouble with honing your reflexes to a fine edge. You can act fast, hit hard, shoot to kill, but then you have a problem explaining why you acted. Maybe that's why I wanted to tell it to Teresa Aiken. So I could explain what I'd done.

"I'll kill 'em," Billy Bob said. His big football player's face was creased with anger.

"The head guy is already dead," I said.

"What about the others?"

"Some dead. Some in jail."

"Back home," he said, "we'd handle it different, I swear."

220

He whipped out a black notebook and a gold ballpoint. The notebook was edged with gold, and three gold stripes crossed the front cover. "Gimme them names," he growled.

I told him the only names I knew, Fred J. Johnson, alias the cowboy, from Las Vegas, and Lucinda Smith-Travis, of Laguna Beach. I left him alone with his helpless rage in the hospital lounge in El Toro.

So, on midafternoon Saturday, I drove slowly back home. The sun was out, for a change, and the traffic on the Newport Freeway was thick, prelude to summer. My body ached from taking more than its share of punishment. My mind felt like a paper cup that had been pitchforked a hundred times, and then left in the gutter to waste away.

Teresa Aiken waited for me at the bottom of the stairs that led up to my place.

"You look terrible," she said.

"How much do you have already?" I asked.

"Is there something to drink? I was up all night on this story."

"Sure," I said. "Guide me upstairs."

"They tried to shove the story back to Metro," she said on the way up, "but I'm getting the lead on page one, tomorrow."

"What is tomorrow?" I asked.

"Sunday. How's Ms. Kirkwood?"

"She's hurt bad, and still in shock." I followed my plan, to lead Teresa off the track. "You were right about the sister. It was murder."

"I knew it. And you've got proof, right?"

The trick was how to use her eagerness to swerve the story back to Gayla Jean, away from Meg. "You'll get it all."

A spell of the whirlies hit me just as we reached my porch. I grabbed the railing, hung there for a moment between two worlds. Down below, three teenage kids in swimsuits walked arm in arm toward the pier. They were already tanned, and summer was three months off.

"Waddell was making snuff films, wasn't he?"

"Yeah." I unlocked my door. The place looked the same as I had left it Friday evening, when I'd loaded up my arsenal and charged off to save Meg Kirkwood. I took the sofa while Teresa Aiken got us both a Bud.

"And selling them to VC Clubs?" Her voice sounded smug.

"Yes." VC Club would soon become a household word.

She set the beers down, flipped open her notebook and read to me. "In New York, the videocassette club is called 'The Silver Chamber.' In Dallas, it's called 'Dark City.' In Chicago, it's called 'Bathing for Dollars.' There are clubs in every major city in the country. They provide that special technofix for highly paid technocrats, many of whom work for your government, in highly classified jobs. Waddell was a supplier, through Butterfly Productions. My story will blow the whole thing wide open."

"Big story for you," I said.

"There has to be a mob tie-in," she said, glowing with excitement.

"Don't get yourself roughed up."

"If I do, I'll hire you."

I thought of Ellis Dean and didn't answer.

She sipped her beer, then told me what she wanted. "I have a rough idea of what went on in Laguna Canyon, but what I want from you is what happened at Philo's place, later."

"You're keeping my name out of it, right?"

She sighed. "Give me credit. I know how you feel."

"I'm glad someone does." I realized I was feeling sorry for myself. It was the pain, probably. Pain did things to your confidence. I took a long slug of Bud and then told her a version of the real thing.

"Okay. Yesterday afternoon, I get a message from Ms. Kirkwood, telling me to meet her at the Burgoyne place, up above the stables in Laguna Canyon. Couple days out from Fort Worth, she falls in love with Laguna, wants to own a piece. Next thing, Mrs. Smith-Travis shows up here, wanting to hire me to gather dirt on her husband. She's stalling, telling lies, making sure I stay put, so I figure she's here for Waddell. I toss her out, drive to Laguna Canyon to meet Ms. Kirkwood. Three of Waddell's apes are waiting for me. I'm not as good as I used to be, and get shot nailing the apes. One ape tells me they've got Ms. Kirkwood at Waddell's. I drive there, force my way in. In the basement, they're making the ultimate snuff film—a crippled woman with a dull kitchen knife in the ring with a trained fighting cock. I show up, they start shooting. I drop two of them. Mrs. Smith-Travis gets knocked cold. Waddell escapes. Ms. Kirkwood and I find him at his gallery, on Forest Avenue. He pulls a piece. Ms. Kirkwood shoots him."

Teresa Aiken was writing furiously. "Great action piece. I need a quotable source."

"Say you got it from Philo's houseboy, Quan, that Filipino cat in the white coat."

"This will make you famous. Why can't I quote you?"

"Because you promised not to."

"Damn you! This is dynamite! That houseboy's gone. If they do find him, I won't be able to get to him."

"There's always Mrs. Smith-Travis."

"Mrs. Smith-Travis isn't saying much. Not about last night."

"Did you ask her about the snake?"

Teresa looked at me sharply. "What snake?"

"The one around her neck. During Philo's last shoot."

"You're kidding." Now she was really excited.

"Word of honor."

"What happened to it?"

"Got itself shot. Line of duty. This snake something •you can use?"

"You're a devil." She got up from her chair and sat close to me on the sofa. Her eyes danced with the need to know.

"Now, I'm not a reporter, but the big story here is Philo and the dead girl, Gayla Jean. Pretty girl comes to town from Texas, dies in burning car with Latino actor. All the time she was making blue movies, yearning for Hollywood. Sister shows up for funeral, gets kidnapped. Bad guys use her as replacement."

"I already wrote that story."

"Without the ending."

"The snake helps. It might work. It's bigger now."

"If I were you, I'd dig around in Philo's past, see if he knew Modesto."

"That sounds promising."

"A story with social depth." I heaved myself up out of the chair, walked slowly into the kitchen, opened the sliding panel behind the fridge. Inside was some cash, saved for a rainy day. Also there was the small address book from Jaime Modesto's. I handed it over to Teresa.

"Whose is it?"

"Could be Modesto's. Maybe one of his friends. Might help you run down some leads." Sitting down felt better than walking or standing. My face hurt. Sunlight streamed in from the beach.

"There's more. Your part in this. How you figured it out." Teresa crossed her legs. The skirt rode up above her knees. On the burnished shins, a gloss of reddish tan. Everyone was preparing for summer, even busy girl reporters. She leaned toward me, eyes bright. "How did you do it? Manage the timing and all?"

"Trade secret. You were going to leave me out of it."

"Damn you!"

"This is enough for the Pulitzer, if you dig. Now. It's your turn. How will the mighty *Trib* handle this one?"

She thought if she told me part of it, I'd fill in the rest. She flipped the notebook open, to an earlier page. "All right. Here's the plan. Tomorrow, on page one, we're running two photos of Mrs. Lucinda Smith-Travis. One is a society photo, South Bay Garden Club, the lady looking haughty. The other is from jail. Mrs. Smith-Travis is behind bars, looking whipped. After being identified as a walk-on in two films produced by Butterfly Productions, she's decided to turn state's evidence. She gave a group interview, earlier. No mention of a snake. Thanks for that."

"You could probably dicker with her to ghost write an autobiography. Start with college, her life at Bryn Mawr. Photograph her husband. They met in Acapulco. She'll could use the book royalties for her defense. Like Liddy and Dean."

"The husband's back east, won't talk to anyone." She flipped back another couple of pages. "This Fred J. Johnson, who got himself shot on the hill above the Laguna Stables, has to be a hit man for the mob. From him, I got the idea for the tie-in."

"How'd you figure that?" I asked.

"Fred J.'s from Vegas. He's wanted in Texas and Florida. He's worked for two casino owners who have mob connections. He came here only a month ago, to help straighten things out. Mrs. Smith-Travis swears he was ordered by Waddell to kill Modesto and the Kirkwood girl."

"You're already making the connection. You don't need me."

Teresa locked eyeballs with me. "What really went on? In Waddell's office?"

"Philo had a gun, tucked under some airline tickets. He was about to waste me when Meg shot him."

"Noble scenario. But it leaves something out."

"The piece was a Mauser, HSC. Vest pocket pistol. Needed cleaning."

"Don't parade your vast technical knowledge, okay?"

I saluted her with the Bud.

She dipped back into her notes. "The names of the other two men on the hill were John Cacciola, from Vegas, and Alfred Ricci, also from Vegas. When he was alive, Alfred went by the nickname of 'Ace.'"

"Terrific," I said. "What about another beer?"

"What made you go up there, armed to the teeth?"

"Good place for an ambush," I said. "I was getting close. They needed me out of the way."

"Lieutenant Smith said you were wearing body armor."

"It was a cold night."

She brought me the fresh Bud and then settled down on the edge of the sofa, knees uncovered again. She wasn't through with me. I was dead tired. "How much do you think they made off those films?"

"A hot porno tape retails for eighty bucks. Snuff has to go higher. Five bills per tape. If Vegas financed the productions, Philo could have skimmed. Maybe Fred J. was a watchdog."

"Then you agree with my theory?"

226

"Makes sense." Fatigue makes you agree with any theory.

"They're getting a court order to open Philo's safety deposit box, Monday. I want to be there."

"Should be juicy. Old Philo lived high. Cockfights. Upkeep on the pool and the court. Fancy apartments for his stars. That house in Bluebird Canyon's worth a bundle." I yawned again. Two Buds and you're out.

Always thinking, Teresa changed the subject on me. "Your pickup's a stick, right?"

I knew what was coming. "Yeah."

"And you were shot in the canyon, and then you drove in the rain to Waddell's place, in Bluebird Canyon. You invaded the house, rescued Ms. Kirkwood, and then you drove back to town, to the gallery."

"The rain had stopped. I forget the time."

"There's a problem, driving a stick when you're hurt." She looked hard at my left arm.

"I shifted with this one." I raised the beer.

"No." She shook her head. "You need two hands. There was someone else. Someone called in for you. Someone helped you drive."

"How do you know someone called in?"

"I looked at the police log."

"Sneaky."

"Who was it, Murdock? You couldn't drive. Ms. Kirkwood couldn't drive a stick. You had help. Who was it?"

I wasn't giving them Cindy. "What if I taught Ms. Kirkwood to shift? I worked the clutch and the accelerator. She steered."

"In her condition?" Teresa made a face.

I didn't answer. Outside, Saturday sunshine streamed down on the beach.

She sat watching me for a minute, then stood up. This

interview was over. "They're holding the presses. I've got to get this story to bed. Call me, okay?"

"Sure," I said, covering my yawn with the back of my hand. "Luck with your story."

She kissed me on the mouth before she went out. Her mouth tasted young, vibrant, moist. The kiss was meant to welcome me back to the land of the living. I felt welcomed. I listened to her heels tap-tapping as she went down the stairs, seeking fame through the mystery and power of the printed word, and then I went downstairs, to my battered pickup. I got Philo's valise out. On my way back, I checked the mail. I didn't remember checking it Friday.

There was the usual clutter of junk mail, and wedged in between an advertisement for panty hose for the non-existent Mrs. Murdock and a financial planning blurb offering me security forever, I found a printed yellow slip from the postmaster telling me they had tried to deliver a piece of registered mail and had not found me at home. Great, I thought. There hadn't been time to stop to read it anyway. As nothing was open until Monday, I tucked the slip into my wallet, and then I hit the sack, still wearing my killing clothes.

I woke, in the night, to the sound of singing. Some drunk college kids were whooping it up on the beach. Philo's valise was on the floor by the bed. Without checking the contents, I moved it to the secret place behind the fridge. Tomorrow, or the next day, I would count the money and read Philo's book.

Then, at last, I stripped off my sweaty clothes and stumbled to the shower. I had the water running hot before I remembered the bandaged left shoulder, so I ran a tub, and was careful to keep the new wound from getting wet.

228

22

The headline for Teresa Aiken's story was perfect for a sunny Sunday morning in March:

BLUE FILMS IN LAGUNA'S EXCLUSIVE BLUEBIRD CANYON

There were photos of Philo's house and also of the gallery. Photos of the house in Bluebird Canyon showed the room behind the heavy metal door, with the movie equipment, the dead roosters, and the handcuffs attached to the wall. Someone had taken Lucinda's snake away, but Teresa featured it in her prose.

Photos of the gallery showed the mess of burned tapes on Philo's desk, the big wall-size video screen, and a chalk diagram of where Philo's body had fallen. A full investigation was underway, the story said.

Lucinda Smith-Travis stole page one, along with Teresa Aiken, who had the byline. Two photos of Lucinda, before and after. "Before" depicted the Garden Club, upscale society ladies meeting at the Ritz Carlton Hotel in Dana Point. "After" displayed Lucinda behind bars, wearing a gray prison smock, staring at the camera. There was no photo for "During," to reveal her in costume for one of Philo's snuff epics.

A clerk at the 7-Eleven on Glenneyre thought he remembered a kid in a yellow rain slicker making a call Saturday night. He didn't see the kid's face, but thought the kid drove a VW bug.

The cops were still hunting for Quan, the Filipino houseboy.

Since I knew the story, I didn't read all of Teresa's prose. It had the smell of prize-winning stuff. I finished my coffee and went out for some breakfast. Then I drove to El Toro, to check on Meg Kirkwood. Billy Bob was outside her door, jawing with the cop on duty. Beneath Billy Bob's chair was a stack of newspapers. He glared at me as I came up. "You left a couple things out of your story, Mr. Murdock." When Billy Bob said "things," it came out sounding like "thangs."

"How's the patient?"

"Had a purty good night," he said. "Wish they'd let me take her on back home. Got me a friend down to Baylor Med knows just what to do in cases like hers."

"Mind if I take a peek inside?"

"She's asleep just now," Billy Bob said, swelling up like a Texas horned toad. "Maybe tomorrow."

I knew she would be asleep tomorrow when I came, and the next day, and the next, so I walked down to Emergency, where they changed the dressing for twenty-five dollars and said my shoulder was coming along just fine.

When I got back home, I counted $72,000 in cash from Philo's valise. I put it back into the secret place, intact. It was Meg's money, for pain and suffering. It would be there when she wanted it.

The fat leather book was a diary Philo Waddell had been keeping for a long time, apparently since he was a teenager, growing up in Craighead County, Arkansas. His handwriting was tight, controlled. I brewed coffee, paged through some entries. Years weren't important. Philo tracked days of the week, seasons. In winter and fall, entries dried up. In spring, they blossomed. Summer entries were garbled, crazy. Something mad happened to him when the weather turned hot. He was sharp enough to figure it out, to feel it coming. He called it "It." I thought I knew what I was hunting for—some reference to Gayla Jean—and I found it near the end of the book, under a reference to "Monday:"

MONDAY—It has commenced again,.that feeling of heat, or of intolerable burning, and thus today one has grappled with the dread demon and lost. Her name is Kirkwood. She has only recently emigrated from Texas, by way of Los Angeles, that city of wasted dreams, and her speech—random snatches of phraseology such as "you-all" and "bidness"—reminds one of the quaint echoes from a distant childhood. She still possesses "friends" in the City of Angels. Were they to appear, one would gladly throttle all! She was sighted on the beach, accompanied by Mr. Jack Downs, a member from Le Club. Later, she appeared at L's party, with two young beachcombers in tow. Her attraction knows few bounds, and one's jealousy rages. It is March. She resides now in Long Beach, that sewer! By May, one should have lured her southward, with the ineffable stuff of dreams. One is helpless in the grip of things, as it were. She lusts for her image on film, fame, lights. Platinum dreams. In that area, one may perhaps be able to oblige, for she is an actress, and undulates her way through life with total fakery. One detests it when she refers to one as "sir." How aged one feels. She can be lured here, surely. But how soon?

FRIDAY—Interruptions from the powers in Las Vegas continue, as they clamor for more cinematic inventory. La Kirkwood is arriving for luncheon. L will attend, for deceptive female coloration, but one is unable to console poor, depressed Butch, who senses competition for one's attentions. Greedy Georges has promised La Kirkwood a job at Le Club. She will stun them all at Grogan's, for its terrible bourgeois tastes. Jung was right about the anima-figure! Less than a month, and she is drawn into the web. One feels triumphant. Perhaps even gleeful.

TUESDAY—It is night. La Kirkwood has viewed the lodgings at Lido Landing and will take possession in three days. She was busy today gathering appropriate female appurtenances. Her interior life is a shambles, and snuffling, hot-fisted, greedy-eyed males track her every step. Since her first teen signs, life for La Kirkwood has been a dance through a jungle of male desires. She is what all males dream of, and endless profit awaits, in the form of videocassettes for the masses. Each day finds her in perpetual heat. Naughty Butch suggested to willing, rumorous L that La Kirkwood would astound science if she inserted a permanent thermometer, in his gross words, "where the sun don't shine." Butch is testy. Already, they are at war. Arrangements are being made for a "modeling" session. Her portion for this tasteful "beauty" service elicited a wide-eyed look, as she earned far less with her protectors in Los Angeles. She is perfect for the role. One must keep her off the streets and out of random beds of her thousand thousand admirers while the plan proceeds. Filming begins next week on *Masque*.

WEDNESDAY—In the manner of a test, one enjoyed her this noon, in the garden, from behind. She is efficient in sex, wanton, enigmatic. The hair is much her finest feature, especially in that light, where it resembled nothing less than spun gold from a Pre-Raphaelite painting. One was surprised (and pleased) to discover that her buttocks were ample. A technical problem: How can the exquisite textures of her flesh be translated to film? In the right hands, such flesh is worth millions! A rim of freckles dusts her pretty back, breasts,

232

shoulders. A single birthmark or mole graces her supple spine. She is Diana, with Actaeon spying. She is Susanna, amidst gouty Elders. She is ripe, and begs to be plucked. She will be. If she only knew, she possesses the ability to drive one mad.

As I read Philo's diary entries, I kept trying to place them in chronological order. "March" was the only clue I had, and that meant he'd met Gayla Jean about this same time last year. It didn't take him long to discover her secret dream—she wanted to be a movie star. Philo obliged, became the builder of her "platinum dream," loaded her up on drugs and something called "cantharis vessicatoris," his own version of that legendary aphrodisiac, Spanish fly.

Butch, grumbling, shot some footage of her, hopped-up, buzzing through a sex video with no dialogue. She was fresh meat, frisky, just the right mix of innocence and sexuality. The boys in Vegas were delighted. Philo added the mask to hide her face and also to jazz up the porno patrons. He knew she wouldn't last, and planned to snuff her when the market softened. His big decision was whether to keep the mask on or off in the snuff film where she died. When Modesto showed up, Gayla Jean was getting restless about Hollywood. She had made three films for Philo. He hadn't delivered Hollywood. She'd gone up to L.A. for a couple of parties. Angry, Philo had taken her car keys. And that's where things stood when she arrived with Dean at Philo's Saturday party.

SUNDAY—How will she die on film? What market needs can be exploited? Stabbing? Gunshot? Strangulation? Biblical stones? Electrical shock? The prostitute script is as yet incomplete. When it is completed, perhaps her time will have come. She talks incessantly of Hollywood. When? Who? How? It renders one temporarily insane.

Philo was out to get her, to kill her for being sexy. Her power to attract drove him bananas. It was only a matter of time before she got‚Äâsnuffed.

I flipped ahead in the diary, until I found Philo's last few entries. They seemed to have been made about ten days ago, on the Wednesday before the Saturday when Gayla Jean had died.

WEDNESDAY‚ÄîThat same voice again today, obviously disguised, speaking in slow, ironic Spanish, as if to a dull child. Insulting manner! Night of thrills. The firelight. An electric moment outside Culiacan. So long ago, that other life. Memories flood back. It is ironic. Was the voice present during the filming, or has he come into possession of evidence by secondary means? One feels vibrations connecting with Las Vegas. Could he be a messenger from them? He demands $10,000, in U.S. funds. Clearly, this payment is a mere beginning. He must be dealt with, at once. He arrives Saturday. The guest list is complete. He is to be admitted, allowed into the crush, then observed. Whoever crashes is he, with slow Spanish speech.

THURSDAY‚ÄîL was apprehended this morning perusing these pages, which provided an excuse for giving her pain. She bruises so easily. What would happen if L should perish on film as well? Perhaps she searches in these pages for her own execution day? One shall think about that. Butch rages with jealousy. What a bitch he is.

SATURDAY‚ÄîA phone call from the voice, to confirm the cash is ready. Was he able to divine there would be protective bodies around him? One is suspicious of everyone‚ÄîL, Butch, Quan, La Kirkwood, odoriferous Johnson, and even of weak Ellis Dean, who would do anything in his puny power to bring one to one's knees. I have instructed the voice to arrive bearing photos and negatives. The cash rests securely in the safe, but today this book is being transferred to the gallery. Too many eyes pry here.

SUNDAY—Insanity! La Kirkwood has been killed! Butch, with his inane smile, swears it was an accident, but cannot hide his smug glee. It is clear he has conveyed her to darkness. Wretched timing. In life, they quarreled like sisters. Johnson aligns himself, for the moment, with Butch. One assumes they acted in obvious haste, to cover the "disappearance" of the extortion cash. The obvious scenario: envious Butch knew La Kirkwood accompanied Modesto in the car (I did not!) and seized his opportunity. Butch's time will come. Of late, his ego has swelled beyond usefulness. More strategically, La Kirkwood's death alters the timetable on the *Golden Boy* piece.

Thirty percent more footage, yet to be filmed. A suitable substitute must be found! There is a sister in Texas. Will she travel this far to mourn? Can a reception be arranged? What does she look like? Will she resonate à La Kirkwood? Johnson shadows Ellis Dean, who attempts to extort a pound of one's flesh via phone. One would relish the pleasure of dealing with Dean in person.

That was Philo's last entry, on Sunday, a week ago. It was the day after Philo's boys had murdered Modesto, killing Gayla Jean along with him. In the black book, Philo laid the blame for her death on Butch. Motive: jealousy.

Sexually, Philo swung both ways.

Philo made sense. Butch's brains were divided between his shoulders and his crotch. He liked hurting people. Whether an accident or not, the girl was dead.

If you read between the lines, you could see Philo's operation in trouble. Vegas was asking questions, putting on the pressure. He planned to kill Gayla Jean eventually, for one more snuff ending. When Butch burnt her up, screwing up the schedule, Philo thought about killing Butch. When Dean tried his amateur's blackmail, Philo's boys got him with a pitchfork. When Meg Kirkwood arrived, Philo sucked her into the schedule, using his fake society charm.

Philo went for the jugular.

Teresa Aiken called the next day, to tell me that Philo's lock box at the bank held a half a million in Swiss francs, another three-quarters in U.S. greenbacks, plus some bearer bonds that she called "negotiable." The bonds brought Philo's liquid wealth up close to three million—not bad for a fat kid from Arkansas with a taste for art and literature.

After talking to Teresa Aiken, I swung by the hospital to see Meg, but Billy Bob blocked the door again and wouldn't let me in. She was mending, he said. I felt like busting him one, but I was still weak from the gunshot wound, and he was brute-big, and besides, it wouldn't have helped.

I went from the hospital to the post office, to get my registered letter. It was a small manila envelope, addressed to me, and postmarked last Tuesday, the day after Dean had been killed. But the package had been routed to San Francisco first and held there for a couple of days before getting back to Southern California, another sign that the country was going to the dogs.

Inside the envelope were Ellis Dean's photos of the killing of Jaime Modesto and Gayla Jean Kirkwood. There were five photos in all, shot from a distance with infrared film, showing Modesto's Trans Am slammed up against the hill, the red pickup parked in front, Butch's Land Rover in the rear. In the foreground of three photos, a dark figure sprayed the Trans Am with liquid fire from a small flamethrower. Another figure stood off to the side. In the photos, you couldn't tell who was Butch and who was Johnson. None of the photos showed Gayla Jean trying to crawl away from the wreck, but she would have been on the other side, out of the camera's view.

I bought a carton of Camels at the Sav-On drugstore in the shopping center and then I drove up the Santa Ana Freeway to the UCI Medical Center, in Orange. That's where they hold shot-up criminals, in the jail ward. I left my wallet and keys with the deputy at the desk, who said he knew me from a training session at the academy. The deputy said I could keep the Camels and the photographs. A red-haired deputy with a sidearm showed me to a room with two chairs, a metal table, bars on the windows. Sunshine streamed through the bars.

In about four minutes, a burly male nurse wheeled him in. The red-haired deputy came along. Sitting in the chair, foot bandaged, arm in a sling, he didn't look so tough. The male nurse went out.

"I got to stay," the deputy said, giving me a look that meant the man in the chair was dangerous. He walked to the window, sat down in a metal chair, folded his arms.

I turned to the man in the wheelchair, who looked at me, then at the carton of Camels. His eyes were slate blue, cocky.

"Hello, Johnson."

"Hello, Santa Claus."

I handed him the Camels. He bit open the seal, opened a package with his teeth, shook a Camel out with one hand, wrapped his lip around it. I lit it for him. After two drags, he arched his eyebrows at me, smirking. Once a smart ass, always a smart ass.

"Well?" he said.

"Heard you turned."

"They're shipping me back home."

"Where's that?"

"Ennis. Little town outside Dallas. Goddam lawyer thinks they won't get to trial here until a year, mebbe. Them Texas Highway boys got their own shit to stir."

I held the first photograph from Ellis Dean in front of his eyes. He glanced at it, then at me. "*People* magazine?"

"The girl's dead, Johnson. That's your pickup, nosed into the hill. A jury sees this, your ass is electric smoke."

Holding the Camel between thumb and forefinger, he stared at me through the smoke. "How'd you figger I'd like this brand?"

"You're the Camel type."

He leaned forward, kept his voice low, so the deputy wouldn't hear. "Should have wasted you right off. Saved myself a passle of trouble. Old Fatso said wait, see what develops. Shit!"

"Why'd you let Butch do it, Johnson?"

"Do what?"

"Kill the girl."

"Butch who?" He grinned, a dead, prehistoric look.

"She went off with Modesto. You could have waited."

"Prick of a spic." His eyes boiled as he remembered. "No reason for her to do that to a fella. Kept shinin' up to her. Prick cut in on me at the dance. Gave her ever' chance."

"You knew she was in the car. You could have stopped Butch."

"Gave her ever' frigging chance." His voice was almost wistful. "What that heifer needed was a dose of Doc Fred's White Root Tonic." He grinned, then slid his eyes away. "Purty little thing, and put together real good. Too bad she got it, that way. Shouldn't have split with that there spic. Like red Rio Grande mud, right on her."

"Where'd Butch learn to use a flamethrower?"

He shifted in the chair, reminding me how you get bedsores, waiting around in hospitals. "Uncle Sam's army. Butch was down south, for awhile, in El Salvador. Blowing them spics away."

"They sent you over from Vegas, didn't they? To check on Philo."

At the mention of Vegas, he grinned. "Great little town, Vegas. Smart old boys over there, sitting around in shorts and Hawaiian shirts, pulling them strings. Wish I'd stayed. Drove over here, pushed past that Filipino nigger. Hour later I was up to my nuts in fancy society gash." With his middle finger, he pantomined a slow, circular motion.

I figured he meant he'd made some time with Lucinda Smith-Travis. We talked some more, but he kept wandering off the topic. Vegas. Hookers in the Persian Gulf. Houston. Some whoopee in the Jacuzzi with Bunny, a tennis chick who hung around Philo's. Like everyone else, the cowboy had his dreams. Ten minutes with him was all a carton of Camels would buy. I walked out without wishing him a safe journey. Behind me, the red-haired deputy waited for the male nurse to wheel him away.

It was early afternoon when I left the jail ward in Orange and drove to Laguna Beach. The sun was out, the wild spring rains a distant memory. Driving down Laguna Canyon road, I lowered the windows on the Plymouth. The earth smelled ripe, in the grip of rebirth.

At the Laguna Beach station, Lieutenant Webby Smith greeted me with a frown. His face was flushed, healthy. He was fresh from his noon workout.

"Judas Priest," he said, when he looked at Ellis Dean's pictures.

"I just showed them to Johnson, the cowboy over in the jail ward at UCI Med. He reacted different."

"These are evidence. They belong here, in police jurisdiction."

I didn't answer.

"How did he react?" Webby asked.

239

"Thought the girl deserved to burn, for fooling around with a Mexican. Johnson wanted into her pants. She wouldn't let him. So she dies."

Webby brought out a magnifying glass, studied the photos. "Lab boys might drag up a license number. Those shadowy figures could be anyone."

"Yeah."

Webby spoke without looking up. "What surprises me is that anyone survived that firefight at the Burgoyne place."

"I'm getting soft, Webby. Thought I might find a cushy job as a cop."

He laid the magnifying glass down, gave me the once-over. "You look terrible, Murdock."

"Couple of weeks, I'll run around the block with you, get myself in shape to be an Iron Man."

"Ha ha," Webby said. Then he opened his desk drawer and tossed four more photos to me. They were sandwiched in between two pieces of greasy cardboard, held together by a frayed rubber band. "Turnabout."

I wasn't ready for any more revealing photos, but I looked through them, just the same.

The first photograph showed a man holding a pitchfork. He wore a leather mask over his face, and the leather garb of a medieval torturer. Light from a huge bonfire glinted off the buckles securing the mask. The second photograph showed the man in the mask stabbing the pitchfork down into the belly of a half-naked woman. She was spread-eagled on a rough bed in a stand of trees. Her eyes were wide with fear and horror. The third photograph showed three men stabbing the same woman with bloody pitchforks. The three men were dressed in business suits. None of them wore masks. The guy closest to the camera was Philo Waddell, heavy, massive. This was one time he should have worn the alligator mask.

"Who's the photographer?"

"Modesto, is my guess. Or he bought them. We'll never know."

"When do you figure they were taken?"

"Six years ago. Maybe seven. Hard to tell."

"My guess is Mexico."

"Why not? Flame thrower's turned up. Probably the one used to torch Modesto's car."

"Where?"

"Butch Denning had himself a room in Huntington Beach. Probably went there for surfer contacts. Wicked-looking equipment. Israeli made, accurate for maybe fifty feet."

"Prints?"

"Just Butch's."

"Swell guys, in the porno business."

"There's an interesting social sidelight to all of this."

"What?"

"Waddell was subsidizing half the art colony around here. We surmise he connected through Mrs. Smith-Travis. The calls to City Hall have tied up lines all morning. Protests. Questions. Lots of surprised, stuffy, upper-middle class shock from the good citizens. Tomorrow, there'll be a funeral parade, guys in smocks and berets. The mayor's very unhappy. I could lose this job of mine."

"Throw in with me. We're a tough team."

"Who'd keep you out of jail?"

"Good thought." I stood up, moved to the door. "Anything new on those Nevada plates?"

Webby smiled wearily. "Company car, on a three year lease, to Gold Farm Properties, Ltd. Last year, Gold Farm engineered a posh condo project out in Sunrise Manor, but stopped after they put in curbs and fireplugs. There are rumors Gold Farm's into making profit on human vice—prostitution, drugs, porno—but no proof."

241

"And no one's claimed the car?"

"Not yet." Webby opened a drawer in his desk, brought out two cassettes. "Two more films have surfaced. One's S&M. The other's a snuffer. No titles."

"Can you connect them to Waddell?"

"Maybe. A fat guy resembling Waddell does the snuff job, at the end. The kid who gets snuffed was a beach bunny, blonde, pretty, and there's a good chance she's local. Last October, a blonde of the same age and build was reported missing by her parents. Prominent Laguna-ites."

"Making that connection should secure your job."

Webby nodded. "If this investigation goes down just right, I'll apply for that new special investigator slot with the county. I'll even hire you on to help out." He leaned back, put his feet on the desk. "I wish we could have stopped him sooner." It was Webby's way of thanking me.

I opened the door. Standing made me shaky. With effort, I could make it to the car.

"How's Ms. Kirkwood?" Webby asked.

"Her Texas linebacker bodyguard won't let me in to see her."

"Jealous, probably."

"He should be."

"She'll come around. They breed them tough in Texas."

"How would you know?"

"Just one of the myths I live by."

23

Meg Kirkwood left town without saying goodbye, and I figured she had too much to handle, with Billy Bob standing guard at the gate and all that medication and her nightmare memories. I was part of those memories, and I understood that she would block out the whole scene. I wasn't happy about it, but when you have decided not to own anyone, then you give up some rights. I had decided that a long time ago, not to try to own someone. So far, it was working, barely.

I did hear from Meg's lawyer, a couple of weeks after she'd left town. Instant spring had come to California. The rain was warmer now, and it wouldn't last as long. Beach people ventured out with their blankets and suntan oil to work on browning up their bodies. On the freeway slopes you saw color, red, yellow, pink, life bursting up, flowering.

The lawyer wanted me to handle the closing of Gayla

Jean's apartment, at Lido Landing. I would get paid my fee, forty bucks an hour, plus expenses. I told him I'd do it for nothing. Being a lawyer, he didn't believe me. "Just send the bill, Mr. Murdock." I didn't tell the lawyer I'd already taken care of Meg's rented car, which one of Webby's officer's had found backed into a culvert in Laguna Canyon.

So I got the apartment closed, and I took on a divorce case (not my favorite way to pass time) and I did a little construction work to help out a friend of mine, and as spring drifted on toward summer I even tried taking up where I'd left off with Teresa Aiken, thinking intimate contact with her smooth tanned flesh would help heal me, make me whole. It was almost fun. She was ardent and artful and her flesh was salty, with a sun and sea tang that would have driven me up the wall ten years back. But we both sensed it was no good, so we let it drop, softly, with a whisper.

In June, I took a case that led me a merry chase down to Mexico, where I had to shoot a guy before he shot me. I got the money back for the client, and since I was working for thirty percent of whatever I recovered, my bank account would be healthy until midautumn.

I still kept on working, because that kept my mind off Meg Kirkwood.

The telegram arrived on a Tuesday in mid-July. Summer was building toward the high white heat of August, the beaches were packed with oiled, smoking flesh, and almost every day I had the sweet pleasure of calling my friend Joe Lopez to bring his big blue tow truck and haul a car away. Inevitably, there was a scene, because the cars that parked in my personal slot always belonged to (or were driven by) an endless succession of sultry squealing beach belles from Irvine or Tustin or San Bernardino or

Phoenix, Arizona. They come a long way to hit this beach. They promised Joe Lopez the moon if he wouldn't tow them away. A couple of them wound up in Joe's bed. He was a guy with a high body odor, and tattoos. For an inland belle who can't read a big No Parking sign, it is not the worst introduction to beach life.

Here's what the telegram said:

ARRIVING AMERICAN FLT 83 TUESDAY EIGHT PM
CAN YOU MEET PLANE.
MEG

I was there, waiting for her, when she came off the plane. I wasn't prepared for the wheelchair. Her face was grave and solemn, but she lit up when she saw me. A flight attendant walked behind her, carrying crutches. Meg held out her hand and we shook. She wore tan slacks and a soft blue blouse.

"I have a new prosthesis," she explained. "It takes some getting used to."

"Maybe I can help," I said.

"I certainly hope so," she said.

Her voice had a new quality, less poised, more sexy. It's hard to explain. I had never been attracted before to a lady in a wheelchair. But Meg was special. And desire was pounding in me, hard. We waited for her luggage—three hefty suitcases and a hanging suit bag—and then I wheeled her out to the parking lot.

"How's the pickup?" she asked, when she saw the Plymouth.

"Runs good. Why do you ask?"

"I dream about it," she said. "I dream about it smashing through that gate, so you could come rescue me."

"You okay?" I asked.

"Um," she said, nodding. "Therapy gets suffocating. You focus inward. You need to look out, at the world."

When I got her baggage stowed, I lifted her out of the wheelchair into the passenger seat. Her thighs were solid and warm where I held her, and I smelled perfume mixed with her own special body scent. A strand of hair brushed my shoulder. "God," she said. "I'm so glad to be here."

"Where are you staying?"

"At the Newporter," she said. "They should be expecting me."

"What are your plans?"

"I'm not sure," she said. "I came back to face things. I've been having dreams, and therapy, and then more dreams. Billy Bob is taking care of things, and I've found a manager that I trust, to run the word processing business. I feel really dumb, really lucky. I want to go over it inch by inch, look at it, where Philo lived, what he did, try to understand Gayla Jean, myself, why we were—" She didn't finish.

I started the car. "Sounds good," I said. "I'm glad to see you." Some days, I believed in facing things, myself.

When we were in traffic, heading south on Jamboree, toward the Newporter, she said, "Could we go to your place first? I'd love to smell the sea."

I was surprised. "Sure."

"Is there—" She began. "Is there someone else there?"

"Nope."

She laid a hand on my thigh. It made me nervous, having it there while I drove, but I left it there. After awhile, she took the hand away. "I'm glad to see you, too."

When we got to my place, she asked me to bring her carryon, and then she used the crutches to climb the stairs. "I'm just getting used to these. The new leg is lighter, but it has to get used to me."

"What happened to the old one?"

She made it to the porch before she answered. "He touched it, soiled it, made it ugly. I wanted something new. You understand?"

"Sure."

She looked around. "It's lovely here. The breeze is glorious. It's been merciless at home. So hot."

I wondered if she was talking about more than the weather. "Want to come inside?"

She spotted the director's chairs and the old plastic chaise, which a lot of ladies had used for sunning. "Could we sit outside awhile? It's so nice here."

"Sure."

When I came back with a couple of beers, Meg was sitting on the chaise with her eyes closed. "Thank you," she said. "And here's to you."

"How long can you stay?" I asked.

"As long as it takes. How long can you stand me?"

"Long," I said.

"Sure I'm not interrupting a serious love affair?"

"Yep."

"What about that pretty girl reporter? The one who wrote us up for everyone to read about?"

"I tried with her. She's very young. It didn't work out."

"I'm sorry."

"I'm not."

"All right." She let out a sigh, and I realized for the first time she'd been holding her breath about me and Teresa Aiken. We sat there awhile, chatting, taking in the ocean breeze. "Can you help me to my feet?" she said. "I need to go to the bathroom."

247

I helped her up.

"Can you bring my little carryon?" she said.

"Sure."

She was in the bathroom a long time. I finished my beer and thought about getting a fresh one. I wondered if Meg wanted a beer. I wondered if her plan would work, the one about facing things. I heard the bathroom door open, and the light went out behind her. When she didn't come back out to the porch, I went to the door and called.

"You okay?"

"Yes." Her voice came from the direction of my bed.

"You sure?"

"Positive. Just a little tired, that's all."

"You're welcome to take a nap."

"Thank you."

There was something new in her voice, something sleepy and sexy, a hum that sent a charge of electricity through me. I went into the kitchen, rolled the fridge aside, opened the secret place. The valise was there. I took out the money, put the valise back. Holding the money, I stood at the bedroom door. The lamp was turned on low. Meg Kirkwood was in my bed, with the sheet pulled up to her neck.

"Sure you don't mind?" she said. "I could go on to my hotel."

"Positive," I said.

"If I could walk," she said, "I'd lead you over."

"Over where?"

"Over here." She patted the bed. One side of the sheet fell away. She wore a pair of my pajama tops, unbuttoned. She did not hurry to close the front. Seeing her brought a lump to my throat.

I walked over, showed her the money.

248

"What's that?"

"Seventy grand. In cash."

"Impressive. Where did it—" Then she knew. I could see it on her face, a flicker of that killing look. "You've been keeping it."

"In the insurance trade, they call it pain and suffering."

"How much did you say?"

"Seventy thousand."

The smile started slowly, then crept across her face. She held out her arms, beckoning me. "What a lovely present."

I sat on the bed and took her in my arms. The money plopped on the bed. Some dropped to the floor.

"You're already starting, aren't you?" Her mouth was warm on my ear.

"Starting what?"

"Starting me facing things."

"I could have spent it. Liquor. Women. Wild parties."

She laughed. "Oh, how I've needed you."

"The same goes for me, double."

"Can we talk about the money tomorrow?" Her voice was hoarse.

"Sure. Or the next day."

She brought her mouth around for a kiss. It was exploratory, getting to know you. I felt her heart beating. Beneath the thin pajama fabric, she was soft, yielding.

"Can you wait for me?"

"Sure." She was talking about sex, making love.

"Just until tomorrow. Or the day after. I need to . . . walk around, hold hands, be with you."

"No problem. Like I said, it's nice to have you here."

"I'm already thinking of how we can spend it."

"Good. That's what it's for."

"Have you ever been to bed with a one-legged woman?"

"No." My voice was choked.

"They say it's an experience." She was smiling, trying to have a sense of humor about herself. It was a lovely try.

I nodded, held her close.

"I just . . . want to wait." She gripped my arm. "Do you understand?"

"Hell, yes."

"You've got to help me get well. That's why I came back."

"You'll make it. You're tough."

"I want to go there, look at the house."

"Okay."

We didn't talk for awhile. I listened to her heart beating. Outside, voices carried up from the summer beach.

Meg stirred. I was aware of shoulder blades, softness. Underneath the sheet, I was aware of the empty place, where her leg ended.

"It's funny," she said.

"What?"

"I'm very excited. And yet I'm terribly tired. How can that be?"

"Long trip."

She looked at me. Her eyes studied the room behind me. "I feel like I'm home."

"Good."

"It is good."

In the soft light from the lamp, she smiled, and then she began to cry.